"I want a chance, Tamara."

Before she could do more than stare in surprise, Sam stepped closer and knelt beside her chair. "Tamara, I'm not going to con you by saying I'm madly in love with you. Hell, I don't even know what love is. But we're married, we're going to have a baby, and shouldn't we at least try and make it work?"

The sincere plea in his eyes touched Tamara, but his past attitude toward her had been devastating to her pride. Tamara was weakening, and she wasn't sure she should. It would be so easy to be taken in again, to make another mistake with Sam.

"I don't know, Sam," she whispered. "What if it *doesn't* work?"

"Would we be any worse off than we are right now?" he asked.

I might be. If I let myself fall in love with you and it doesn't work out, I would be a lot worse off....

Dear Reader,

At long last, summertime has arrived! Romance is in full bloom this month with first-time fathers, fun-filled adventure—and scandalous love.

In commemoration of Father's Day, award-winning Cheryl Reavis delivers this month's THAT'S MY BABY! *Little Darlin'* is a warm, uplifting tale about a cynical sergeant who suddenly takes on the unexpected roles of husband—and father!—when he discovers an abandoned tyke who couldn't possibly be his...or could she?

In these next three books, love defies all odds. First, a mysterious loner drifts back into town in *A Hero's Homecoming* by Laurie Paige—book four in the unforgettable MONTANA MAVERICKS: RETURN TO WHITEHORN series. Then fate passionately unites star-crossed lovers in *The Cougar*—Lindsay McKenna's dramatic finish to her mesmerizing COWBOYS OF THE SOUTHWEST series. And a reticent rancher vows to melt his pregnant bride's wounded heart in *For the Love of Sam* by Jackie Merritt—book one in THE BENNING LEGACY, a new crossline series with Silhouette Desire.

And you won't want to miss the thrilling conclusion to Andrea Edwards's engaging duet, DOUBLE WEDDING. When a small-town country vet switches places with his jet-setting twin, he discovers that appearances can be *very* deceiving in *Who Will She Wed?* Finally this month, *Baby of Mine* by Jane Toombs is an intense, emotional story about a devoted mother who will do *anything* to retrieve her beloved baby girl, including marry a handsome—dangerous!—stranger!

I hope you enjoy these books, and each and every story to come!

Sincerely,

Tara Gavin
Senior Editor & Editorial Coordinator

Please address questions and book requests to:
Silhouette Reader Service
U.S.: 3010 Walden Ave., P.O. Box 1325, Buffalo, NY 14269
Canadian: P.O. Box 609, Fort Erie, Ont. L2A 5X3

JACKIE MERRITT

FOR THE LOVE OF SAM

SPECIAL EDITION®

Published by Silhouette Books
America's Publisher of Contemporary Romance

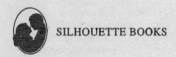

SILHOUETTE BOOKS

ISBN 0-373-24180-1

FOR THE LOVE OF SAM

Printed in U.S.A.

Books by Jackie Merritt

Silhouette Special Edition

A Man and a Million #988
*Montana Passion #1051
*Montana Lovers #1065
*†Letter to a Lonesome
  Cowboy* #1154
‡For the Love of Sam #1180

Silhouette Books

Montana Mavericks

The Widow and the Rodeo Man #2
The Rancher Takes a Wife #5

Summer Sizzlers Collection 1994
"Stranded"

*Made in Montana
†Montana Mavericks:
  Return to Whitehorn
‡The Benning Legacy
**Saxon Brothers series

Silhouette Desire

Big Sky Country #466
Heartbreak Hotel #551
Babe in the Woods #566
Maggie's Man #587
Ramblin' Man #605
Maverick Heart #622
Sweet on Jessie #642
Mustang Valley #664
*The Lady and the
  Lumberjack* #683
Boss Lady #705
Shipwrecked! #721
Black Creek Ranch #740
A Man Like Michael #757
Tennessee Waltz #774
Montana Sky #790
Imitation Love #813
**Wrangler's Lady #841
**Mystery Lady #849
**Persistent Lady #854
Nevada Drifter #866
Accidental Bride #914
Hesitant Husband #935
Rebel Love #965
Assignment: Marriage #980
*Montana Fever #1014
*Montana Christmas #1039
Wind River Ranch #1085

JACKIE MERRITT

and her husband live in the Southwest. An accountant for many years, Jackie has happily traded numbers for words. Next to family, books are her greatest joy. She started writing in 1987, and her efforts paid off in 1988 with the publication of her first novel. When she's not writing or enjoying a good book, Jackie dabbles in watercolor painting and likes playing the piano in her spare time.

Chapter One

Tamara Benning's closest friend in the company for which she worked, Rowland, Inc. of Dallas, Texas, was one of the receptionists for the sales department. A good seven years older than Tamara, who was twenty-three, Natalie Cross was a woman with an upbeat attitude, and Tamara enjoyed her company. They often ate lunch together, and were presently in the process of devouring delicious hot pastrami sandwiches in Henry's Deli, which was within walking distance of the Rowland Building.

"So anyhow," Tamara said after a sip of iced tea, explaining the significance of a conference that morning with her immediate supervisor, Elliot Grimes, vice president in charge of sales, "each assistant was assigned specific field representatives. Instead of the reps delivering their sales orders to whichever assistant is available at the time, they will be seeing the same assistant every time they come in. I think it's a sensible policy, and I'm surprised Rowland hasn't implemented it before. In the five months I've worked here I've dealt with numerous field reps, but I can't say I know any of them. Mr. Grimes thought a closer working relationship between the field reps and their co-ordinator might help departmental efficiency, and I fully agree.''

''I figured something like that was going on,'' Natalie said. ''Reception was notified to direct any phone calls from reps to certain assistants. We were given an alpha-betical list of the reps' names, with an assistant's name beside each one.'' Natalie grinned rather impishly. ''I no-ticed you drew Stoneface Sherard.''

Tamara sat back, mystified. ''Are you talking about Samuel Sherard?''

''Sam Stoneface Sherard,'' Natalie said with laughter lurking in her dark eyes. ''You haven't heard his nickname before?''

''No,'' Tamara replied. ''Who calls him that?''

Natalie shrugged. ''Almost everyone.''

''Why?''

''Because the man never smiles.'' Natalie started laugh-ing. ''You haven't met him yet, have you?''

''No, I haven't.'' Frowning, Tamara attempted to link Sherard's name with the personnel and production records that she had requested after the meeting, so she could be-come acquainted with ''her'' field reps' company history. ''If memory serves me,'' she said thoughtfully, ''Mr. Sher-ard is one of Rowland's top producers.''

''Could be,'' Natalie said with another shrug. ''That kind of information rarely reaches reception. All we do is answer the phones and direct traffic.''

''I take it that you've directed Mr. Sherard.''

''Many times. Tamara, all kidding aside, he's just about the most unfriendly person I've ever met. You know me— I talk to everyone. When I first started working at Row-land, I tried talking to Sherard when he came in. He did everything but stand on his head to avoid conversation. Believe me, he's the coldest fish in the sea.''

Tamara looked at her friend. Natalie and she couldn't be further apart in appearance and personality. Natalie was a petite woman who literally bounced with energy. Her hair was a rich brown color, short and curly, and her dark eyes had a permanent twinkle, even when her personal problems seemed overwhelming. Natalie was divorced with two small children, and she had an admittedly prejudicial attitude toward men because her husband had deserted his family. Neither she nor the state of Texas had been able to locate him to force him to pay child support, and Natalie often had a hard time making ends meet on her own.

Tamara was tall, blond and serious-minded. She doubted that her green eyes ever twinkled like Natalie's. While Natalie dressed in bright colors and sometimes outrageous outfits, Tamara's work clothes were sedate and understated, as were the styles she forced upon her thick mane of long, naturally curly, sun-streaked blond hair.

Regardless of their many differences, the two women had hit it off from their first meeting. Natalie seemed to know something about everyone working in Rowland's vast sales department and was more than willing to pass on information. Tamara discouraged out-and-out gossip, but she had learned a lot about her co-workers from Natalie, which had been most helpful in the first few weeks of her job.

Her career, actually. She hadn't started at the bottom with Rowland, Inc.—she'd been hired during recruitment week at her alma mater, the University of California at Berkeley, and her position was that of assistant to Elliot Grimes. Granted, she filled the lowest notch on the assistants' totem pole—there were four others with the same title—but she loved her job, took it seriously and fully intended to advance in the company.

As close as she felt to Natalie, Tamara didn't always agree with everything her friend said. This was one of those times. ''It seems strange that Sherard would be such a successful salesman with a cold personality, Natalie. The people in sales that I've worked with all seem to have a naturally gregarious nature. If anything, some of them talk too much."

Natalie looked skeptical, her expression suggesting she knew what she knew and that was that. "Believe me, Tamara, Sam Sherard marches to a much different drummer than his counterparts."

"Possibly," Tamara said thoughtfully. "Well, it really doesn't matter, does it? He's a top producer and that's what counts." She paused, then added, "I can't say I like his nickname. I never have liked jokes at other people's expense."

"Maybe not, but I would bet anything that you'll agree it's appropriate once you meet him."

"Possibly," Tamara murmured again. They talked about other things while finishing lunch and walking back to the Rowland Building. Tamara's curiosity about Sam Sherard had definitely been whetted, however, and the minute she returned to her office, she took another look at his files.

He was thirty-two years old, single, and he had a rural address. In case of an emergency, the company was to notify someone named Stubby Draco, same address as Sam's. Other than production records and payroll data, that's all there was.

Tamara closed the files. Sam Stoneface Sherard would obviously remain a mystery until she met him face-to-face.

For some reason she was looking forward to doing exactly that, probably because she'd hadn't yet met anyone who *never* smiled.

That thought caused her to smile herself. "Stoneface, indeed," she said under her breath, doubting that anyone deserved such a label.

Especially a man with Sam's impressive sales record.

It was almost five—normal closing time—on the following Friday when Tamara's intercom line beeped. It was

Natalie, speaking in an exaggeratedly formal manner. "Miss Benning, Mr. Sam Sherard is in reception."

"Nat, you rat," Tamara said with a laugh. "Send him back."

"Yes, ma'am." Natalie kept the line open, and Tamara heard her say, "Mr. Sherard, you are to go to *Miss* Tamara Benning's office."

A deep male voice said, "Which is where?"

Natalie gave him directions, waited in silence a moment, then said to Tamara, "He's on his way. Let me know what you think of him."

Tamara grinned at Natalie's curiosity. "Why on earth would you care?"

"You'll know a whole lot more about that when you see him. Bye. Gotta run."

Natalie's mysterious comments began to bother Tamara. What kind of man was going to come walking into her office? she wondered uneasily, while clearing a portion of her desk to make space for whatever paperwork Mr. Sherard might be bringing in.

Her office was small but nicely situated. One wall was constructed of glass panels, through which she could see the enormous room of cubicles and desks filled with busy sales department operatives. When concentrating on an important task she usually closed the blinds to avoid distractions.

Today the blinds were open, and she spotted a tall man heading her way. Instinctively she knew he was Sam Sherard, and she took this golden opportunity to look him over. He was dressed in jeans, a neatly pressed blue shirt, cowboy boots and a tan suede vest. He was carrying a worn leather case and a hat. His hair was dark, almost black, and he was, she realized with a most peculiar sinking sensation, unusually handsome.

For some reason she tensed. Probably because of Natalie's remarks, the last thing Tamara had expected Sam

Sherard to be was handsome. Not that masculine good looks turned her into a gibbering idiot, but there was something in Sherard's bearing, in the way he walked, in the stern expression on his face, that set off alarm bells in her system. She was leery of labeling her spine-tingling reactions to this man as instantaneous physical attraction, but she didn't know what else to call them. In the very brief time it took him to reach the door of her office, she remembered, with a deluge of disoriented emotions, that she had not had one real date with a man since her move to Dallas.

He stopped at the glass door to peer in at her, and she rose from her chair behind her desk, smiled and beckoned him in, vowing in the back of her mind that she would *not* let her nervousness show.

The door opened and he stepped in. "Ms. Benning?"

"Miss...it's M-Miss Benning," she stammered, embarrassing herself with her very first words. It flashed through her mind that Natalie had addressed her as "Miss" on the phone and Sherard must have heard her. Unless he'd been paying no attention to Natalie's theatrics, that is.

Tamara took a furtive little breath and felt slightly calmer. "Please come in, Mr. Sherard." She held her hand out across the desk.

Sam shut the door, took the few steps to her desk and shook her hand. It felt small in his, and warm, full of life and vitality. Her gorgeous green eyes conveyed the same zest, and her smile was the most beautiful he'd ever seen. Although he knew very little about women's clothes, he was positive that Tamara Benning's were stylish. She was not at all what he had expected.

Actually, he had arrived with no expectations whatsoever. He'd been notified by company memo about the new arrangement, which hadn't mattered to him one way or the other. Meeting his coordinator changed things considerably. He was not accustomed to doing business with a woman with stunning blond hair—even if it was trussed into an unnatural style—green eyes that could knock the underpinnings from any man, and a face and figure that dreams were made of.

His expression became tighter as their hands broke apart, and tighter still when she said, "Please call me Tamara. I'd like to be on a first-name basis with my field reps." When he made no response, she asked, "You don't mind if I call you Sam, do you?"

Would it matter if I did? "That's my name."

Tamara ignored his gruffness and smiled as though he had exuberantly agreed with her suggestion. "Wonderful. Please sit down." She gestured at the two chairs in front of her desk.

Sam placed his hat and leather case on one and sat in the other. Tamara slowly sank into her chair behind the desk. Her heart was beating a little too fast. She still felt his hand around hers. Talk about chemistry! Sam Sherard positively exuded sex appeal, and apparently she *was* overly susceptible to it.

She tried to think of the negative aspects of this meeting and was only partially successful. So far Natalie was right—Sam Sherard had not even come close to a smile, and it was discombobulating for Tamara to realize she would much rather say something clever and make him smile than sit here and talk business. *He's too good-looking. It's all I'm seeing, all I'm thinking about. Get yourself together, for heaven's sake!*

Sam's thoughts were startlingly similar. *She's too young, too beautiful. What in hell is she doing working in a stuffy office like this?*

"Well," Tamara said brightly. "Shall we get down to business?"

"It's the reason I'm here," Sam said brusquely. He reached for his leather case and pulled out a stack of papers, which he shoved across the desk. "Take a look at these orders. If you have any questions, now's the time to ask 'em."

Tamara wondered if he knew how rude he sounded. *Maybe he doesn't care,* she thought with a pang of disappointment. She turned the papers around so she could read them, then found it difficult to grasp what she was reading. It was impossible to tear her thoughts away from the man sitting across her desk. *Thirty-two years old, single, rural address. And who is Stubby Draco, the man living with him—a relative, a friend?* She was curious enough about Sam Sherard to want to know the answer to that question.

As she worked her way through the sales orders, a method of finding out occurred to her. Putting it on hold until she finished perusing the orders, she came to one that requested immediate delivery.

She lifted her gaze. "How immediate is immediate on this order for the stainless steel pipe?"

"Like yesterday," Sam drawled.

"I see." She picked up the phone and dialed the inventory department. "Jim? Tamara Benning. I have an order for 500 lineal feet of one-inch stainless steel pipe, contingent upon immediate delivery. Do we have it in inventory?" After a moment she said, "Thank you," then looked at Sam. "He's checking."

Sam folded his arms across his chest and sat back in his chair. While he glanced around Tamara's office he felt her eyes on him. He sensed more than normal curiosity from her, but he wasn't sure that he wanted to examine it too closely. For one thing, he didn't do a lot of dating, and for another, he had never become that friendly with anyone working for Rowland. Just didn't seem smart to him. But he'd never before met anyone in the company like Tamara Benning, either. He would bet anything that if he asked her out she wouldn't say no.

But then what would happen? If they didn't click it would be tough dealing with her, and if they did it would be even tougher. Let sleeping dogs lie, he told himself as Tamara began speaking into the phone again.

"All right, Jim, thanks." She put down the receiver, looked at Sam again and nearly choked. A lock of dark hair had slipped down over the right side of his forehead, and her fingers itched to smooth it back in place. She cleared her throat. "The pipe is in inventory. We can deliver first thing in the morning. Will that satisfy your customer?"

"It's what he's come to expect from Rowland." Sam himself smoothed his hair back.

Tamara licked her lips, which suddenly felt sandpaper dry, and forced herself to finish going through the orders. She'd had two sexual relationships, both in college, and neither man had impacted her so overwhelmingly as Sam Sherard did without even trying.

At least he didn't appear to be trying. He wasn't flirtatious; he wasn't even friendly. No, he definitely wasn't trying to impress her.

With an inward sigh she turned over the final sheet of paper. "That's that," she said. "You have some very good orders here."

"Just doing my job."

"Doing it very well, if these sales are any measure. Oh, by the way, when Mr. Grimes instigated this new program, he stressed his desire for a closer working relationship between the assistants and the field reps. I pulled your files, and I have a question."

Sam narrowed his eyes on her. "A question about what?"

"Just a moment." Tamara opened a drawer of her desk and drew out the reps' files. "As you can see, your files weren't the only ones I read." She found Sam's and set the others aside.

Before she could get one word out of her mouth, however, Sam asked, "Is your question connected to my job?"

Startled, she looked up into a pair of glowering, dark blue eyes. "Uh…no."

"Then don't ask it. My personal life is no one's business

but my own." Sam got to his feet. "Is there anything else?"

Tamara could feel the heat of embarrassment in her cheeks. Obviously she was not going to learn from Sam who Stubby Draco was. "No, nothing else."

Sam picked up his hat and leather case. "Then I'll be going." He walked out the door, and Tamara stared in shocked disbelief as he crossed the big room—almost vacant now because it was past five—and vanished.

She sat there for a long time, pondering Sam Sherard, recalling his rudeness and icy personality and wondering if she hadn't lost her mind at some point during the last thirty or so minutes. The problem was that she found herself rationalizing his disinterest, knew she was doing it and couldn't seem to stop herself. Something had happened to her the second she'd laid eyes on him, and while she couldn't—or wouldn't—give it a name, it had seemingly become a permanent part of herself. That idea scared her. She had no experience with the kind of emotional upheaval Sam Sherard had caused within her, and she honestly didn't know what to do about it.

Especially when the focus of this chaotic feeling was a man whose nickname, Stoneface, fit him like a glove.

When Tamara graduated from college she'd had about a hundred dollars in her checking account. Her mother, Myra, had flown from her home in Coeur d'Alene, Idaho, to California for the graduation ceremony, and the two of them celebrated the event that same evening with a lovely dinner in a very expensive restaurant. Myra's treat, of course. Tamara had dressed up for the occasion, taking pains with her hair, using makeup, and even she had noticed how many men did a double take when she walked in.

Myra commented on it after they were seated. "I have never gone anywhere with one of my daughters without men tripping over their own feet gawking at them. The three of you are very beautiful women.''

The compliment surprised Tamara. While she'd been growing up, her mother had stressed good grades, proper behavior, a spotless reputation and good manners. As long as her daughters were scrupulously clean, their looks had never seemed to matter to Myra.

''Thank you, Mother,'' she said, expressing her pleasure with a radiant smile. In the next instant she became pensive. ''Wouldn't it have been nice if Sierra and Blythe could have been here?''

''They're busy with their own lives,'' Myra replied rather absentmindedly as she scanned the menu.

Tamara sighed quietly. Myra and Dr. Harry Benning had produced an unusual family; each of their daughters had been born ten years apart. With such a vast difference in their ages, they had never been close. They heard news of each other through their mother, if at all. Tamara was the youngest, Sierra was the middle child and Blythe the eldest. Tamara sometimes longed to know her sisters better.

But they were from three different decades, and maybe more important, they were very different women. Sierra was talented artistically; her medium was oil paints. Her career in art had been progressing nicely when she married a lawyer, Mike Findley, a young man she had met in college some years before. His family was very wealthy, and Sierra and Mike lived in a modern-day mansion in San Francisco. To Tamara's knowledge her sister was ecstatically happy.

Blythe, being twenty years older than Tamara, was more of a mystery. She had married within months of graduating from college. Five years later, Blythe's husband had died after a year-long battle with cancer. When Tamara did see her oldest sister, she was always struck by the sadness in her lovely blue-gray eyes. Blythe was a gentle woman, soft-spoken and intelligent, and since her husband's death she had taught at the elementary level of education at an exclusive private institution.

Tamara was drawn from her reverie by her mother's voice. "All three of you graduated from college with honors," Myra said, still studying her menu. "Your father would have been very proud."

Dr. Harry Benning had been dead for fifteen years, but Tamara knew Myra still mourned the loss of her husband. Peering over the top of her own menu, Tamara studied her mother. She was sixty-five years old and still very attractive, her pale blond hair perfectly coifed, her clothing stylish, her makeup tastefully done. Tamara could not remember ever having seen her mother with curlers in her hair, for instance, or dressed in old clothes, except for gardening. Myra had a passion for roses, and her backyard rose garden was her pride and joy.

Myra laid down her menu. "Tell me about your job in Dallas. I know you're excited about it."

Throughout the delicious meal Tamara related what she knew about Rowland, Inc., and her reasons for accepting their job offer. Myra seemed pleased at her daughter's success story, except for Rowland's location.

"You've never been to Texas, Tamara. What if you don't like living in Dallas?"

"I really don't think that will be a problem, Mother. Dallas is a beautiful city with a great deal to offer."

"And, of course," Myra said after a moment of contemplation, "we all do what we must, go where the opportunities are, live our own lives."

Tamara had heard that philosophy from her mother before and wondered, not for the first time, how Myra had come by it. Blythe lived in Connecticut, Sierra in San Francisco, her mother in Idaho and now she herself would be living in Texas. Didn't Myra get lonely living in that big house in Coeur d'Alene all by herself? Yes, she missed her husband, but didn't she ever miss her daughters?

Tamara suddenly had to know. "I'm sure you get lonely, Mother," she said gently.

"Tamara, I am not one of those mothers who refuse to let their children grow up. I'm very busy with my civic committees and church activities. Same as always, dear."

Tamara was disappointed in her mother's response, but kept a smile on her face. Her spirit brightened as an idea occurred to her. "When I'm settled in Dallas, I would love it if you came for a visit."

Myra smiled, reached out and patted Tamara's hand. "Not during the summer months, dear. I've heard that Texas can be very hot and humid." They were eating sherbet, having foregone the rich desserts offered by the splendid restaurant. "Tamara, I know you don't have the money to relocate. Have you any idea how much you will need?"

Tamara's eyes dropped to her dish of sherbet. As guarded as Myra was with her emotions, she had always been generous with money. Tamara had often wished it were the other way around. For one thing, she didn't like taking money from her mother. She had gotten through college mostly on scholarships and part-time jobs. There'd been times when she'd had to rely on Myra's largesse, but not many. This was different. There was no way she could make the move to Dallas without financial help, and she found the subject distressing.

But there was no way to avoid it. "Around two thousand dollars, Mother," she said quietly. "And it would only be a loan. My salary is going to be good, and I insist on paying you back."

Myra nodded. "As you wish. I'll write you a check before I leave tomorrow."

They finished their meal with cups of hot tea.

Five months later, Tamara sat in her office and contemplated the best-looking but strangest man she had ever met—Sam Sherard—long after he'd gone. Mingled with images of Sam was the memory of that postgraduation

dinner with her mother, and all that Tamara had accomplished since her move to Dallas.

She had repaid her mother, furnished her apartment and
had a respectable savings account, mostly slated at present
for the purchase of a car. She'd been relying on buses and
taxis for transportation and knew that had to stop. But she
didn't know which she disliked more—riding buses or
shopping for a car.

Putting both Sam Sherard and the car issue out of her
mind with a sigh, she started clearing her desk for the day.
Elliot Grimes rapped on her door, then walked in. "I'm
glad you're still here, Tamara. I've been meaning to speak
to you all day, but time got away from me. May I keep
you here a little longer?"

"Of course. Please sit down, Mr. Grimes."

"I studied that report you turned in last week," Grimes
said as he took a chair.

Tamara felt a quick flash of anxiety. On her own time,
after normal working hours and on Saturday mornings, she
had devised a new format for the monthly sales evaluation
report. No one had requested she do the extra work, but
she had found the present structure of the monthly reports
to be cumbersome and difficult to follow. There had been
a lot of room for improvement, she'd decided, and she'd
taken it upon herself to clarify the crucial data.

"Yes?" she said calmly, belying the quickened beating
of her pulse.

"It's an exceptional piece of work, Tamara. I've passed
it on to Tom Rowland for his opinion. I thought you'd like
to know."

Rowland, Inc. was a family-held corporation, and Tom
Rowland was its current CEO. Tamara had met Mr. Rowland, of course, but she certainly couldn't say she knew
him. It was very exciting to think that a report into which
she had put so much time and brain power was now in the
hands of the head man himself.

"Thank you, Mr. Grimes. I'm very pleased."

"Let me say that so are we, Tamara. Overall, your work is exemplary. I must admit to having had some doubts about filling that vacant assistant's position with someone just out of school, but you've proved your worth many times over," Elliot Grimes told her. "I predict a long and successful career for you, Tamara. Hopefully, it will be right here, at Rowland." Mr. Grimes smiled and got up. "That's all for now, Tamara. I just wanted you to know how highly I rated your report."

"Thank you, sir," she murmured, and watched him leave.

This was very exciting news. She'd been career oriented all during college, maybe even before that, and her willingness to go the extra mile in her job was paying off. If nothing came from that report except what she had already received, Mr. Grimes's recognition of a job well done, it would be enough.

But it was in the hands of Tom Rowland! *Imagine that.* Tamara's excitement increased as she thought about it.

Well, today had brought two surprises—meeting Sam Sherard and recognition of her keenly thought out sales report. She felt very proud of herself for having contributed something of value to her employer's methods of record keeping.

Rowland, Inc. was an old company, having been founded in 1920. Its home base was Dallas, but it had a branch in Alaska and another in Mexico. It manufactured and sold oil-field equipment and supplies, and its customers ranged far and wide. The field reps were every bit as important to the ongoing success of the company as those people in sales who sat at desks and took orders over the phone. In 1920, in fact, the company had depended solely on direct contact with customers through field reps. Now, of course, sales also came in from mail-order catalogs, by telephone, fax and E-mail.

Those thoughts brought Sam Sherard, successful field

rep that he was, to mind again, and Tamara sat back in her chair to once again ponder his unusual personality.

In a moment she decided that rather than wasting time in trying to understand Sam, she should be worrying about herself. After all, *he* wasn't the one who'd gotten overheated and giddy in that simple business meeting, she had.

The question, of course, was why? Discounting Sam's incomparable good looks, was there anything else about him to plant him so firmly into her thoughts that she feared he would remain there for some time?

"Not one damn thing," she mumbled, opening the top drawer and clearing the surface of her desk with one sweep of her arm. *He's rude and probably dull as dishwater when not talking about sales. Forget him. Sam Sherard is definitely not your type.*

It was darned good advice, she decided as she reached for her coat.

She rode an elevator to the ground floor, left the building and walked the two blocks to her bus stop feeling good about herself.

Things were falling into place very nicely in Dallas. She had made a wise decision when she had accepted Rowland's job offer.

During the bus ride home, however, she realized that forgetting Sam was not going to be easy. There was no telling how often she would have to see him, and the mere thought of seeing him again, of having him seated across her desk again, made the fine hairs on the back of her neck get all prickly.

Now, just what should she make of that?

Chapter Two

Sam's sales expertise lay with the small, independent oil companies, those with one to a hundred wells and the land or leases to punch additional holes whenever the fluctuating crude oil market looked good. Sam had grown up all over Oklahoma, Texas and Louisiana. His father had been an oil-field drifter, rarely working more than a few months at any one job. In Sam's estimation it had been a lousy way to grow up, but he'd learned the jargon and knew how to talk to men obsessed with the oil business. He could lean against the bed of a pickup truck and discuss geology and ground formations with the best of them—and the worst. Oilmen liked Sam and bought their supplies and equipment from him, scarcely giving two hoots that they were really buying from a Dallas firm called Rowland, Inc. It was Sam they dealt with, Sam who dropped in and asked how the new well was progressing or how the family was faring, Sam with whom they felt a special rapport. When oil prices dropped, Sam listened to their complaints, and when they were up, it was Sam who slapped them on the back and drank a beer with them in celebration.

Sam's unstable youth had shaped him into a cynical man. He had absolutely no pretensions about life; it was hard and you only got out of it what you were willing to put into it. He rarely visited his parents, who lived in Tulsa, as they had both become alcoholics, and he couldn't bear seeing the slovenly hovel they called home and what they had settled for. When he thought of his family he got an ache in his gut, so he tried *not* to think about them. He'd even been in Tulsa without letting them know he was there. What really hurt were the memories of how he'd tried to make them see what they were doing to themselves, and of how they had turned on him and told him to mind his own damned business.

How he had escaped that same self-destructive pattern he would never know, but he was cautious with alcohol and fanatic about cleanliness. He was *not* going to end up like his parents, and that was a vow he'd made to himself at the tender age of eighteen. He'd gotten through high school, only God knew how, but that was the end of his formal education. He had packed his things, left his family in some little berg in west Texas and set out on his own.

And he hadn't done badly. He had worked at various jobs until landing his present position with Rowland, Inc. He'd been with them for ten years now, and he liked that he was making good money and doing something worthwhile with it. Six years ago he had bought a rundown ranch—eight hundred acres—near the Oklahoma-Texas border, and gradually he had cleaned it up, hauled away mountains of junk, repaired the shaky barn and modernized the house. He hadn't done it alone. After the second year, an old fellow named Stubby Draco had come along one day when Sam had been reinforcing a fence under a broiling sun, working without a shirt and sweating rivers.

Stubby had been looking for work. "Been a ranch hand all my life," he'd told Sam.

Sam had already decided he needed a hired man. His job with Rowland took up most of his time, and he wasn't fixing up the ranch as fast as he'd like. But he had thought twice about hiring someone as old as Stubby, who looked to be pushing seventy. They sat on the front porch of the house, drank lemonade and talked. Stubby told him that he was alone in the world and a teetotaler. Sam couldn't help liking the older man's wry personality and ready grin, and he'd hired him. "The house is still in bad shape, but it has three bedrooms. You can use one of them."

Stubby had moved in, and after that every time Sam went home he was amazed at the changes in the place. Now, after four years of working with Stubby, relying on him to tend the ranch in his absence, Sam was concentrating on stocking the Double S Ranch with horses and cattle, and it was the one truly satisfying aspect of his life. Oh, he liked his job with Rowland well enough. It was a good company to work for, and Elliot Grimes permitted him to do his job in his own way. Sam punched no time clock and he set his own schedules. But sales put money in his pocket, and he couldn't hang around the ranch very often. Someday he was going to live there on a permanent basis, but not for a long time yet. He was thirty-two years old and figured he'd have enough money accumulated to retire at fifty. That was his dream, and it didn't bother him an iota that his dream did not include a wife. If his parents' marriage was any measure, the institution was highly overrated. In analytical moments he had to admit he liked being a loner. He knew hundreds of people and had only one real friend, Stubby, which was fine with him.

Actually, Sam got a kick out of a rather ironic distinction between himself and Stubby. At thirty-two he spent very little time thinking or talking about women; Stubby, at seventy, adored the opposite sex and couldn't compliment them enough. He loved the smell of feminine cos-

metics and called women "sweet little flowers" and
"God's gift to mankind." How he had sniffed out so many
widow ladies in the sparsely populated area where the
ranch was located Sam would never know, but every Saturday night Stubby had a date. If Sam happened to be at
the ranch on a weekend, he spent Saturday night alone, as
Stubby, all slicked up and smelling of cologne himself,
would go off around five and not get home until the wee
hours. Sam wondered if his old friend was still sexually
active, but Stubby never offered that information and Sam
couldn't bring himself to ask.

As for himself, sex wasn't a high priority. He ran into
a willing woman occasionally, and that was enough. He
had never had even one serious relationship with a woman
and didn't feel as though he'd missed anything. In truth,
it wasn't a subject he spent time thinking about.

Considering the misery of the first eighteen years of his
life, he figured he was as happy as could be expected. He
had a home he loved, one very good friend, a steady job
and his health. What more should a man hope for?

Sam thought of all that as he left Dallas after dropping
off his sales orders at Rowland. He was driving north,
heading for his ranch for the weekend and happy to be
doing it.

But there was a pocket of confusion in his system like
none he'd ever before encountered, and he didn't much
care for the feeling. It had to do with Tamara Benning. So
she was beautiful. He'd met up with many good-looking
women in his adult life and hadn't gotten confused over
them.

He couldn't come up with an answer as to why she was
different, he just knew she was. Worse than that, though,
after spending thirty minutes with the woman, *he* was different. He shook his head in abject disgust. He'd walked
into Rowland today contented with life in general, and had
walked out a half hour later with a knot in his gut because
of a woman. It made no sense.

Sensible or not, he got warm all over just thinking about her. Yes, he'd like to take her to bed; what man wouldn't?

But he knew in his soul that there was a hell of a lot more to Tamara Benning than sex appeal, and maybe that was what confused him most.

Several weeks passed, and Tamara noticed—with mixed emotions—that Sam was faxing in his orders instead of delivering them personally. She'd had a brief conversation with Natalie about Sam, only because Natalie was so avidly curious about Tamara's opinion of him after their Friday afternoon meeting.

"You have to admit he's an odd duck," Natalie had persisted when Tamara tried to shrug off the subject. She'd been thinking of Sam an awful lot, but preferred not to disclose that fact to anyone. She was, after all, long past the crush stage, and since Sam had given her absolutely no reason to think he might be interested in her, she didn't want anyone, not even her best friend, thinking *she* could be interested in *him.*

Somehow she had managed to throw Natalie off the scent, and they again settled into their normal routine of chitchatting about everything from Natalie's kids to Tamara's car shopping to world affairs during their lunches together.

Tamara didn't go out for lunch every day, however. Sam wasn't the only field rep she had to deal with, and that was on top of her work with the in-house salespeople, an almost constant connection with the inventory department and the never-ending reports and letters to clients she generated on her computer. Many days Tamara ate lunch at her desk, on occasion skipping it altogether.

She had a nice surprise one morning. Tom Rowland came to her office to discuss the sales evaluation report she had devised. He praised her work so highly that Tamara felt very good about herself—and her progress in the company—for days.

Whatever else was going on, though—however busy she was—Sam Sherard kept lurking in the back of her mind. She might not have impressed him, but he had definitely made a lasting impression on her. It didn't make her happy. On the contrary, thoughts of Sam brought a discomfiting sinking sensation.

Regardless, she couldn't help wondering when Sam would stop by again. It was bound to happen sooner or later, and every morning she got ready for work thinking that this might be the day.

Halloween rolled around. From her desk Tamara gazed out onto the floor through the glass wall of her office. Orange and black decorations were everywhere. Rowland, Inc. encouraged recognition of holidays and always planned some sort of social function for their employees. There was a costume party scheduled for this evening, and it was to be a family affair. Natalie had been working on her children's costumes for weeks and was excited about the party. Tamara had been planning to attend and had put together a Davy Crockett costume.

But this morning she had awakened with a killer head-ache and an upset stomach. She hadn't yet missed a day of work and had forced herself out of bed and into the shower. But sitting here now at her desk, she knew she was going to have to miss the festivities. Her flu symptoms were getting worse; she felt miserable.

Sighing fitfully, she dialed Mr. Grimes's office number. He answered as he usually did on an in-house call. "Yes?"

"Mr. Grimes, this is Tamara. I'm feeling ill and have to go home."

"Ill as in what?" Grimes spoke sharply, as if immediately concerned.

"I'm sure it's just the flu."

"Oh. Well, it's been going around. By all means, go home and take care of yourself. Sorry you won't be here for the party, though."

"Yes, I'm sorry, too. I've been looking forward to it."

All week she had been wondering if Sam would attend, and regardless of feeling like the dregs at the bottom of a barrel, she suffered an almost painful disappointment that she wouldn't be there to find out.

"Stay home for as long as it takes," Mr. Grimes told her.

"Thank you. Goodbye." Tamara hung up, then fell back in her chair. It was an effort to move at all. Every bone in her body ached. She wished there were some magical way to transport herself from this chair to her bed. One thing was certain—she was going to take a taxi home rather than put herself through the ordeal of that long bus ride.

Before she could leave at all, however, she had to clear her desk. Moving in slow motion, she went through the process of turning off her computer. Papers, file folders, pens and pencils were shoved into a drawer. She would sort everything out when she returned, she decided through the sickish fuzz in her brain.

Finally she got her purse and walked out through the maze of desks and cubicles to the exit. She stopped in reception to speak to Natalie. "I'm going home, Nat."

"Girl, you look terrible! What's wrong?" Natalie exclaimed.

"The flu."

Nat's face fell. "You're going to miss the party."

"I know and I feel bad about it." Tamara began edging toward the elevators. "You have a good time, okay?"

"*You* take care of yourself and get well fast."

"I intend to. Bye."

Tamara weakly leaned against a wall of the elevator during the ride down. She followed the corridor leading to the employees' entrance and parking lot to leave the building, rounded a corner in the long hallway and collided with someone.

A pair of strong hands grabbed her shoulders, and she found herself looking directly into Sam Sherard's electric blue eyes. Her heart sank clear to her toes. She'd been hoping so much to see Sam again, but not like this.

"Sorry," he said, then noticed the paleness of her face and eyes, the feverish blotches in her cheeks. "Are you all right?"

She saw not a dram of genuine friendliness on his face, and her spirits dropped another notch. "I'm *perfectly* all right," she said, unable to keep the sarcasm out of her hoarse voice. He hadn't used her name. Was it possible he didn't remember her? Was she *that* forgettable?

Sam heard the sarcasm and internally winced. He'd been faxing his orders in, deliberately delaying another meeting with Tamara. Today he'd had no choice. Several of the orders in his leather case required discussion and some decisions. He'd braced himself to face Tamara again, but literally running into her like this was a shock he hadn't counted on. Apparently she wasn't overly thrilled with it, either.

He released her shoulders and bent over to pick up his case, which he'd dropped in the collision.

Bleary-eyed, Tamara watched him. If she felt better, she'd ask him right out if he remembered her. Make him squirm a little.

But she didn't have the strength for even normal conversation right now, let alone a confrontation. Moving around him, she walked away.

Sam turned and watched her with a frown. What in hell was wrong with her? He hadn't wanted to see her again, but he hadn't expected her to feel the same about him. He walked on toward the elevators.

Outside the building, Tamara managed to hail a taxi. She endured the ride home with her eyes closed, and when she finally stumbled into her apartment, she undressed and crawled into bed.

She fell into a deep, exhausted slumber the second her head hit the pillow.

* * *

When Tamara awoke, her bedroom was silvery with early evening shadows. She stirred and realized that she felt much better. It was enormously relieving to know that the bug she had caught wasn't going to keep her down for long. She would stay home tomorrow to be on the safe side, but considering the improvement she'd made in one afternoon, she should be back to work the day after.

Getting out of bed, she went to the kitchen and drank a tall glass of cranberry juice while heating a can of chicken noodle soup. She had just sat down to eat it when a horrifying thought struck her: Sam hadn't arrived that early for the party! He must have had orders in his leather case. She had missed seeing him!

Groaning, she put her head in her hands. Not only had she missed a second meeting with Sam, she had treated him rudely because he hadn't said her name.

How ridiculous to think he didn't remember her. He wasn't stupid, for Pete's sake. It was possible that her name had slipped his mind in the shock of their collision, but he'd been on his way to deliver orders to her office. Of course he remembered her. Why, oh why, had she contracted the flu today of all days?

The first day that Tamara returned to work, she and Natalie ate lunch together in the employees' lunchroom. "So," Tamara said, "how was the Halloween party?"

Natalie's eyes lit up. "Absolutely wonderful. My kids had a ball, and so did I. I think everyone did. Do you know that every child there was given a prize for some trumped-up reason? The toddlers got stuffed animals, and the older kids got those little hand-held computer games. The food was great and some of the costumes were hilarious. Oh, yes, it was a wonderful party. I'm really sorry you missed it."

Tamara nodded. "So am I. Who attended?" *Was Sam Sherard there?*

"Goodness, so many I couldn't begin to name them.

Besides, there were a lot of masks. Mr. Grimes wore one, and I didn't know who he was until he took it off to eat.''

Tamara wanted so badly to know if Sam had been there that she could hardly contain herself, yet she couldn't bring herself to mention his name. But neither could she drop the subject. There must be a subtle way to approach it.

She sipped her soda. "Were any of the field reps there?'' She'd already learned that Sam had delivered his orders to another assistant that day, but that wasn't what was eating her alive. Had he stayed for the party? Had he relaxed and enjoyed himself? Had he worn a costume?

"Oh, I'm sure there must have been, but picture that huge room with hundreds of witches, goblins, pirates and harem girls milling around. I stayed close to my kids, since I was worried they might get frightened in such a strange crowd.''

The party had been held in the huge convention room on the first floor of the building. Tamara had no trouble at all in envisioning Natalie's description of the event.

"Did they?'' she asked quietly, giving up on the question of Sam Sherard's attendance.

"Not once,'' Natalie said proudly. "They loved every minute of it. And you should have seen their surprise when they were each handed a gift.'' She smiled happily. "The whole evening was a rousing success, I would say.''

"I'm glad,'' Tamara murmured, concealing some very resentful thoughts behind an impassive expression. The flu could not have struck at a worse time. No matter how many people had gathered in the convention room, or how many masks there'd been, if she had been there she would have somehow managed to find Sam and make him talk to her. He probably wouldn't show up again for weeks.

She sighed quietly. It just wasn't meant to be, was it? She might as well accept her fate and forget about Sam Sherard.

"So it's Thanksgiving next, then Christmas,'' Natalie said around the last bite of her salad. "I do love the holiday season. The kids get so excited.'' She laughed. ''Maybe I'm the biggest kid of all.''

''Thanksgiving, yes,'' Tamara murmured, realizing that she wasn't at all thrilled about the upcoming holidays. For one thing, being the newest assistant in the company, she would probably have to work. For another, even if she wasn't called upon to form part of the holiday skeleton crew, she would be alone. Unless she could talk her mother into coming to Dallas for the holiday. *Mom, come for Thanksgiving. We'll have a wonderful day.*

She would worm out of working somehow, and she'd cook a turkey. She and Myra *could* have a wonderful day.

She glanced at her watch. There was twenty minutes remaining of her lunch hour. Standing, she gathered her dishes and stacked them on her tray. ''I'm going to run, Nat. I have a very important letter to write to my mother.''

Chapter Three

Tamara thought nothing unusual about a summons to Elliot Grimes's office, since he often called meetings in his private domain.

To her surprise, when she walked in, Tom Rowland was present. Both men stood, said good morning and smiled warmly. Slightly mystified, she smiled back and said hello.

Mr. Grimes spoke first. "Tamara, Tom has something to tell you. I think you'll be very pleased."

"I wanted to do this myself," Tom Rowland said. "Please sit down, Tamara."

"Thank you," she murmured, taking a chair. The men resumed theirs.

"Tamara, you already know my feelings about the new format you designed for the sales evaluation reports," Tom Rowland said. "Everyone in administration agrees that it's an exceptional piece of work, but more importantly, from the conclusions you incorporated in the report, it's apparent to all of us that in a relatively short span of time you have completely grasped Rowland's sales goals. We've put our heads together, Elliot included, and we would like to advance you to a brand-new position. How does coordinator of sales sound to you?"

"It sounds..." Tamara couldn't find the appropriate word and gave a rather nervous little laugh. They were inventing a new position just for her? This was not at all easy to digest. "I don't think I know *what* to say," she admitted.

The two men looked at each other and smiled. "I can see we've surprised you," Tom said. "Let me explain. No matter how much education some people attain, they will go only so far in their careers because they do not have the talent required to see beyond the duties assigned them. You have that unique, enviable talent, Tamara, and I for one will not have it wasted. Elliot agrees with me. Since he's operated his division with assistants—and they're very important, don't misunderstand—we had to come up with a new position and job title. Coordinator of sales seems appropriate."

"But...what would I be doing?" Tamara's mind was spinning. She felt elation, although it was nearly smothered by confusion. Was it possible that she was being groomed to take Mr. Grimes's place when he retired?

Elliot intervened. "Tamara, you have an insight into this division of the business that Tom and I find remarkable, and we want to give you the time to develop that perceptiveness to its full capacity. We want you sticking your nose into every nook and cranny of the entire sales department, taking a look at what everyone else is doing and finding out if there's room for improvement."

Tamara gulped. "I...see."

Tom Rowland eyed her keenly. "Think you can handle it?"

Tamara sat up straighter. She hadn't exactly been projecting confidence in herself, had she? She was tingling with excitement, but kept her expression cool and businesslike.

"Yes, sir," she said firmly. "I can handle it."

Tom nodded. "I'm sure of it. Now for the logistics of it all. We're going to relieve you of some of your current responsibilities so you may put some time in on planning. Elliot will be available for conferences, of course. One duty we are going to delegate to other assistants is dealing with the field reps."

Tamara felt a pang of disappointment. She would not be seeing Sam in the office again; he would be delivering his orders to someone else. But then, did it matter? He hardly knew she was alive, and she had no reason to think that would change.

Tom was still talking, and she shoved Sam Sherard from her thoughts to listen. "We're going to have to hire someone for your present position, which will take some time. Elliot and I are going to strive to have everything in order by the first of the new year. Your promotion will be announced at that time. Of course, you will receive a sizable increase in salary." He looked at her intently. "Do you have any questions?"

Tamara was certain a hundred questions would arise once her mind cleared, but right at the moment she felt in a daze. "No, sir, but if something occurs to me later on, I'm sure Mr. Grimes will help me out."

"You may count on it," Elliot Grimes said. He stood. "Well, I think that concludes our business for today."

Tom Rowland rose, also. "I would appreciate your not mentioning this to anyone yet, Tamara."

She, too, got up. "*You* may count on that. Good day, gentlemen." She walked out of Elliot Grimes's office feeling ten feet tall. What a coup! Had it really happened or was she dreaming?

By Friday Tamara was able to think of her promotion with a modicum of composure. Difficult as it was, she kept her promise to say nothing about it, but she found herself smiling at the oddest moments. She was glad this weekend was free for her, as she wanted to do something to celebrate. With a "sizable" raise in salary on the horizon, she might even check out *new* cars.

Late that afternoon she swiveled her chair around to look through the window on her outer wall. Her eyes widened when she saw rain coursing down the glass. Getting up, she went to the window, looked up at the sky and realized this wasn't merely a shower. Heavy, dark clouds hung over the city, appearing firmly entrenched.

She'd been so involved in her work the weather was the last thing that might have penetrated her concentration. How long had it been raining? How long would it last? She had a two-block walk to the bus stop, and getting drenched wasn't a particularly appealing prospect.

Well, she thought logically, she had already planned to stay past closing, and maybe the storm would have passed by then. She returned to her desk and took up where she had left off. Every three months the firm sent out updated catalogs to clients, and form letters were a definite no-no. Although similar in content, each letter accompanying a catalog had to contain something personal, a message that Rowland, Inc. was aware of each customer's special requirements.

How could she improve on *that* sensible policy? Tamara asked herself as she started another letter. She bit her lip for a moment, worried suddenly that she would not be able to live up to Tom Rowland's and Elliot Grimes's expectations of her "enviable" talent.

But no one advanced in any endeavor without taking risks. Her new job would be her first real challenge in the business world. There was room for improvement in any routine chore—these letters, for instance—and she would find it.

"I can do it, and I will," she whispered ardently, and looked though the client list for the history of the company she was now addressing so she could come up with that "personal" message.

She was aware when five o'clock came around and people began leaving, but she had only a handful of letters left to write and she kept working. At 6:15 she turned off her computer, stood up and stretched. Through the glass wall she could see just a few people still at their desks. The place was all but deserted, but she had worked past closing many times and leaving late didn't bother her. What did bother her was the rain; if anything, it was coming down harder than before.

"Oh, well," she said. Maybe she would look for a taxi, or call one from downstairs rather than brave the rainfall to the bus stop. She wished she had an umbrella.

After clearing her desk, she gathered her purse, turned off all but one of the lights in her office and left. She rode an empty elevator down to the first floor, then followed the corridor to the employees' entrance.

"Oh, damn," she said under her breath when she reached the heavy glass door. It wasn't just raining, it was pouring. Taxi or bus? Oh, goodness, did she have enough cash in her purse for a taxi? Quickly she dug through her handbag and found eight dollars and change. The taxi ride to her apartment complex the day she'd been ill had cost twenty-two dollars plus tip. So much for that idea, she thought grimly. Well, so be it. She checked her watch: 6:25. The next bus came through at seven. She would wait here until 6:55, then make a run for it.

Watching the rain pelting the asphalt parking lot, which contained about a dozen vehicles widely spaced among numerous puddles, she leaned against the wall, thinking that if it rained all weekend she wouldn't be doing much of anything, especially not car shopping. She heaved a disappointed sigh. Since the meeting with Tom Rowland she had been keyed up and looking forward to a celebratory weekend, even if all she did was some more sightseeing. The Dallas-Fort Worth area was rich with museums, parks and art galleries. She had visited many, some of which she planned to show her mother should Myra accept her Thanksgiving invitation.

Sighing again, feeling a sense of poignancy because she really had no one with which to celebrate her promotion, she became vaguely aware of distant footsteps. Someone else was leaving late, undoubtedly the owner of one of those remaining vehicles in the parking lot. Darn it, she *had* to find a car to buy. She had ridden the bus long enough. Rain or no rain, she was going car shopping tomorrow!

The footsteps grew louder and more distinct, approaching the corner in the corridor where she and Sam Sherard had collided the day she'd gone home with the flu. She hadn't seen Sam since and had more or less relegated him to the lost-cause bin. He might have come in with orders, but now that she wasn't seeing field reps there was little chance of her even knowing about his visits. It was really quite strange how progress in her career had affected her personal life, she mused with a dull ache in her chest. If one could call an attraction for a man who didn't reciprocate a personal life, that is. But Sam was the only man she'd met in Dallas who had piqued her interest, and while she was still thrilled with her promotion, her feminine side couldn't help wishing things had happened differently.

The person treading the corridor came around the bend, and Tamara glanced over her shoulder to see who it was. Her curiosity was casual, of no real import, so when she saw Sam striding toward her, her swift shift in mood felt like a shock. Her pulse was suddenly fluttering and her mouth went dry. She pushed away from the wall to stand under her own power and braced herself to speak to him.

Sam saw Tamara waiting near the door and felt himself become tense. He'd gone through a disturbing array of emotions when told she would no longer service his orders, but then had decided it was for the best. He had not expected to run into her like this, and realized that the tension in his body was not due to annoyance but to the fact that she was suddenly in sight.

He stopped a few feet from her. "Hello."

"Hello, Sam." How she could sound normal when her entire body felt tight as a drum was beyond her understanding. My Lord, he was handsome! Tamara's pulse was racing double time.

He glanced through the glass door. "It's really coming down."

"Pouring," Tamara agreed.

He turned back to her and narrowed his eyes slightly. Pretty. More than pretty, beautiful. Hair like sunshine and eyes the color of a turbulent sea. A small, straight nose. A sensually full bottom lip.

He directed his thoughts away from her looks. "You must be hoping it will slow down so you can get to your car."

"I don't have a car."

"Then you must be waiting for someone to pick you up."

"No, I ride the bus."

"Why?" he asked bluntly. "Don't you drive?"

She smiled. "I drive, but I haven't yet bought a car. I've been looking for one, rather sporadically, I admit, but looking nonetheless. I'll find something I like soon, I hope." He still hadn't used her name, and she still didn't know if he recognized her.

Sam frowned suddenly. "The day of our collision...you weren't feeling well, were you?"

Tamara's eyes lit up. He *did* know who she was! "The flu. It was only a twenty-four-hour bug, nothing serious."

"How did you get home that day?" Sam asked. If he'd known she used public transportation, he would have offered her a ride, same as he would have done for anyone who was feeling under the weather and had to ride a damned bus to get home.

"By taxi, which, of course, I can't do everyday. Why?"

"Just wondering." His eyes drifted left, to the storm outside. "You're waiting in here for your bus?"

"Yes." Sam actually talking to her was so thrilling she didn't care what subject they discussed, even one as mundane as this. She was subtly taking in every inch of Sam— the way his blue shirt and jeans fit his sinewy body, the expensive-looking boots on his feet, his black hat with its cockily rolled brim, even the size and proportion of his hands.

Sam was again looking outside at the rain. He wanted to get going. He hadn't been to the ranch in three weeks, and he was planning to spend the weekend there. He was anxious to be on his way.

But Tamara was tweaking his conscience. He'd never had reason to rely on public transportation in Dallas and knew nothing about bus schedules. Did she wait in this hallway two hours every afternoon for her bus? He couldn't imagine being without a car, but supposed it was harder for a woman to buy one than it was for a man.

Hey, that's none of your affair. Say goodbye and leave. Sam cleared his throat and turned his gaze on Tamara. "I've got to go."

"Yes, it's getting late. Dark as well." An explosive clap of thunder and a brilliant flash of lightning made Tamara jump. "Oh, no," she groaned. "Not that, too." Maybe she could borrow twenty dollars from Sam and call a taxi. It was a sensible idea, but she couldn't get the words out of her mouth. Why had she let herself get so low on cash? Hiking to the closest ATM machine would be as bad as walking to the bus stop. Obviously she was destined to get drenched this evening and she may as well accept it.

Her nervous reaction to the thunder and lightning made Sam frown. She *was* a member of the fairer sex, after all, so how could he leave her standing there to jump a foot every time lightning bolted from the clouds? "How far is it to your bus stop?"

"Two blocks."

"I'll give you a lift."

"You will?" She couldn't conceal her surprise. He *could* be nice! Why on earth did he walk around with that stony face and give everyone such a false impression? "I'll take you up on that offer," she said quickly. "Thank you."

"If you'd like to wait here, I'll get my rig and pick you up. You won't get so wet that way."

Why should he get soaked and she stay dry? His consideration was so startling that Tamara said the first thing that popped into her mind. "Let's just make a run for it. Which vehicle is yours?"

Sam frowned, then shrugged. If *she* didn't care if she got wet, why should he? He pointed to the parking lot. "That tan Jeep is mine. It isn't locked, so go directly to the passenger door and get in. Ready?"

"Yes."

Sam pushed the glass door open and rain immediately blew in. They didn't tarry a moment before dashing out into the storm. Splashing through puddles, Tamara ran for the Jeep. It wasn't close to the building, indicating that Sam had arrived before closing time and had taken the first available space he could find. Tamara could feel the rain soaking her cotton-and-linen-blend taupe suit and the hosiery on her legs. Her taupe fabric pumps might withstand getting wet, but she had some doubts about that. The wind loosened the combs holding her hair in place, and one of them went flying. She didn't stop to look for it. Squinting against the driving rain, she finally grabbed the door handle of the Jeep, yanked it open and climbed in. *You dunce,* she thought in total self-disgust. *He offered to pick you up at the door. What's wrong with you? Now you look like a drowned rat, and you didn't have to. He probably thinks you're a half-wit.*

Sam got in, slammed the door and muttered, "It's a gully washer." Another lightning bolt and an earsplitting clap of thunder drowned out his comment, and he saw

Tamara flinch again. She was dabbing at the water on her face with a tissue she must have had in her purse. Her clothes were blotched and sticking to her skin. Her prim hairdo was gone; her hair was dripping, and he almost said she should wear it down like this. Not wet, of course, but the way it was framing her pretty face right now was so much more becoming than it had been before.

His own clothes were as wet and sticky as Tamara's, but he ignored his discomfort and sat there admiring his passenger. When he realized what he was doing, he faced front, feeling disgruntled, and started the engine.

"Tell me how to get to your bus stop," he said rather gruffly.

"Make a right at the street and drive two blocks." The tissue was soaked, and it was the only one she had. Rolling it into a soggy ball, Tamara held it in her hand. She closed her eyes, condemned herself again for getting so wet when she could have avoided it, and then shuddered when lightning lit up the sky again.

Sam put the vehicle in Drive and got it moving toward the street. "Are you afraid of electrical storms?"

"I'm certainly not fond of them."

"This is a bad one, all right. It won't last long, though."

"From what I can see of that sky, it doesn't look to me like it's going to suddenly turn sunny."

"No, but it's getting late. The storm will pass soon, Tamara, believe me."

He had finally said her name. Regardless of the unnecessary misery of sitting in wet clothes, a tingling excitement went up her spine.

They had reached the street. Sam took off his hat and tossed it into the back seat before taking that right turn. The windshield wipers were on high, but sheets of wind-driven rain kept visibility at a minimum. He switched on the headlights, then cautiously drove into traffic. He started thinking of that long trip to the ranch in this kind of storm and decided it might be wiser to get a motel for the night and drive up in the morning.

"There's my bus stop," Tamara said. "You can let me out here."

Sam pulled over to the curb. The bus stop was an uncovered bench. Good Lord. "How long till your bus comes along?" he asked tensely. He didn't want to dawdle in the city one minute more, but how could he let her off to sit on that damned bench in this rain, and just drive away?

Tamara checked her watch. "About fifteen minutes. If it's running on time." She lifted her gaze from her wrist to him. "Thanks for the lift."

He snorted derisively. "Lot of good it did. You'd have been better off waiting in the building than on that bench."

"Sam, I appreciate the ride. Really, I do."

Sam didn't feel like smiling himself, but he stared at her and felt a familiar stirring in his groin. This was what he'd been leery of from their first meeting—feeling desire for her even while knowing that intimacy between them would be a mistake.

"Where do you live?" he asked abruptly. "I'll drive you home." Hell, what was another half hour or so? He was probably going to stay in a motel tonight, anyhow.

Tamara blinked in surprise. "It's about ten miles from here. Are you sure? I mean, I really don't want to put you out. You've already been more than generous with your time, and—"

He bluntly interrupted. "What's your address?"

For goodness sake, he sounds angry, Tamara thought in alarm. Had she said something to offend him? In the next heartbeat a gleeful understanding hit her: he *wanted* to drive her home and she, out of consideration for his time, had argued against it.

Well, there would be no more of that. "Stay on this street until you come to..." Tamara recited directions to her address. "I live in the Sunset Apartments complex, number 212," she finished.

Sam nodded, checked traffic and pulled away from the curb. Tamara was so thrilled with this turn of events, she knew she must be glowing. Had Sam noticed? The question made her smile. In her present damp and disheveled state, an inner glow couldn't possibly be outwardly visible.

She wanted to say something so witty that Sam would laugh, then start to talk. She would ease into conversation, of course. She certainly wasn't going to start throwing jokes at him. "This is awfully nice of you," she said in a pleasantly inviting way.

"Thanks," he mumbled, more aware of the way she flinched at every flash of lightning than of anything she might say. In fact, he was *completely* aware of Tamara, and would be if she didn't speak at all. It was all physical with him, though. He had no wish to learn about her background, likes, dislikes, family or job. The two of them were together purely by accident, and he fully intended to keep things casual and impersonal.

Hmm, Tamara thought. Sam's "thanks" had obviously been the end of that subject. But she was far from giving up on him. Racking her brain for a topic of conversation that he had to respond to with more than a one-word reply, she murmured, "Traffic is lighter than usual."

Sam said, "Yeah."

"The storm, I suppose."

"Right."

Next she stated, "You were at the office late."

"I'd like to know something," he said, surprising her. "Did you ask that I be transferred to another assistant?" The question had arisen the second he'd been told to report to a different assistant, but he certainly had never expected to put it to Tamara.

She was so startled that she couldn't immediately come up with an answer. All she could think of was that she had given Mr. Rowland her word not to tell anyone in the company about her promotion.

"Uh…n-no," she stammered. "It was…Mr. Grimes's

idea. I don't deal with any of the field reps, uh, these days.''

Sam thought a moment. ''I wonder if that's a demotion or a promotion?'' he said. ''Either you're on your way up in the company or moving down. In your case I would have to say you're moving up.''

She turned her head to look at him. ''You're…very perceptive.''

Sam felt like biting off his own damned tongue. He'd decided that it was in his best interests to keep this ten-mile drive impersonal, and then he had started questioning her. What in hell was wrong with him?

Even though she couldn't talk about her job, she felt it was safe enough to talk about his. ''How long have you worked for Rowland?''

''Ten years,'' he said flatly.

''Really. Then you must like your job.''

''It's okay.''

''Have you always worked in sales? Even before Rowland, I mean?''

''Nope.''

She wasn't getting very far with conversation, was she? Sighing quietly, she studied Sam out of the corner of her eye. He was the most handsome man she'd ever seen, let alone met, but wasn't he also one of the strangest? Should she have some qualms about being alone with him? She didn't, she realized. What she did have were some very personal thoughts about Sam Sherard. And feelings that she recognized as physical attraction, a very *strong* physical attraction. Right now she'd like nothing better than to smooth that lock of wet hair from his forehead.

Recalling that she'd had the same idea the first time they'd met, she clutched her purse on her lap with both hands and told herself to cool down. He was giving her a ride home and that would undoubtedly be the end of it. He might say hello the next time they ran into each other or he might not. She simply could not read Sam as she could most people. Without question Natalie had him pegged—Sam marched to a different drummer.

Tamara wished she didn't look like the wrath of God, and remembered again, disgustedly, that it was her own fault. Regardless, she knew that given the opportunity, she could make him look at her again. Not at the office, of course, but if she could get him to ask her out for dinner, for instance, he would be mighty surprised by her appearance.

After miles of silence, Sam pulled into the Sunset Apartments' parking lot. "Which way to 212?" he asked.

"Go left and make a right turn at the first cross street."

Sam hated apartments, but had to admit this complex was darned impressive. Well-tended lawns, fall flowers, trees and shrubs were everywhere. The buildings were a creamy, smoothly textured stucco with red tiled roofs. It looked to him as though each unit had a garage and maybe a walled-in back patio. Tamara was paying a pretty penny to live here, he would bet. He braked to a stop in front of number 212.

Tamara smiled and looked at him. "Well, thank you very much. You saved me from a thorough soaking."

"Not entirely." Sam took his hands from the wheel and turned slightly toward her. "But you're welcome."

There was something in his eyes that caused her heart to skip a beat. He wasn't nearly as impervious to her as she'd been thinking. Her courage rebounded. "Would you like to come in? I could make a pot of coffee and you could dry off."

He looked at her until her cheeks got pink, then nodded. "A cup of hot coffee? How could I refuse?" He *should* refuse; dammit, he knew he should. There was a terrible battle going on inside him. He was so attracted to this beautiful woman that he wasn't thinking straight, and yet he had enough common sense to put up a fight.

"Great!" Tamara exclaimed. "Oh, no one can park on

the streets in this complex. I'll go inside and open my garage door. You can park in there.''

Irritated with himself, Sam merely nodded. He could park in her driveway, but if she wanted his vehicle in her garage, so be it. She probably had her reasons.

"See you in a few," Tamara sang out as she opened her door. An enormous flash of lightning illuminated the sky, followed immediately by a roll of thunder. Tamara wanted to crawl over to Sam and bury her face in his shirt. Shuddering, she forced herself out of the Jeep. The wind tore at her clothes and the rain was instantly beating against her face, saturating her hair and clothing. Giving the door of the Jeep a push to close it, she dashed up the walk, unlocked her front door and went in.

Dropping her purse on a table, she hurried to the bathroom, grabbed a towel and then continued on to the garage, wiping her face as she went. Pushing the button to open the garage door, she watched it go up.

And that was when it really struck her—Sam Sherard was coming into her apartment for coffee!

How very incredible.

Chapter Four

When Sam was finally standing in Tamara's living room, she called, "Make yourself at home. I'm going to put on the coffee."

She went around a corner—into the kitchen, Sam presumed. He stood where he was and frowned at the white sofa and pale beige chairs. His jeans were too damp to sit on such pristine furniture. The entire room was done in pale colors, except for some green plants, throw pillows and a couple of multihued paintings on the walls. On a small round table with skinny little legs resided prettily arranged pictures in white ceramic frames. Sam took a peek at the photos and decided he was looking at Tamara's family.

Well, he thought, the color scheme in here was easy on the eye, but it sure as hell wasn't a man's room. He remained on his feet.

Tamara came sweeping in, saw that he had barely moved from where she'd left him and flushed at her thoughtlessness. "I'm sorry," she said. "I'll get something to lay over a chair. Be right back." She dashed away to get her one extra blanket, and returned a minute later with the blanket and a better idea. "Sam, I'm going to have to dry off, and you should, too. Why don't you get out of those wet clothes, use this blanket for a cover-up and put your things in the dryer? It shouldn't take more than ten, fifteen minutes to dry them, and I'll do something with myself in the meantime. We'll both feel much more comfortable." Besides, if getting soaked and chilled made one a candidate for a cold or the flu, neither of them should take the chance.

He thought a moment, then nodded. "Where's the dryer?"

"Come on, I'll show you."

He followed her into the kitchen to a folding door, which she drew back to expose the washer and dryer. "I'll set it for you and all you'll have to do is push in that one button." Tamara fiddled with the dials. "There, it's ready. Just toss in your clothes and push the button. I'll leave you now."

As soon as he was alone, Sam sat on a kitchen chair and yanked off his boots. They'd gotten wet before and he knew no real damage had been done to them. He peeled off his socks, then stood up and undressed. Placing his wallet, his belt and the loose change in his pockets on the table, he carried his damp clothing to the dryer, shoved them into the machine and pushed the button.

As Sam wound the blanket around himself, the whole thing suddenly struck him as funny. Here he was, stark naked except for a blanket in a woman's apartment, a woman he hardly knew. It *was* funny.

But wasn't it also a little dangerous? His urge to laugh died a sudden death. For some reason he could not put Tamara in the "willing woman" category, that place where every other female he'd known and bedded resided as a vague, shadowy figure, and it worried him.

His lips thinned. He should have dropped her off and made a quick getaway. One cup of coffee, then he'd go. Just one, he told himself.

Tamara had fully intended on a quick cleanup for herself, but one thing kept leading to another—a shower to a shampoo, then makeup and one of the prettiest casual things she could find in her closet, an ivory-colored, pleated caftan that left one shoulder and arm bare.

"Yipes," she whispered when examining herself in the mirror. If *this* didn't knock Sam's socks off, nothing she could do to herself would. Her hair was down, curling around her face, and the unusual caftan was absolutely stunning.

Her heart fluttered. Exactly what kind of message was she attempting to communicate to Sam? Was she falling for him? Did she want *him* falling for her?

Oh, he did make her feel…alive! And very female. Why wouldn't she be sending him messages? She was in this lovely, romantic mood because of Sam, and it felt wonderful having him under her roof. They would eat and talk, and maybe, just maybe, before he left he would ask her for a date. For another evening, of course. Tonight was already in motion, so they would spend it getting to know each other.

She frowned suddenly. *Stop planning, worrying and analyzing every little thing. Wondering if you're falling for Sam, or if he's developing feelings for you, is childishly premature. Relax and go with the flow.* Deciding that was very good advice, she slipped her bare feet into a pair of ivory sandals and left her bedroom.

Sam literally gulped when she walked into the living room. She wasn't just pretty anymore, she was gorgeous. A temptress in that dress or gown or whatever it was, with her hair a froth of curls, expertly applied makeup and a scent that immediately assailed his senses. *She wants a lot more from you than drinking coffee together.* More uncomfortable than he could ever remember being in a woman's company, he got to his feet to acknowledge her entrance.

She smiled at his courtesy. He was fully dressed and so handsome she felt breathless. "All dried out?" she asked.

"We both are, it seems." Sam's mouth felt as dry as his clothing. She looked sinfully sexy and it was difficult to think of anything else.

"Yes," she agreed. "Didn't you help yourself to the coffee?" She could tell he liked how she looked. It was in his eyes, in the very air they were breathing. In truth, there was so much electricity in the room she marveled that her hair didn't crackle.

"I waited for you," Sam replied, trying very hard to speak casually. Actually he felt almost choked from sexual excitement, and his voice came out low and husky.

It slithered into Tamara's system, wriggled under her skin and penetrated clear to the core of her womanhood. Her knees were suddenly weak, and she strove for composure. She cleared her throat—daintily, she hoped. "I think we should have more than coffee. I'm hungry and so must you be." She didn't have the ingredients to prepare a first-class meal, but soup and sandwiches were better than nothing.

Sam knew when a woman was coming on to him; Tamara's efforts were obvious. But he wasn't thinking as clearly as he had in the kitchen a short time ago, and he heard himself saying, "Yes, I'm hungry."

Tamara read much more into Sam's words than he'd intended to convey. But instead of blushing or playing it coy in response, she acted as though she hadn't noticed the sexual nuance underlying his very ordinary words.

"How about some hot soup and a ham sandwich?" she said.

"Sounds good," he replied.

She couldn't help smiling, simply because he was here, in her apartment, and they were going to eat together. She blinked in surprise when he smiled back at her, and thought happily, *He's as human as I am, so why is he so unfriendly with people in the sales department that they call him Stoneface behind his back?*

Tamara could only conclude that he was rarely as friendly as he was this evening, which said something positive about her, in her estimation. That idea pleased her immensely.

But then another possibility wormed its way into her thoughts. His friendliness this evening could be a business-versus-pleasure thing. It could be that away from the job he let down his guard and became the man he really was. If that was the case, great. Whatever, she was thrilled with the way the evening was progressing. It was still raining, but, as Sam had predicted, the violence of the storm had diminished. The apartment was cozy and comfy, she had an exciting guest and Tamara's spirits were running high.

"Why don't I get you a cup of coffee and you can sit in here while I fix us something to eat?" she said.

"Why don't I have my coffee in the kitchen and keep you company?" he returned. Sam had finally decided to play her game. Any man who turned down a woman like Tamara would have to have rocks for brains. He wasn't sure just how far she would go, but it sure would be interesting to find out.

Sam's suggestion was unnerving. Tamara had been thinking of hurrying through the simple supper preparations, and now he'd be watching her every move.

But what else could she say except, "If that's what you prefer, fine."

Watching her in that slithery thingamajig she had on was *exactly* what Sam preferred. It wasn't tight fitting, not a bit. But the way those little pleats flowed over her figure when she moved just might be fatal to a man with a weak heart. Sam's heart was strong and healthy, as was every other part of his very masculine body.

They went into the kitchen. Tamara poured a cup of

coffee and set it on the table. Sam sat down to drink it. "Sugar or milk?" she asked.

"I like it black," Sam replied.

Tamara began taking out canned soup, ham, bread and condiments from the refrigerator and cabinets, placing them on the counter. She was fully aware of Sam's eyes following her every movement, and she was doing her level best not to let it fluster her. It wasn't easy.

"Let me know if you want some help," Sam said.

She sent him a smile over her shoulder. "Thanks, but I can handle it. Everyone knows his or her own kitchen best, don't you agree?" She turned back to the counter. "You must have a kitchen somewhere, don't you?"

He was silent a moment, then said, "You don't know much about me, do you?"

"All I know is what's in your personnel and production files."

Amusement entered his voice. "Do you usually accept rides from strangers, then invite them in for coffee?"

She slowly turned to face him. "Do you consider yourself a stranger, Sam? I don't. We work for the same company. We've seen each other before, and…" Her voice trailed off as his tongue-in-cheek expression registered. "You're teasing me, aren't you?"

His gaze held hers. "Am I?"

She gave her hair a sassy flip, but his teasing thrilled her as nothing else could have at this point of their burgeoning relationship. "Drink your coffee," she said pertly, turning back to the food on the counter. The soft laughter behind her made her feel as though someone had just given her a gift. Her responsive smile was one of total happiness, complete abandonment.

Any awkwardness she'd previously felt over his staring at her vanished. Moving around her kitchen, she quickly put the meal together and set the table. She could feel the attraction between them growing by leaps and bounds, and she reveled in the sensation.

Finally everything was ready. She sat down and smiled at Sam. "It isn't gourmet fare, but we won't go to bed hungry."

His response was a full-blown smile, which made him so stunningly gorgeous Tamara nearly choked...and she hadn't even put a bite in her mouth yet. She knew if she'd been standing her legs would have grown limp. As it was, her whole body suddenly felt weak. A smile like Sam's should be outlawed.

But no, definitely not. That drop-dead smile just might be his best feature, and if anything, he should flash it more often.

She picked up her spoon, indicating they should begin eating. Sam followed her lead, and after a few minutes she noticed that he seemed to be enjoying his food. She liked that he could do that with a virtual stranger, but then she tried to recall if she'd ever known a man who couldn't eat because he was nervous about being with her on a first date.

Never, she thought emphatically. It was *her* stomach churning, not Sam's, *her* throat attempting to close off and refuse food because the man at her table excited her so.

She made a small throat-clearing sound. "You didn't say whether or not you had a kitchen," she said.

He looked at her peculiarly. "Pardon?"

"I guess what I'm really asking about is your home."

He snorted. "It's not an apartment, that's for sure."

"Oh? You don't like apartments?"

"Rabbit warrens. Not to insult your preferences, you understand, but for myself I can't stand being cooped up."

"I'm not the least insulted. To each his own, Sam. I happen to like apartments and believe they're sensible for a single woman. We have good security in this complex at night, and a lot of rules that keep things on the straight and narrow. No wild parties, only so many guests per unit for any event—"

"You have *got* to be kidding," Sam said.

"About what?"

"Are you saying if you wanted to invite—what's the permitted number of guests you can have?"

"Ten."

"So, if you wanted to invite eleven or twelve friends over, you couldn't do it?"

"That rule is for the benefit of one's neighbors, Sam. The complex has a beautiful clubhouse, and large dinner parties, for instance, can be held there."

Sam shook his head in disgust. "I hate the whole damned concept. I'd go crazy in a place like this."

"In that case you must live in a house."

"With lots of space and land around it," he confirmed.

Tamara smiled. "You know, I could have predicted that about you."

"You could have, huh? You admitted a few minutes ago that you didn't know much about me."

"I don't, but you have the aura of a country man." She smiled again. "Where's your house, Sam?" A rural address was so vague, especially to a newcomer to the area.

"You wouldn't know the place. Just believe it's not in Dallas or any other big city."

"You don't like cities, either?"

"Do you?"

"I've never lived anywhere *but* a city. My hometown isn't a large city, but it's a lot more city than country."

"And your hometown is where?"

"Coeur d'Alene, Idaho. Have you heard of it?"

"Can't say that I have. So, you were born and raised in Idaho."

"In the panhandle, which comprises northern Idaho. And I was raised there, but I was born in Colorado." Tamara stopped to frown. It didn't happen often, but every once in a while she thought of her birthplace and got a very odd feeling. Her family had always lived in Coeur d'Alene; her two older sisters had been born there. She had asked her mother why *she'd* been born in Colorado and had heard the strangest story.

Tamara, your father and I had a falling out. I'm not going to tarnish his memory by explaining what caused it, but I left him and went to Colorado. I was only there a short time when I discovered I was pregnant. I had a lot to sort out and didn't tell anyone, not even your father. Over the next eight months we gradually solved our problems—mostly through phone conversations. I finally told your father about my condition when I was five months along. He was delighted to have another child and wanted me to come home immediately. But I had to be sure everything was all right between us, and I stayed in Colorado until you were two months old.

Something about that story didn't ring true for Tamara. For one thing, even though she had only been eight years old when her father died, she could not remember one cross word ever passing between her parents. For another, while Blythe had been in college at the time, Sierra had been just nine. Tamara could not see her mother leaving her nine-year-old daughter for a year, no matter how furious she might have been with her husband. No one would ever convince Tamara that there wasn't more to the whole thing then Myra claimed, but though she'd initiated the subject several different times through the years, her mother had not deviated in her explanation, even slightly.

Tamara had her birth certificate, of course, and it cited Colorado as her birthplace and Myra and Harry Benning as her parents. What choice did she have but to believe everything her mother said was true? No matter, she always got that odd, almost suspicious feeling whenever it came to mind. It was something she would like to discuss with her sisters someday. *Haven't you ever had the feeling there's something Mother can't talk about?* She just couldn't help thinking there were secrets in the Benning family, or at least one secret, and she suspected it had something to do with Myra's year in Colorado.

Sam noticed Tamara's introspection and went on eating without interrupting her thoughts, though he kept watching her. Damn, she was pretty, and she must have a thing for him or he wouldn't be in her apartment, sitting at her table. But what precisely were her expectations for this rainy evening?

He knew what his were now—how could he not when his blood was doing a slow boil? Tamara just might be the best-looking woman he'd had the honor of meeting, but equally as important as good looks to him, she was a grown-up, a mature woman despite her age, which he estimated to be no more than twenty-five, perhaps even younger. She'd proved her adulthood by dressing like a siren and acting like a lady. Obviously she was highly intelligent along with having a good education. Bottom line: she'd known what she was doing when inviting him in.

Tamara suddenly realized that she'd been lost in the past and gave her head a small shake to clear it. "Goodness, I seem to have drifted off. Where were we? Oh, yes, we were talking about my hometown. Where's yours?"

"I was born in Laredo."

"So you're Texas born and bred." A teasing twinkle entered her eyes. "I could tell by your accent."

"*I* don't have an accent, you do."

"Mr. Sherard, your drawl is thick enough to cut with a knife," she retorted.

The soup and sandwiches had been consumed. Tamara got up for the coffeepot and brought it and a plate of cookies to the table. "They're fat free," she explained while refilling their cups.

Sam made a face. "Fat free?"

"They're good. Try them." She resumed her place at the table. "The ham was low fat and it was good, wasn't it?"

"The sandwiches were good, yes."

"Don't you watch your fat intake?" He had to, she

thought. Either that or he was one of those enviable, naturally lean people. Lean but muscular. But even lean people could develop a cholesterol problem. He should be made aware of that.

However, she wasn't going to start preaching good health practices. Not tonight, for heaven's sake. She wanted to know about his thoughts, his life-style, what he did for fun. She wanted to know *him!*

"So you grew up in Laredo," she said after a sip of coffee.

"I didn't say that."

"No, I guess you didn't. Where did you grow up?"

Sam's lips thinned. He was *not* going to talk about his family or his abominable childhood. Hell, he barely let himself remember it, so he certainly wasn't going to discuss it with Tamara Benning.

"Texas, mostly," he said flatly, with a cold expression on his face that said the subject was closed.

A sense of panic seized Tamara. She had annoyed him with her questions and he was going to leave! A discomfiting picture flashed through her mind—Sam walking out the door and herself alone for the remainder of this rainy evening.

Hastily she pushed her chair back and got up. "I have some very good brandy. Let's have coffee and brandy in the living room."

Sam almost said he didn't drink, but changed his mind. He did have a drink once in a while, not for himself and never alone, but there were times when a situation called for a relaxation of his attitude toward alcohol. This was one of them. Tamara was obviously prolonging the evening by offering coffee and brandy. He would play along.

"Sure, thanks," he said, rising from his chair. "Dishes first?"

"Pardon? Oh, the dishes. No, I'll clean up later." She picked up the plate of ham and put it in the refrigerator, then went to a cabinet for a small bottle of brandy. Sam watched as she poured coffee and a splash of brandy into their cups. She picked up her cup and he followed suit. They left the kitchen and entered the living room.

"Sit anywhere," Tamara said. She sank onto the sofa. Sam chose one of the pale beige chairs. "It's still raining," she murmured after a sip of her drink.

"The storm's passing, though," Sam replied. He took a swallow of his own drink, which tasted more of coffee than of brandy. She'd gone light on the liquor, which told him she wasn't much of a drinker, either—definitely a point in her favor. He looked at her and thought what a lovely woman she really was. Friendly, beautiful, independent and bright. And sexy, he added to that complimentary list. Very, very sexy.

On top of all those positive attributes, she was attracted to him. It wasn't something he had to question, not when he could sense her feelings so well. He'd always found it easy to tell when a woman found him attractive, and it was especially obvious with Tamara. Her warm smiles and sensuous demeanor were a dead giveaway. He wondered in an offhand way how she would react if he told her he had to be going.

But he'd definitely changed his mind about leaving at the first possible opportunity, and smiled at her to prove it, if only to himself. "So, Miss Tamara Benning, what brought you to Dallas and Rowland, Inc.?" he asked.

Her smile was cute and slightly teasing. "Rowland, Inc. brought me to Dallas."

"Oh, you came here specifically to work for Rowland."

"Precisely."

"Do you like Texas?"

Tamara hesitated before answering. "To tell you the truth, I don't know. I like Dallas and I certainly like my job. But other than the Dallas-Fort Worth area, I haven't seen much of the state."

Sam nodded. "It's a mighty big state."

He saw that her eyes had taken on a dreamy cast, maybe

because of the brandy, maybe because of him. He narrowed his own eyes slightly. Was she really taken with *him,* or was this standard operating procedure for Tamara? Envisioning her smiling and flirting with a parade of other men was a surprisingly discomfiting image, and he shied away from it.

"You hold quite a position at Rowland for someone your age," he said.

The urge to tell him about her promotion was so strong that Tamara could hardly contain it. "It's a good job," she said instead. Setting her cup on a coaster on the end table, she got up. "How about some music? What do you like?"

"I'm easy. You choose." Sam watched her select a CD and insert it in the player. He took in a quiet breath, although he really needed a huge gulp of air. Was it possible she wanted him to do nothing more than sit in this chair, listen to music and talk? If so, why hadn't she just thrown on a pair of jeans and a sweatshirt? No, he thought, answering his own questions. She wanted the same thing he did. God knew he hadn't driven her home in search of opportunity, but when it stared a man in the face, how could he help reacting?

With pleasant background music wafting from the CD player, Tamara returned to sit on the sofa and smile at him. "This is nice," she said.

"It could be nicer," he said softly.

Tamara's heart missed a beat. "Could it?"

Sam set his cup on the small table next to his chair and moved to sit beside her on the sofa. He laid his arm on the back of the sofa behind her head and purposely let his thigh press into hers. "Now, I personally think this is much nicer," he said, speaking low and intimately. "What's your opinion? Tell me what you're thinking."

She cleared her throat and turned her face toward him. "Right this second I'm thinking that you wear the most incredible aftershave or cologne I've ever inhaled."

He crooked his arm to touch her hair. It was silky and

soft, just as he'd thought it would be. "I don't use cologne, so it must be my aftershave. But it can't begin to compare with your scent."

They were looking into each other's eyes from a distance of about eight inches. "I want to kiss you," Sam said huskily.

"I know," she whispered. Her whole body was in a state of anticipation, her heart pounding, her pulse racing. "So what's stopping you?"

A hot light entered Sam's eyes. He laid his free hand along her cheek and slowly brought his head closer to hers. Her lips parted at the same time she raised a hand to his chest. His heat radiated up her arm and mingled with the flames in her own system, creating an explosive desire within her. This man was dynamite and she knew in her heart where a kiss would lead them.

Getting off this sofa and putting a halt to what was happening was not an option, however. She wanted Sam's kiss more than she'd ever wanted anything. When his lips brushed hers softly, gently, her breath caught in her throat. "Sam," she whispered. "Oh, Sam."

It was a plea for more if he'd ever heard one. He pressed his lips to hers in a kiss of utter possession. His tongue toyed with hers, and her mouth opened wider. His pulse went crazy, and he turned her so her back was against the overstuffed arm of the sofa, then leaned into her. She responded by wrapping her arms around his neck and taking his tongue deep into her mouth.

The passion between them was mind-boggling. For both of them. Sam's head was spinning at such a fast pace he couldn't think of anything but having her. Tamara was in another world, one totally occupied by delicious, erotic feelings she had only come close to with other men.

It never once occurred to her that they might be moving too fast, too soon.

Chapter Five

Tamara was on her back on the sofa, snuggled so closely to Sam that he was virtually on top of her. Oddly, there wasn't a smidgen of alarm anywhere in her system. In fact, along with the curves, dips and angles of his marvelous body pressing into hers, she was feeling glorious, dreamily beloved and so emotionally connected to Sam Sherard that she sent silent thanks heavenward for today's storm. Without it she would have left the building before Sam showed up, ridden the bus home as usual and now be in her apartment alone.

While he nuzzled her throat, murmuring unintelligible words that sounded to her like the very essence of masculine appreciation, she ran her hands up and down his back and absorbed the heat of his skin through his shirt. She yanked the bottom of his shirt free of his belt and slid her hands under the garment to explore his bare back.

Sam's desire was reaching the frustrated stage. That thing Tamara was wearing had no evident openings, and there wasn't enough space on the sofa to wriggle around and find one. He touched what he could through fabric—the soft mounds of her breasts, her small waist, her hips and thighs—but that wasn't enough. He wanted her naked, wanted *himself* naked, but not here, not on this blasted sofa.

He raised his head and probed the glassy radiance of her eyes. "Let's move this to your bedroom," he said hoarsely.

If she was going to say "No deal, Sam. This has gone far enough," it would be now. He didn't think she would say anything even remotely in that vein, but he had to give her the chance.

Tamara thought him adorably blunt. Her responsive smile was flirtatiously female. "My bedroom," she murmured. "Yes, it would be more comfortable, wouldn't it?"

He kissed her and whispered, "It would be for our first time, at least."

Her pulse went wild. He was talking about making love more than once. She had never known a more exciting, more vital man, not ever. That their feelings for each other were advancing at such a rapid pace was exhilarating. Her imagination took wings and the future suddenly looked brighter. There was so much to see and do in the Dallas area, but doing it alone wasn't one-tenth the fun it would be with a handsome escort. Besides, being a native Texan, Sam must know about places to go and things to do that a newcomer like herself would never unearth.

Still, she realized, none of that would matter if she wasn't so dizzily attracted to Sam. Maybe it had started the second she'd seen him walking toward her office the day they'd met. Whatever, it had progressed to this, to her lying under him on her sofa and knowing she was going to make love with him.

But he was right; a bed would be so much more comfortable than the sofa.

She traced his lips with her fingertips until he took them

into his mouth. Holding her gaze with his, he sucked on them, and she saw desire—strong, potent desire—in the dark depths of his eyes. She wanted exactly what he did, and there wasn't a reason in the world to deny either of them.

"Yes," she whispered raggedly, so lost in the magic of what was happening that she couldn't speak normally. "Let's go to my bedroom."

Immediately Sam got up. He held out his hand to her and she took it. Then, arm in arm, staying as close together as possible, they walked to her bedroom. There was no reason to close the door behind them, but Tamara did it anyway, causing Sam to wonder if she felt some sort of need to shut out the rest of the world. Or maybe it was to shut them in more securely, to make this as intimate as she could. He liked privacy in situations of this nature, but it suddenly occurred to him that Tamara might be reading more into his passionate attentiveness than she should.

But no, he told himself, she was a worldly woman and knew the score. Innocents or disinterested women did not invite men they hardly knew into their home. Nor did they dress the way Tamara had for a cup of coffee. He'd been around enough to know that.

His opinion was reinforced when Tamara started unbuttoning his shirt, and he shoved the entire subject from his mind.

"Baby doll," he whispered gutturally. "This is going to be some night."

Tamara blinked at his choice of endearments. She was *not* a "baby doll" and never would be. But she didn't want to ruin the mood they were in by even hinting that he might be doing something wrong, so she let it pass with a hope that he wouldn't use it again. She undid the last button on his shirt and pushed it from his shoulders.

Her breath caught at the sight of him shirtless. "You're so tan," she murmured while her gaze roamed his nude torso. His belly was rippled with muscles and looked hard as rock. His chest broadened from his narrow waist and had a small triangle of black hair between his nipples. His shoulders and upper arms were heavily muscled. He was, in a word, beautiful.

He smiled. "Let's see if *you're* tan. How do you get out of that dress?"

She had to laugh, because she'd known he had tried to find an opening during their time on the sofa. "Like this," she said, and swept the caftan up and over her head.

It was Sam's turn to stare. Clad in an ivory lace bra and bikini panties, Tamara was a sight to behold. "You're beautiful," he said.

"You sound surprised." Tamara took a step closer to him, and he reacted by putting his arms around her and holding her in an embrace that felt almost fierce to her.

"I'm not surprised," he said into her hair. "Thrilled is a better word."

Her lips moved against the smooth skin of his chest as she said softly, "I'm thrilled, too, Sam. This is important, isn't it?"

"Right now it's damned important, baby." He flipped open the clasp at the back of her bra and slipped it from her shoulders. It fell to the floor, unnoticed.

Before Tamara could assimilate the meaning behind his comment about "importance," he was kissing and gently suckling her breast. The delectable sensation of his mouth and tongue on her nipple rippled throughout her body, culminating in an almost unbearable ache between her legs. Sam had to know what she was feeling, she realized, because he slid her panties down past her knees, where they, too, fell to the floor. Tamara stepped out of them at the same moment Sam's right hand took their place.

"Oh," she gasped. At some point while they'd been kissing and petting on the sofa she had wondered if, in the end, he would disappoint her. She knew now from the way he was caressing her that she would definitely not be disappointed. In fact, if he stroked her the way he was doing for very long, it would all be over for her.

"Sam...Sam...I'm going to...and I—I don't want to," she stammered. "Not like this."

"Go with it, baby. It'll happen again, I guarantee it," he whispered, and took her mouth in a hot, wet kiss that carried her even closer to the brink. Her legs were getting so shaky she had to cling to him to stand, and his hand kept moving and his kisses just got hotter.

It happened. It consumed her. She cried out. "Sam...oh, Sam!"

"That's my girl," he said, satisfied that he'd done what he'd set out to do. She was leaning into him, weak as a newborn kitten. Tenderly he brought her to the bed. "Lie down, sweetheart. I'll be with you as soon as I get rid of the rest of my clothes."

Glassy-eyed and dazed, she watched him shed his boots, socks and jeans. Completely naked, he faced her and again felt satisfaction at the awestruck way she was looking at him.

Tamara dampened her dry lips with the tip of her tongue. He was...he was incredible! She held up her arms, inviting him, wanting him so much she was dizzy from it. Nothing in her life had prepared her for the power of over-whelming desire or for a man like Sam, who knew exactly what he was doing and how to do it to assure total and complete fulfillment for both him and his lady.

He lay beside her, took her into his arms and very gently began kissing and caressing her. In moments Tamara couldn't lie still. Almost greedily she ran her hands over him, up and down his body, back and front, wherever she could reach. It astonished her that she felt edgy and achy so soon again, burning with internal pressures. Women fell in love with men who made them feel this way, she thought. Was that what was happening to her?

She frowned over that idea for a moment, then let it slip away as a maelstrom of emotions overcame her. Sam's kisses were no longer gentle, and she kissed him back with all the hunger he had brought to life in her on this most magical of evenings. They rolled this way and that on the bed, gasping in air when they could, arms and legs tangled, becoming more aroused by the second.

"Sam...Sam."

He recognized the plea in the way she moaned his name, and he moved on top of her. Her legs opened without direction from him, and he heeded the invitation and slid into her with a groan of supreme pleasure.

It wasn't easy, gentle or especially loving. It was sex at its rawest. He took her by storm, and it didn't even occur to her to demand anything else, not when she was somewhere in outer space, soaring far beyond the world of mundane activities. Nothing penetrated her rapture, not the rain hitting the windowpanes nor the headboard of her bed bumping the wall in a hard, steady rhythm. She heard him mumble "sweetheart" and "baby" several times and she was vaguely aware of calling him "darling" and "my love." She knew when she began weeping, and when in a raspy, tear-clogged voice she begged him not to stop. She liked it when he took her hands and held them over her head, their fingers entwined, and minutes later let go of them to burrow his own hands under her hips, lifting her higher for his driving thrusts.

And then they were moving faster, bonded together and climbing the pinnacle to the final bliss. She clutched at his back and turned her head when he tried to kiss her, because she needed air so badly. He was heavy, pinning her to the bed, and she caught a glimpse of the concentrated pleasure on his face. She closed her eyes just as she went over the edge. He roared her name and collapsed on her, but she continued to move her hips, drawing every delicious sensation from him that she could. Tears were coursing down her temples and all she could do was whisper his name. "Sam...Sam..."

It was over. Neither moved. Sam was so spent he

wanted to fall asleep right where he was. Tamara was the most exciting woman he'd ever made love with—uninhibited, free spirited, giving as much as she took. With his head on the pillow next to hers, he thought of how great sex was with her, and how much alike they were—independent, asking nothing of anyone, taking their pleasure where they happened to find it. She was the best kind of woman for a man of his nature—generous with her favors and expecting nothing from him afterward.

At least he hoped he had her figured out. So far he'd been right on every point. She'd invited him in for sex and had participated eagerly. The aftermath would tell the tale, however, and he might as well ferret out her mood right now.

He raised his head and looked into her eyes. A slight grin tipped one corner of his lips. "Was it as good for you as it was for me?" he asked lightly, already knowing it had been.

Tamara stared back at him without answering for several long moments. He could have said something nicer, she thought with a sudden ache in the vicinity of her heart. But what had she hoped for? If she could have chosen his very first words herself, what would they have been?

She let out a sigh. "It was the best, and I think you know it."

A warning bell went off in Sam's head, but he told himself not to judge too hastily. He really didn't want to get up and leave. In fact, he'd like to spend the whole night in her bed. An image of reaching for her while half-asleep was amazingly arousing, considering how physically drained he'd felt only a few minutes ago.

She spoke again. "You're a wow with the ladies, aren't you, Sam?"

He answered cautiously. "I haven't had any complaints, if that's what you're getting at."

She sighed again. "Please let me up." It struck her then

like a bolt of lightning. They hadn't used protection! She pushed against his chest. "Sam, let me get up!"

He didn't understand the panic in her voice. "What's your hurry?"

"If you've been thinking I'm on the Pill, think again."

He stiffened, then hurriedly rolled to the side of the bed. Tamara got off of it and ran for the bathroom. He lay where she'd left him, frowning slightly and pondering fate. He was never negligent about protection, and tonight he had been. Tamara assumed he'd thought she was on the Pill, but the subject had never once entered his mind. There was no question that he'd been thinking with a part of his anatomy that wasn't anywhere near his brain, but why? As satiated as he was now, it was difficult to recall the driving force behind such unnecessary recklessness as had occurred this evening. There simply was no acceptable excuse for taking such a risk.

But even though the misstep made him nervous and edgy, he still wanted to stay the night, make love with her again—with protection, of course. He would not forget a second time. Or a third, he thought with a rather self-satisfied grin, caused by a positive feeling that Tamara would cooperate with any idea he came up with, as far as making love went.

After Tamara refreshed herself in the bathroom, she lingered to brush her hair and put on a little makeup. She, too, was doing some rationalizing. For one thing, Sam was no more at fault than she was, and blaming him could cause a rift that she didn't want. Truth was, she was thrilled to death over their relationship. She'd been lonely and now she wasn't. Having Sam for a lover also meant having a friend, someone to talk to and go out with. Why on earth would she deliberately destroy what they had created this evening?

"No way," she said out loud and in an adamant tone. She was going to forget their carelessness this one time, making sure, of course, that it didn't happen again. She suddenly became anxious that Sam might be getting dressed and preparing to leave, so she threw on the terry robe that hung on the bathroom door and hurried back to the bedroom.

She went all weak and relieved when she saw him still in bed. Regrouping her wits and smiling warmly, she crossed the room and sat down next to him.

He took her hand. "Everything okay?"

She dismissed that topic with a nod of her head. "How about a pizza?" It was a spur-of-the-moment idea to delay his departure.

He laughed. "A pizza! Are you hungry?"

"I'm not empty—we ate only an hour ago—but a pizza sounds good. There's a pizza place not far from here that delivers. How about it?"

"A fat-free pizza?" he drawled with a raised eyebrow.

She laughed, then gave him a coy look. "I fall off the wagon every so often. Twice in one night is a record, but..."

"You're intimating that you fell off the wagon with me?" He couldn't quite believe her, or maybe he just didn't want to. She was much too worldly-wise in bed to live a totally celibate life. He knew she hadn't been a virgin before they'd made love, and he had absolutely no curiosity about the previous men with whom she'd gone to bed. But he wasn't a liar himself, he didn't like people who were and Tamara's attempt to make him think tonight was a rare occasion rubbed him the wrong way.

She caught Sam's change of mood and felt her pulse flutter in alarm. She wanted him to know *her*, the woman she really was. It was suddenly crucial that he didn't see her as promiscuous, just because she'd been so free and easy with him.

"Sam," she said quietly, "there have been three men and you're one of them. Do you want to hear about the other two? I have no qualms in talking about them. They were—"

"No," he said sharply, interrupting her. Realizing that he sounded angry, he lightened the tone of his voice and gave her hand an affectionate pat. "What's done is done. I don't want to talk about your past any more than I want to discuss mine. Let's leave it at that, okay?"

Obviously she had no choice but to agree. Getting to know each other was going to take more time than they had this evening. He didn't want to hear her war stories, nor did he intend to tell her his. It was a sad, almost painful moment for Tamara, as she had hoped for so much more than Sam was willing to give.

But she was not going to let his attitude get her down. She had romantic feelings for this man and had been telling herself he cared for her in the same way. She knew she couldn't stray from that belief and still feel good about herself, so she deliberately clung to it.

"I'll call for the pizza," she said, pulling her hand from his and getting to her feet. "The number for the pizzeria is by the kitchen phone." She started away, then stopped. "Oh, I forgot to ask. What do you like on your pizza?"

Sam grinned. "I've never met a pizza I didn't like. You choose." She was halfway through the door when he asked, "Is it okay if I use your shower?"

"Go ahead," she called over her shoulder. He would relax and talk while they ate pizza together, she told herself, simply because she had to believe he wanted more from her than sex.

But she felt troubled as she dialed the pizzeria's number to place her order, and strange, uneasy thoughts roiled in her mind. She had never in her life experienced anything remotely close to making love with Sam, but what if that's all there was? Could she participate in a relationship based solely on sex? Didn't she need more from a man? Her nature was pragmatic and sensible. Even as a child she had thought things through before jumping into risky undertakings. While Tamara was growing up, her mother had praised her sensibility many times and had teasingly told her she'd been born an adult. On top of those positive traits she had an exceptionally high IQ. That was the side of her that kept questioning the logic of tonight.

But she was learning that intelligence and emotion could function independently. Should she listen to her heart or her brain? Sam was so exciting. She'd never met anyone like him before. Could she rout him out of her life simply because he couldn't seem to talk about himself?

Even while placing her order she was rationalizing again, talking to a stranger on the phone and thinking about Sam at the same time. Hanging up, she sat there and told herself that Sam was entitled to his privacy. *Give him time, for heaven's sake. So he's different. Isn't that what you like most about him?*

Her glance fell on the table, still bearing the residue of supper. Quickly she got to her feet and rushed around the tiny kitchen, cleaning up. Finished with that chore, she put on another pot of coffee and laid out some fresh napkins and plates, wishing that her apartment had a fireplace. It was a perfect night for a fire, and she spent a minute or so thinking of how romantic eating pizza together in front of a fire would be.

But the kitchen would have to do.

Or would it? she thought in the next heartbeat. A slow smile curved her lips. Yes, why not? she decided, dashing to the hall linen closet. Grabbing a clean white sheet, she brought it to the living room and spread it over the carpet. Then she hurried into her guest bedroom and took the large decorative pillows from the bed. There were four, patterned in bright hues of aqua, purple, rose and blue, and she returned to the living room and tossed them on the sheet.

She heard the shower stop running and suddenly felt choked at the mental image of Sam naked and wet. She could have joined him! Why had she wasted time cleaning the damned kitchen and worrying about pizza and where to eat it?

Self-annoyance pursed her lips. True, she wasn't used to having a sexy, hot-blooded man in the apartment. It was also true that she had never joined *any* man in a shower before, but she'd seen it in movies and it always looked exciting to her. She had let a golden opportunity to experience it for herself slip by.

On the other hand, did she know Sam well enough to predict his reaction to a woman entering the bathroom while he was using it? He might not have been as thrilled as she would have hoped.

"Oh, well," she said under her breath, admitting that she felt on tenterhooks with Sam. She really had no idea what would happen next between them. Sam might eat a little pizza and leave. Sam might leave *without* eating any pizza. He could very likely think her "picnic" area, devised by the sheet and throw pillows, to be utter nonsense. Or kid stuff.

She suddenly felt like a kid—there had to be at least ten years difference in her and Sam's ages—and nearly stumbled over her own feet while gathering up the pillows and sheets and rushing the armload to the guest bedroom. Depositing everything on the bed, she closed the door behind her with a sense of relief. A picnic in the living room, indeed. What on earth had made her think *that* had been a good idea?

And she should get dressed. A pair of jeans and a T-shirt would do—anything would, actually, just so she wasn't still wearing a robe when Sam walked out of the bathroom.

She was in the hall, about to go into her own bedroom, when the bathroom door opened and there was Sam with a towel around his hips. Tamara's mouth went dry. His hair was wet and looked finger combed. A few beads of water he'd missed while drying off glistened on his skin. She got absolutely weak-kneed again. Sam affected her as no man ever had, and she wanted to take the few steps between them and melt into him.

Sam did it for her. "I was just thinking about you," he said as he untied the sash of her robe and slipped his hands inside to encircle her waist. "And here you are." He brought his head down to whisper against her lips, "I'd bet anything we've both been thinking about the same thing."

His kiss, hot and hungry, stopped her from answering, and in the next instant it didn't matter if she answered or not. The way Sam kissed destroyed any and every inhibition she might have had with another man. His hands under her robe turned her from an ordinary human being into a total wanton. Pushing her against the wall, he flipped away his towel and then lifted her to fit them together.

The doorbell pealed. They froze where they were. Thickly Tamara mumbled, "The pizza."

Sam was breathing hard. He didn't give a damn about pizza or anything else right this minute. He was inside her and that was where he wanted to stay.

Tamara was regaining a modicum of sense. "I have to answer the door, Sam. I use that pizzeria all the time, and I have to pay for what I ordered."

His expression darkened, but he untangled their bodies and let her feet slide to the floor. Hurrying down the hall, Tamara retied the sash of her robe.

Sam bent over and picked up the towel, thinking that the interruption was just as well, as he had again forgotten to use protection. Shaking his head and marveling at how strongly Tamara affected him, he entered her bedroom, located his jeans and put them on.

He'd eat some of that damned pizza, but then the rest of the night was going to be *his!* The way he felt right now it would *take* the whole night to satisfy the desire racking his body.

And he knew, as well as he knew his own name, that Tamara would rather make love than sleep. A more willing woman he'd never met.

Wearing his jeans, socks and shirt, the last unbuttoned and with the tails hanging out, he left her bedroom and went to join her in whatever room she intended to hold her little pizza party.

Chapter Six

"Enjoyed it, baby doll. See you around."

Tamara stood at the curb, frozen with shock, and watched Sam's Jeep drive away. That was it, all he could give her—a nonchalant "see you around"? And he'd used that awful term "baby doll," to boot. Anger suddenly exploded within her. What in hell kind of fool was she? What kind of chauvinistic bastard was Sam? He'd used her!

And she'd let him!

The bubble had burst.

Turning abruptly, she marched into her empty garage and pushed the button to close the door. Fury burned a hole in her stomach. All during Sam's time in her apartment, while they had made love, eaten, made love, slept a little, made love—from his very first advance, to be factual—she had waited for him to bring up the subject of their next meeting. It had seemed so crucial, their first real date, signifying endurance, perhaps. Not that she'd been hoping for a one-on-one commitment from Sam, for pity's sake. But some sign of his feelings for her—other than the obvious—wasn't too much to hope for, was it?

Well, she'd gotten her sign, hadn't she? He'd left without even hinting they should get together again. Not within the next few days, or two weeks from now, or a year from now! He hadn't said one blasted word about ever seeing each other again. And she, like a mindless moron, had left it up to him, knowing in her heart that he cared as much for her as she did for him.

So much for premonitions of the heart, she thought bitterly. Sam Sherard cared for no one but himself. Slamming things around, Tamara stripped her bed and threw the sheets in the washer. When had she gotten so stupid? she kept asking herself. How could she mistake lust for affection? Sam was deadly, the snake. There was probably a trail of broken hearts clear across Texas because of his bedroom tactics.

Tears suddenly spilled from her eyes, and she fell into a chair. She could curse Sam from now to doomsday, but the truth was that she should be cursing herself. Sam hadn't forced or coaxed her into anything. She'd behaved like a starry-eyed girl instead of the mature woman she deemed herself. And what really hurt was that she *knew* she was mature and intelligent, and still she had succumbed to a predatory male's fatal charm.

She had never, ever thought such a thing could happen to her. In the first place, Sam was *not* charming, not at all like the smooth-talking rogues who so easily seduced women in novels and movies. Getting Sam to talk about anything was darned near impossible. He had finally spoken some about his ranch, but only after she'd brought up the subject of where he lived for about the tenth time.

I hate him, she thought while wiping her eyes. But even while thinking it she knew it wasn't true. She didn't hate him at all and suspected deep down that she was going to be living with emotional pain for a very long time.

Considering how easy she'd been, dare she even think *never again?*

When Tamara got home from work on Thursday of the following week, there was a letter from her mother in her mailbox. She sat down to read it. The first page started with family news:

I received a nice letter from Blythe. She is already knee-deep in her school's plans for its annual Christmas pageant. As I'm sure you know, the pageant is a longtime tradition of Brockton Hall and sounds like a marvelous affair. Sierra sent a postcard from Bermuda. I don't know if she's there alone or if Mike is with her, as her only message was about the perfect weather and the incredible scenery.

The letter rambled on about Coeur d'Alene events, various friends and neighbors, and finally Tamara reached the paragraph most important to her:

Your invitation to come to Dallas for Thanksgiving was a lovely idea, Tamara, and I hate disappointing you. But weeks ago I volunteered to help cook dinner for the needy in our church. I'm sorry, dear, but perhaps you can come here for Christmas. I know your time is highly regulated by your job, but if it's at all possible…

Tamara lowered the letter to her lap with a heavy sigh. She'd already been assigned to work on Christmas Day. She would be alone for both of the upcoming holidays. Was it selfish to feel sorry for herself? She tried for several minutes but couldn't remember the last time her family had gotten together for any reason. How sad, she thought with misty eyes.

But then, didn't most things strike her as sad these days?

* * *

Thanksgiving came and went. The highlight of that dismal week was the modest, two-year-old car Tamara bought. Having the freedom to come and go as she wished perked up her spirits considerably. Driving to and from work was enjoyable, however congested the streets might be. She started her Christmas shopping and truly appreciated being able to linger in stores and malls without worrying about bus schedules.

But however busy her days, when she turned off the lights and got in bed for the night, she saw Sam's face. Clear as a bell, too. Without fail, her stomach churned and acted up as the anger began. The apparently permanent emotional wounds inflicted by Sam indeed made her angry, like it or not, and although she knew what a fool *she* had been, she was hard-pressed to take full responsibility for that weekend. Plus the fact that she hadn't even caught sight of Sam in the Rowland Building, let alone had the chance to snub him or give him hell, drove her up the wall. She couldn't decide which he deserved more, or what would most effectively convey what a jerk she thought he was, but she knew she could never be smiling and pleasant to him again.

Christmas was only a week away when Natalie eyed her critically during their lunch break. "Are you feeling all right? Frankly, my friend, you look like hell."

Tamara blinked in surprise. Were her restless nights and queasy stomach actually leaving visible traces? They were mostly because of Sam, of course. She might never really get over his treachery. But she'd also been doing some thinking. As much as she liked her job, was she happy living in Dallas? Had she made any important friendships, other than with Natalie? All she had done was work, even refusing offers from co-workers to meet someplace after closing for a drink. The "drink" might be nothing more than water with a high-toned name and special packaging, but it meant socializing, laughter, silly conversation, *fun!* The truth was that other than her job, which she found stimulating and interesting, life was dull. Maybe that was the reason she'd stumbled so badly with Sam.

She wished she could tell Natalie everything, but it was such an embarrassing incident she doubted that she'd ever be able to talk about it with anyone. Besides, knowing Natalie as she did, Tamara decided she might find the whole thing funny. An affair, short-lived as it was, with Stoneface Sherard? Yes, Natalie just might laugh about it, and Tamara didn't think she could bear any amusement over something that was nearly eating her alive.

"I've had a little trouble sleeping lately," she said with a calmness she certainly didn't feel. That, at least, was safe enough to admit, she thought.

"Which indicates a problem of some sort," Natalie replied matter-of-factly. "I've had bouts of insomnia, believe me, and there was always an underlying problem."

"I suppose it's happened to most people, at one time or another," Tamara murmured.

Natalie's eyes narrowed on Tamara's face. "But I don't remember getting pale and drawn over it. How long has this been going on? Maybe you should see a doctor."

Tamara forced a laugh. "Goodness, Natalie, it's not *that* bad."

Later in her office, however, Tamara wondered. She'd been blaming all of her physical discomforts on raw nerves because of Sam's perfidy, but what if there was more to her upset stomach and restless nights?

Her gaze fell on her desk calendar. She did so quite absentmindedly, but the date suddenly leaped out at her. Panic seized her as she began calculating time since her last period.

"Oh, my God," she whispered weakly. This couldn't be happening to her. She *wasn't* pregnant!

But there was no escaping the fact that it was entirely possible.

* * *

Tamara thought the day would never end. All afternoon she tried desperately to concentrate on her work, but in reality she accomplished very little. There was no working late today, not with so much on her mind, and when five rolled around, she grabbed her coat and purse and hurried to the bank of elevators, squeezing into one that was already packed for the ride down to ground level.

Her hands were shaking when she put the key in the ignition of her car, and she sat there with the motor running to get hold of herself before driving. The parking lot gradually emptied, and finally she felt controlled enough to brave the rush hour traffic. But she didn't go directly home. Instead, she went to a shopping center with a large drugstore. Inside, she found the feminine products aisle and quickly picked up three different home pregnancy tests. Looking around to make sure there wasn't anyone she knew at the checkout counters, she hurriedly paid for her items and breathed again only when they were bagged and out of sight.

During the rest of the drive home, her mind raced from one thing to another. *I can't be pregnant, I can't! What would Mother think? My God, my job! The gossip. What will I do if I test positive? Oh, I can't. I won't! I'm worrying over nothing.*

But the nausea she had been blaming on emotional upheaval and her late period were very substantial reasons for worry. *A missed period is not proof positive of pregnancy,* she thought frantically. *I haven't always been regular.*

That was true, and she clung to that bit of hope like a lifeline. Pulling into her garage, she took her purse and package and went into her apartment. It felt like a haven, but only for a few minutes. Removing the boxes from the drugstore sack, she set them on the kitchen table and sat down to read the instructions on each. Maybe three tests were overkill, but she was not going to rely on the results of only one.

Her heart beat fast with fear. Her mouth was dry and her palms sweaty. She chewed on a thumbnail and stared at the three boxes. She knew she should take the tests right away and get it over with, but she was so afraid of the results that she kept sitting there and putting off the awful chore.

"Enough!" she finally said out loud. Worrying herself into hysteria and imagining the worst possible scenario was just plain stupid. "Take the damned tests and find out for sure before you go crazy."

She got to her feet, picked up the three boxes and headed for her bathroom.

Long after night had fallen, Tamara sat in the dark on her living room sofa and stared at nothing. She felt dazed, frightened and insecure. All three tests had come out positive. There was no longer room for doubt; she was pregnant. Very alone and pregnant.

She finally dragged herself to bed around midnight. Emotionally exhausted from hours of mental torture, she fell asleep almost at once.

At 3:00 a.m. she awoke from a disturbing dream. She'd been in what had felt like a well. The water had been a beautiful, pale aqua color, and there was a glow throughout. The water had sparkled with light. She had not been drowning, nor did she seem to have any trouble breathing, but she had definitely been underwater. And in her arms was an infant. Tamara had not been frightened and, in fact, had calmly accepted the situation: she couldn't get out of the well while holding the child, and she couldn't let go of the infant.

Tamara lay there and tried to find meaning in the unusual dream. Did the well represent her sense of entrapment? Was the infant the speck of life developing in her womb? Why couldn't she let go of the child and swim to the surface of the water? And why had it been such a beautiful color and so brightly lighted?

Her hand crept below the covers to rest on her lower abdomen. For the first time she thought of the child as a living being. Tears filled her eyes and her lower lip quivered. And because of the light in that pure, lovely water, and because there was no fear in the dream, Tamara knew that everything would be all right. She would come up with a feasible plan to *make* it right. She was positive of it.

By the following Monday morning—Christmas Eve, actually—Tamara had a plan in mind. The minute she got to work, she went to the personnel department for a form, which she brought to her office and sat at her desk to fill out. It was a request for transfer to the Alaska branch of the firm, relatively easy to complete.

Until she got to the part that read: *State in your own words why you feel a transfer is necessary.*

Because I'm pregnant and don't want anyone in Dallas to know it, she thought wryly, then tried to come up with a response she could actually use. *Make it short,* she told herself. *The shorter, the better. Say what you have to in the fewest possible words.*

She finally wrote, *I am getting married to a man who lives and works in the Northwest. If I transferred to Alaska, I would be able to see my husband much more often than if I stayed in Dallas.*

Tamara had deliberately put her fictitious fiancé in the Northwest rather than in Alaska, as she didn't want any Rowland people in that branch wondering why they never got to meet her husband. Signing and dating the form, Tamara felt she had covered all her bases quite well— except for her promotion, of course. She would deliver the form to Elliot Grimes, and if he mentioned the promotion, she would naturally say that she didn't expect it to follow her to Alaska.

Her plan was really quite simple. She would transfer to the Alaska branch as a married woman. No one there would be curious about dates when she announced her pregnancy about a month after the transfer. She would have the baby, work for seven or eight months, then request a transfer back to Dallas, returning as a *divorced* woman with a baby. Admittedly, Tamara was nervous about the whole thing, but she had thought about it for days, and this plan seemed at least achievable.

It hadn't even occurred to her to seek out Sam and tell him about her condition. She wanted nothing more to do with Sam Sherard, and he was the last person on earth she would ever ask for help. Help for what, anyway? *She* was the one who was pregnant. What could he do about it? He sure wasn't the type of man to say, "Don't you worry about a thing, sweetheart. We'll get married and make a home for our baby."

Besides, she wouldn't marry Sam on a bet. When she did think of him, it was with bitterness and intense resentment. Not because they had made a baby, but because he'd been so damned cavalier about their "romantic" weekend. It hadn't meant a thing to him, and it was tough to admit to herself that she'd fallen hard and fast for him.

That was in the past, she thought adamantly as she took the form, put it in a large manila envelope, sealed it and wrote "Elliot Grimes" on the front.

Her gaze went to the central office beyond her glassed-in office. Christmas decorations were everywhere, and people were dressed up. At noon their children would arrive— some employees had to go and pick up their youngsters, of course—and so would Santa. Natalie had told Tamara about the gifts every child would receive, and the photos with Santa, the games and good food.

Tamara's Christmas spirit was so low she could barely detect it. She had mailed a package to her mother and cards to her sisters. Cards to about thirty other people, as well. But she hadn't put up a tree, and the package she'd received from Coeur d'Alene was her only gift. She and her sisters hadn't exchanged presents for years, probably because they didn't know each other well enough to pick out something any of them would like.

Tamara knew there would be little work done today, although everyone would try to look busy until noon. And, of course, some people *would* actually be working because of the telephone calls from oil company managers and troubleshooters frantically needing a part or a piece of equipment to keep their operation running. Since she was the unfortunate associate chosen to work tomorrow, her calendar was pretty empty today.

Taking the envelope containing her transfer request, she left her office and wended her way to the desk of Elliot Grimes's secretary.

"Good morning, Tamara," Nancy said cheerfully.

"Good morning." Tamara laid the envelope on Nancy's desk. "Would you please see that Mr. Grimes gets this?"

"Of course. I'm not sure when he'll look at it, but I'll certainly give it to him at the first opportunity. I'm not sure where he is right now. Today's going to be pretty hectic, what with the Christmas party and all."

"I understand. I'd like him to see it as soon as possible, but it's not an emergency or anything like that."

Nancy smiled. "Don't you just love Christmas?"

Tamara managed to smile, too. "Doesn't everyone? Thanks, Nancy. I have to run."

"See you at the party," Nancy called as Tamara walked away. "And Merry Christmas."

"Merry Christmas," Tamara said over her shoulder. It was a purely automatic response; she felt about as merry as a mop handle.

The party was in full swing at one o'clock. The entire floor was crowded and noisy. Tamara sipped from a cup of fruit punch and watched the kids. Some of them were barely old enough to walk, and absolutely adorable in their fancy Christmas clothes. Parents were hovering, Santa was ho-hoing all over the place and Christmas carols added to the din. Tamara spotted Elliot Grimes in the middle of the melee and wondered if he'd read her transfer request yet.

Alaska. Lord above, she didn't want to go to Alaska, but what else could she do? She was not going to stay in Dallas and endure raised eyebrows and furtive looks as her co-workers discussed her situation.

"Hello, Tamara."

She whirled and felt a wave of utter fury nearly knock her off her feet. Before her stood Sam, wearing an adorable little half grin and holding a cup of something red. Her own drink was orange, but there were several punch bowls on the serving table.

"No 'hello, Sam'?" he asked when all she did was stand there and glare at him.

Her mind raced with all that she'd like to say to this jerk, but she couldn't do it here, even if there was so much going on probably only Sam would hear her. She turned her face away from him and mumbled, "Hello."

"Nice party," he said.

She felt his eyes go up and down her body and flushed. Because of the party, she was wearing a red dress and matching pumps. She knew she looked good, but she didn't want him studying her like a bug under a microscope.

"I'm surprised you like *nice* parties," she said with all the sarcasm she could muster. "In fact, I'm surprised you're here at all." His good looks irritated her so much she wanted to scream, and how dare he approach her and say hello as though she should be glad to see him?

"I'm a surprising guy," he said.

"You won't get an argument out of me about that," she said through gritted teeth.

He tried to peer into her face. "Are you mad at me about something?"

She was not going to stand next to him one second longer. "Let's just say that I loathe the ground you walk on and leave it at that, okay?" She walked away.

Sam's party expression became a serious frown of perplexity. "What'd I do to deserve that?" he called, but Tamara never heard because she was already twenty feet away and part of the crowd. He stood there for a long time and thought of what had just happened. He rarely attended these holiday functions, and deep down he knew he was here today because of Tamara. She'd been on his mind a lot, and however much he had mentally argued against it, he had finally been forced to admit that he wanted to see her again. The Christmas party had seemed like the perfect opportunity.

He had not expected anger from her, and he felt so shook up over it that he moved through the crowd to a quiet corner and leaned against the wall to wait for her to appear again. He was going to *make* her talk to him, *force* her to explain herself.

There was more than one set of rest rooms on the floor, and Tamara hurried to the farthest ladies' room. As she'd hoped, no one else was in it. She was trembling from rage and frustration, and it took a good five minutes to calm herself down, accomplished finally by an acceptance of the fact that saying more to Sam than she had would only have made her look like a fool to him and anyone else who might have heard her. Far better to just completely forget Sam and what he'd done. Put him out of her mind once and for all. Live her life as though he didn't exist.

She looked in the mirror and saw a woeful, self-pitying expression on her face. Completely forgetting Sam would be easier to do if she weren't carrying his child, wouldn't it? "Damn him!" she cried aloud as her former anger returned full force.

Well, the party was over for her. She did not want to see Sam again, let alone talk to him. It should be easy to slip away. Everyone was so busy having fun, who would notice her absence?

She returned to the din and was about to go into her office for her coat and purse when the music faded and an announcement came over the sound system. "It's gift time for our employees." Applause and whistles came from the adults. "Santa's elves will pass out envelopes with your names on them, so stay put and make it easy for them."

The bonus checks, Tamara thought. She'd forgotten Natalie's excitement over this segment of the annual affair, and she shouldn't have because it was the one and only reason Sam was here.

At that very moment she saw him across the room, and her desire to get out of there became so dominant that she hastened into her office, grabbed her coat and purse and all but ran for the elevators. Her envelope would be just as available tomorrow as it was today, and she personally didn't give a damn right at the moment how much her bonus would be.

Sam saw Tamara pushing through the crowd toward the elevators, and he frowned again. She was leaving. He would not be able to ask her anything. What in hell was wrong with her? She loathed the ground he walked on? For hell's sake, why? What had happened between that memorable weekend and today to change her attitude so drastically?

She was one very peculiar lady, wasn't she? Sexy as sin one time and cold as ice the next. Strange. Very, very strange.

Chapter Seven

Spending Christmas Day at work wasn't nearly as bad as Tamara had feared. At least she wasn't alone, as she would have been in her apartment. Four other people were on the floor, and when they weren't busy with one thing or another, they congregated to share snacks and conversation. Their mood was upbeat and casual, and Tamara actually found herself enjoying the day. One man, Drake Collins, kept coming by her office and telling her jokes to make her laugh.

"What did the flasher say when asked if he was ready to retire?" Drake said with his head just inside her door.

Tamara smiled. "I have no idea. What did he say?"

"Oh, I think I can stick it out for another year or so."

Tamara broke up. The dumb joke was funny and Drake himself amusing. He was one of the men who had asked her out for a drink after work during her first month on the job, and she had refused. He was nice looking—tall and well built with sandy hair and brown eyes. What's more, he had a great sense of humor and a ready smile. What a dolt she'd been to turn him down, she thought in abject self-disgust.

Now it was too late to encourage Drake or any other man. Every time she thought of her personal situation, she felt like sinking to her knees and wailing. The sooner she got out of Dallas, the better. Apparently Mr. Grimes hadn't read her transfer request yesterday, which was understandable what with the party and all. He wasn't here today, of course, and she could only hope that he would open that envelope first thing tomorrow morning.

Quite a few calls came in during the morning hours, but the phone rang very little that afternoon. Around four, everyone was grouped in the main room, anxious for the relief crew to arrive so they could go home.

That was when someone mentioned Mr. Grimes's vacation. Tamara sat up straighter. "Is Mr. Grimes on vacation?"

"He always takes a week or so at Christmas, Tamara," Drake volunteered. "Didn't anyone tell you?"

"No," she said in a thin little voice. It was a miracle she could speak at all considering the shock she felt over Drake's information. Grimes wouldn't see her request for transfer for a week or more? Oh, no!

"I'm surprised he didn't tell you himself. He didn't give you any special instructions about your work or anything?"

"No," she repeated. There was no need to wonder about that question, however. Her promotion was coming through shortly after the first of the year, and Mr. Grimes had probably seen no good reason to load her with assignments she wouldn't be available to finish. She couldn't tell these people about it, of course, even though they were all looking at her curiously, as though she was out of the loop because they'd known something she hadn't.

That was the least of her concerns, however. Her plan was not going smoothly and she had honestly believed it would. A headache began throbbing in her temples. What if Tom Rowland announced her promotion before Mr. Grimes returned to work? Dare she go over Elliot Grimes's head and present her transfer request to Mr. Rowland?

She got up from her chair. "I have a few things to do," she said by way of explanation to her co-workers. What she needed to do was escape their scrutiny so she could worry in private. Seated at her desk again, she covered her face with her hands and groaned quietly. Her plan was deteriorating before it had gotten started.

Wait a minute, she thought. Tom Rowland was not apt to announce an important change in the sales department with its vice president on vacation. She was panicking unnecessarily. *Get hold of yourself. Everything will work out. Have a little patience.*

But not only did she lack patience at the present, her nerves were so frayed she constantly teetered on the brink of hysteria. What had just happened—going a little crazy because Mr. Grimes wouldn't see her request for transfer for a week or so—was proof of her state of mind.

Lowering her hands, she took several calming breaths. The phone rang, and since the others were still grouped and chatting, Tamara picked it up. "Merry Christmas. Rowland, Inc. How may I help you?"

There was a second of silence, then a male voice said, "Tamara?"

She recognized Sam's voice at once. "Yes," she said flatly. Was he working on Christmas, too? Damn fate for the sequence of events that had put her nearest a phone for this call. Sam Sherard was the last person she needed a reminder of right now. "What can I do for you?" she asked politely but coldly.

"I have an urgent order for a 100-amp engine." Sam recited the particulars, technical information that pinpointed the exact engine his customer needed. "Can you get it out immediately?"

"I think so, but hold on and I'll check with inventory

and delivery to be certain.'' Tamara pushed the Hold button and used an in-house line to call the inventory department. She had her answer in minutes and returned to Sam's line. ''It's a go,'' she told him. ''Give me the delivery address.'' She wrote while Sam talked. With the customer's address on paper, she felt the conversation was over. ''Goodbye,'' she said.

''Wait! How come you're working on Christmas?''

What bloody gall! What made him think he had the right to question her about anything? And why would it even occur to him to ask? ''You've worked for this company long enough to know *someone* is always here.'' Her voice was not even close to being friendly.

''Yes, but why you?''

Tamara's whole body tensed. ''Why not me?'' she snapped. ''Goodbye. Tell your customer his engine is on its way.''

Sam winced when Tamara slammed the phone down. She was ticked at him about something, and he wished he knew what it was. They'd had a great weekend, and when he'd driven away from her apartment he would have sworn everything was fine between them.

Women, he thought with some disgust. Did a man ever really understand them?

On her way home, Tamara stopped at Drover's, a very good restaurant only a mile from her apartment complex, to pick up the take-out order she had called in before leaving the office. She was making the best of things, she thought with a rather martyred, lonely feeling. The entire holiday season had been the pits, and this was one year she would never forget.

An understatement, she thought wryly, thinking of her pregnancy. With a child as a reminder, how would she forget any portion of the final months of this year?

Arriving home, she pulled into the garage, gathered her insulated dinner boxes and purse from the front seat and went into her apartment. She changed clothes quickly, donning a light fleece sweatsuit and house slippers. She ate her dinner in front of the TV, although she barely registered the news of the day, as her mind was on her own problems.

She needed contact with her family, she decided wistfully, and after the remnants of her dinner were discarded, she dialed her mother's number in Coeur d'Alene. When Myra's phone rang the fourth time, Tamara frowned. She was about to hang up when a weak, wispy little voice said, "Hello?"

Tamara's heart missed a beat. "Mother?"

"Tamara?"

"Mother, what's wrong? You sound terrible. Are you ill?"

"Just tired, honey. I was lying down."

Tamara wasn't convinced. "Did you have dinner with the Dunns?" During a previous conversation Myra had said that Eva and Frank Dunn, longtime friends, had invited her to have Christmas dinner with their family.

"I canceled, honey."

"You mean you've been home alone all day?"

"Tamara, it's all right. Frank and Eva have so many grandchildren, and I—I...well, I just didn't feel like dealing with children today."

Myra loved children and had said many times in the past that Christmas just wasn't the same without them. Fear rose in Tamara's throat. Canceling a dinner invitation wasn't at all like her mother, who had always enjoyed socializing and get-togethers of any kind. And Myra spending Christmas Day all alone broke Tamara's heart.

But she couldn't be sentimental here. Something more than being "tired" had kept her mother home today. Tamara's nerves were jangling with dread.

"Mother, I want the truth," she said firmly. "Are you really only tired, or are you ill?"

"Tamara, I don't want you worrying about me. Heavens—"

Tamara broke in. "I want details, Mother. Is your stomach upset? Do you have any pain?"

There was silence in Tamara's ear for several seconds, then a sigh. "All right," Myra admitted. "I don't feel well. Does that satisfy your curiosity? Honey, everyone has a day now and then when they'd rather not get out of bed in the morning. You really mustn't make a mountain out of a molehill simply because I'm a little under the weather."

"Were you well yesterday? The day before? Mother, how long have you been feeling 'a little under the weather'? Have you seen your doctor?"

"Goodness, so many questions. I saw Dr. Bergstrom just last week. I'm in very good hands, Tamara. Please, let's change the subject. How did your day go?"

Tamara wasn't interested in discussing anything but her mother's health, but apparently Myra had said all she was going to about it. "I worked, as I told you would be the case the last time we talked. I received a nice bonus check—a thousand dollars—from the company, and everything is..." She faltered for a heartbeat "...fine." If she told her mother how things really were with her, Myra would have a heart attack.

Guilt suddenly struck Tamara. One of them, at least— Blythe, Sierra or herself—should have been with their mother today. Damn jobs and responsibilities and personal problems! Were any of those things more important than Myra alone and not feeling well on Christmas?

Tamara gritted her teeth. She should fly north and see for herself how her mother was doing. How else would she learn the truth? Not from telephone calls, that was certain.

After a bit more conversation, Tamara said goodbye and hung up. Her mind was racing. If she took Friday off, she could fly to Spokane, Washington, rent a car and drive to

Coeur d'Alene, spend Saturday with her mother and fly back on Sunday. It was apt to cost a small fortune, as airlines normally did not provide low-rate fares for spur-of-the-moment trips, but her bonus check should cover it.

She felt so driven to do it, and that in itself worried her. Something was wrong in Coeur d'Alene—she knew it in her soul—and she would not rest until she saw her mother with her own eyes.

Tamara reached for the telephone book with her lips set in a thin, determined line. She would make a reservation with one of the airlines tonight and tomorrow morning notify someone—who, with Mr. Grimes gone for the week?—that she was going to be absent on Friday. In truth, she really didn't care how her employers viewed her decision. She was dealing with an emergency situation, and nothing was going to stop her from doing what she could about it.

It was already dark and close to 5:00 p.m. when Tamara drove into Coeur d'Alene in her rental car on Friday. It was freezing cold, and there had been patches of ice on the roads from Spokane, making driving hazardous and reminding Tamara of how really nasty northern Idaho winters could be at times. She had brought her warmest clothes with her and was wearing wool slacks, sweater and jacket, but it had been years since she'd been in Coeur d'Alene in weather like this and she wasn't at all comfortable with it.

There was an agonizing anticipation within her as she drove familiar streets to Lakeside Avenue, where the Benning home was located. It was one of the older areas of the city, a fashionable district of large, old-fashioned, two-story houses near the lake. Myra had often told her daughters how thrilled she had been when she and their father had decided to go into debt and purchase the house. *Your father's medical practice was really just getting off the ground, and we had to scrimp and pinch pennies to make the payments for the first few years. But then everything evened out, and it was such a joy to have this house.*

In truth it was a beautiful house. White with black shutters, it was imposing on the outside, and inside had a multitude of large, high-ceilinged rooms that Myra had tastefully decorated. It had been a wonderful neighborhood to grow up in, Tamara recalled. She and her friends had spent many long, lazy summer days on the beach. And she could not remember ever being warned about not talking to strangers, or worrying about riding their bikes anywhere that she and her friends chose to go. It had been a different era, Tamara thought. Coeur d'Alene had been a much smaller town then, and the crime rate had been very low. Now, according to Myra's reports, she kept her doors locked and practiced safety precautions just as Tamara did in Dallas.

There was more snow on the ground in Coeur d'Alene than Tamara had seen in Spokane. *Which is normal,* Tamara thought as she cautiously crept down Lakeside Avenue. The surface was hard-packed snow, making Tamara realize the street wasn't used very much anymore. Probably only the residents drove it with any regularity, and it was low on the list of plowing priorities for the city.

It's still a lovely neighborhood, she thought with a nostalgic sigh. Most of the houses were bright with Christmas lights. Driveways and sidewalks had been shoveled. Interior lighting shone through windows.

And then she was within viewing distance of her mother's house and it was completely dark! Tamara's stomach sank. No Christmas lights? To Tamara's knowledge, Myra had always hired a man to put up her holiday lights. Good Lord, there were no lights at all, not one lighted window!

With her heart beating a mile a minute, Tamara turned into the driveway, her attention locked on the dark house. If Myra had gone somewhere, she certainly would have left some lights on for her return. Something *was* wrong here.

Tamara was suddenly afraid, too afraid to even put an image with her fears. It took all the courage she could muster to get out of that car and go up the walk to her mother's front door. She had her old house key with her, but she rang the doorbell instead. She vaguely noticed the cold. Her breath was fogging in front of her face, and her fingers felt stiff from the low temperature. She pushed the doorbell button again, then dug the key ring out of her purse.

Bile rose in her throat when she finally inserted her key in the lock with a shaking hand and pushed open the door. The silence and blackness of the house felt ominous. Quickly she felt around for the wall switch and turned on the ceiling light. Her voice cracking, she called, "Mother?"

Any remnant of adolescence Tamara might still have possessed suddenly disappeared from her system. Myra would not have gone out without leaving lights on, even if she had left at noon. She must be in the house, in the dark with something terribly wrong. An unnatural calm replaced Tamara's previous panic. Hastily she began going from room to room, turning on lights and repeatedly calling, "Mother?"

When she turned on the kitchen light, her heart nearly stopped beating. Myra, fully clothed, was lying on the floor near the refrigerator. Her eyes were closed and she looked as though she were sleeping.

For a second Tamara couldn't move. "Mother," she whispered on a sorrowful sob. "Oh, Mother."

Mobility returned, and she hurried over to kneel beside Myra. Tamara felt for a pulse and breathed again when she found it. She gently shook her mother's shoulder. "Mother?" Tears began streaming down Tamara's face. "Mother, wake up, please wake up."

There was no indication that Myra heard her.

Tamara bent over and kissed her mother's cheek, then got up, went to the phone and dialed 911. She gave her name and Myra's address and requested an ambulance. "And please hurry," she added.

After hanging up, she returned to sit on the floor by her mother. Taking Myra's hand in hers, she wept quietly and waited for the ambulance.

The next three hours were emotionally devastating. Doctors, nurses, confusion, answering admittance questions as well as she could, waiting and more waiting... Dr. Bergstrom had been called in, and finally he took Tamara into a small room. They sat down.

"Your mother is being taken to the Intensive Care Unit," he said. "You may see her in about thirty minutes."

Tamara grabbed at hope. "She's conscious, then?"

"No. Tamara," Dr. Bergstrom said gently, "she's in a diabetic coma."

"Diabetes? That—that's impossible. Mother would have said something," Tamara stammered.

"She never told you?" The doctor sighed and shook his head. "Tamara, your mother has several severe medical problems, the most serious being the diabetes, which she developed approximately six years ago."

"Six years!"

"She has never had a heart attack, but her heart is weak, Tamara. Her circulatory disorders were diagnosed at the same time as the diabetes. We've tried to control the latter with insulin, of course, but some people's physiology simply does not respond to—"

Tamara's thoughts overrode Dr. Bergstrom's voice. "The coma," she said abruptly, interrupting him. "When will she come out of it?"

A heavy, saddened expression appeared on the doctor's face. "I don't think she will come out of it," he said softly.

* * *

It was nine o'clock before Tamara managed to arrange a conference call between Sierra, Blythe and herself. Explaining to her sisters what Dr. Bergstrom had told her took every ounce of Tamara's strength. Sierra and Blythe were both shocked and disbelieving, and had questions Tamara couldn't answer.

"That's what Dr. Bergstrom said," she said wearily.

"But why wouldn't Mother have told us?" Sierra persisted.

"I wish to God I knew," Tamara said. "She always said she was fine when I asked. She never once mentioned the word *diabetes*."

"Same with me," Blythe said dully.

"And with me," Sierra said.

"Are you at the hospital now?" Blythe asked.

"I came to Mother's house to make this call. I'm going back to the hospital right away."

"You never got a chance to talk to her at all?"

"She was unconscious when I got here." Tamara began to break down. "I can't talk about it anymore. I've told you both all I know, and I want to get back to the hospital."

"I'll be catching the first flight out," Blythe said.

"So will I," Sierra said.

"Good," Tamara said in a teary whisper. "The sooner the better, I fear."

The ICU staff was kind and sympathetic, and they permitted Tamara to sit in her mother's room. If it weren't for the numerous monitors, tubes and machines Myra was hooked up to she would look as she always had, Tamara realized. She was praying for a miracle, but in her heart knew it wasn't going to happen. All night she alternately wept, paced the small room, got out of the way when a nurse came in, and dozed in a chair.

At one point she thought of her own problems, and then

wept again because her child would never know its grand-
mother. She wouldn't have to lie to her mother now about
why she was moving to Alaska. None of her family would
have to be told anything. Why would she open up to her
sisters, whom she hardly knew? One or both of them might
think her a tramp, and she wasn't any such thing. She'd
made a dreadful mistake, granted, but not because she was
a woman without morals. Sierra and Blythe might think
so, though, and she was not going to risk their derision
with unnecessary candor.

Those thoughts brought Sam to mind. Tamara sat on
that uncomfortable little chair and wondered about Sam.
When she returned to Dallas with a child, would he put
two and two together?

Her mouth pursed. He wouldn't care if he did figure it
out. Men like Sam Sherard used their good looks to get
what they wanted from a woman and then went on to
another foolish female. How many unsuspecting women
had fallen for him as she had? There might even be others
who'd found themselves in the same fix she was in.

What a disgusting idea, Tamara thought. How could she
have been such a fool? The transfer to Alaska would do
more than provide a means to explain the birth of her child;
she wouldn't have to see or talk to Sam for at least a year.
Maybe more than a year, Tamara mused. And who could
tell? She might like working at the Alaska branch and stay
there indefinitely.

Thoughts of Sam fled Tamara's mind as suddenly as
they'd appeared as Tamara looked at her mother and again
felt saturated with grief. How could Myra have kept such
a secret as the serious breakdown of her health? What had
been her rationale for doing so? Tamara had always admitted that she didn't know her sisters very well, but she'd
trusted in the bond between her and her mother. Learning
how flimsy that bond had really been was disheartening.
Myra had lied to her repeatedly on the phone, whenever
Tamara had asked about her health, how she was feeling.

Apparently she'd been doing the same with Blythe and Sierra.

Tamara released a heavy, forlorn sigh. Maybe none of them really knew their mother.

Chapter Eight

When Myra Benning drew her final breath the following evening, her three daughters were standing by her bed, weeping quietly.

Later, Dr. Bergstrom escorted them from the room. "Go home," he told them, speaking kindly. "Try to get some rest tonight. The next few days are going to be difficult."

At the thought of what was yet to be faced, Tamara broke down and was surprised to find herself in Blythe's arms. Her oldest sister smelled of a flowery perfume. Was it lilac? Blythe's concern was comforting, and Tamara was able to get a grip on her emotions.

Finally the three of them left the hospital and got into their rental cars, forming a small caravan for the drive to their mother's home. The cold, dark night did nothing to elevate Tamara's spirits. Blythe and Tamara parked in the driveway, so Sierra pulled her car over to the curb.

The only thing said on their way into the house was

Sierra's remark, "Feels like we could be in for some snow."

They took off their coats and hung them in the hall closet, then Blythe turned up the thermostat, as the house felt chilly. She looked at her two younger sisters. "Is anyone hungry?"

They hadn't had dinner and had barely touched lunch in the hospital cafeteria. Sierra and Tamara couldn't seem to come up with an answer, and Blythe took charge. "I don't think any of us could eat a big dinner, so I'll fix some snacks. Tamara, you look ready to fall down. Sierra, please take her into the family room and *sit* down."

Once there, Tamara gladly sank into one of the large, comfortable recliner chairs. This was the room with the television set and compact disc player. It had cheerful wallpaper and a redbrick fireplace. Although the architecture of the house was of another era, Myra had kept up with the times and the room was nicely decorated in shades of blue and gray. There was lovely woodwork throughout the old house, high ceilings and an aura of elegance even in this room.

"I'm going to build a fire," Sierra said, moving to the fireplace. "Well, for goodness sakes, it has a gas log. When did Mother have that put in? We used to build wood fires in here."

"There was a gas log while I was living at home," Tamara said.

Sierra turned. "Really?"

"Do you know how to turn it on?"

"Yes. It's what we have in our fireplaces in San Francisco." She turned on the gas and pushed the button for the automatic striker. Instantly there was a blaze among the artificial logs.

Tamara had been watching her middle sister. Sierra was the prettiest of the three of them, she thought. Blythe and herself were blondes, like their mother. Sierra had dark hair and eyes. She wore her hair long and straight, and there was an exotic cast to her face. Eyes slightly tilted upward at the outer corners, naturally tawny complexion, full lips and the most perfect nose Tamara had ever seen—indeed, Sierra was a beauty. Small wonder she had drawn the attention of an educated, rich, handsome man like Mike Findley.

"How is Mike?" Tamara asked out of courtesy.

Sierra didn't answer right away. Her back was still to Tamara as she watched the fire. Finally she said, "He's fine." She got up from the hearth and sat on the sofa to stare broodingly at her own feet.

Tamara didn't feel much like talking, either, and what was there to say to a sister she barely knew, anyway? Sierra had her life, she had hers, and there wasn't much chance of their paths ever doing more than crossing occasionally.

Blythe came in with a large tray, and Tamara immediately thought the same about her. There was even less chance of getting close to her sedately beautiful eldest sister, since Blythe lived on the other side of the country. Actually, the three of them couldn't live farther apart and still be in the mainland United States if they'd deliberately aimed for that goal. *How sad,* she thought.

Blythe set the tray on the coffee table in front of the sofa. From her chair Tamara could see small plates of crackers, various cheeses, green grapes, some kind of sliced sausage, pickles and olives. Nibbling food. Also on the tray was an open bottle of white wine and three glasses.

"I thought a little wine might help us sleep," Blythe said in her naturally soft voice.

"Sounds good to me," Sierra said.

Tamara became slightly uncomfortable. She hadn't yet seen an obstetrician, but she knew what she should and shouldn't drink. "None for me, Blythe. I—I'm not very fond of wine." It wasn't altogether an untruth. She enjoyed a glass of wine with meals on occasion, but it was far from a necessity.

"Really? I think you might like this wine, Tamara. It has a wonderful flavor, not too sweet, not too dry."

"No, but thank you," Tamara said quietly. A strong urge to tell her sisters the truth took her by surprise, and she repressed the impulse by firmly shutting her mouth. But wasn't it odd that she would suddenly want to share her innermost thoughts with two women who were practically strangers, albeit sisters? She sighed and chalked it up to the instability of her emotions right now.

"There are several bottles of juice in the refrigerator. How about one of those?" Blythe asked. Tamara started to get up. "No, no, you sit still. I'll get it. Cranberry okay?"

"Cranberry would be fine." Tamara sank back in her chair. "Thank you." Blythe again left the room.

Sierra took a piece of cheese from the tray. "Aren't you going to eat something?" she asked Tamara.

"Probably," Tamara murmured. She was exhausted, grief stricken and sick at heart. What she really wanted was to go to bed and pull the covers over her head. She had shed so many tears that her eyes burned like live coals.

But there were things the three of them had to talk about, although she hated even thinking of the awful but necessary discussions yet to come.

Blythe returned and handed a glass of cranberry juice to Tamara, who again murmured, "Thank you." Blythe then walked over to a set of wall shelves that contained an assortment of framed photos and knickknacks.

She picked up a picture of her parents and studied it. "I remember when this was taken," she said reflectively. "Twenty-five years ago. How time does fly." She sighed, then added, "They were a very handsome couple, weren't they? Sierra, you look like Dad, and Tamara and I resemble Mother."

"I wish I remembered Dad better," Tamara said.

Blythe returned the picture to the shelf. "You were only eight when he died."

"Yes, but I have memories of my early childhood. I just don't have many that include Dad."

Blythe sat on the sofa and poured wine into two glasses. "I wasn't around during those years, of course, but it's my understanding that Dad put in very long hours with his medical practice."

"That's true," Sierra said. "I was still living at home during that time, and I remember days passing without seeing him. He left the house before I got up and came home after I was asleep." She frowned slightly. "That must have been hard on Mother."

"She never complained about it that I know of," Blythe said. She bit her lip for a moment. "But then, Mother was always good at keeping her feelings to herself."

Tamara stared at her eldest sister. "Good at keeping secrets, Blythe?"

Blythe looked startled. "Why do you think that?"

"I'm not sure. For some reason I've always had the feeling there was something Mother couldn't or wouldn't talk about. I'm almost sure of it now, after learning she kept her...bad health a secret from us." She swallowed the lump in her throat.

"Do you think her secret, if she had one, had something to do with the family?" Sierra inquired.

Tamara thought a moment. "Yes, something about the family. Do either of you know why I would get that impression? Did you have it, as well?"

"No," Blythe said quickly.

Sierra sipped her wine with a thoughtful expression. "Possibly," she said. "What I always thought strange was Mother leaving Dad that time, then discovering she was pregnant with you, Tamara."

"What was strange about that?" Blythe asked.

"Did you ever once hear Mother and Dad quarreling or bickering over anything? I didn't. I never heard a cross word between them, not even once. So what was so bad that Mother left?"

"They never quarreled while I was growing up," Blythe admitted. "But didn't you say a minute ago that Dad was so involved in his work that he was rarely home? That could have caused Mother to leave."

"But she left Sierra as well as Dad," Tamara said. "Who took care of you during Mother's absence, Sierra? Do you remember?"

Sierra nodded. "I was almost ten and remember it all quite well. One day Mother was here and the next she was gone. Dad's explanation was that she simply went on an extended vacation. A woman named Sara Wickham moved in. She kept the house, did the cooking and watched me like a hawk."

"Was there…what I mean is…was there a—a closeness between Sara…and Dad?" Tamara stammered.

"Oh, Lord, no," Sierra said. "Sara Wickham was all-business, as plain as they come and at least twenty years older than Dad. No, there wasn't anything funny in that regard."

"Blythe, where were you when that was going on?" Tamara asked.

"In college," Blythe said curtly. "Look, that's all water under the bridge. Why even talk about it?"

Blythe's unusual tone of voice and dismissal of a subject that was of great interest even to Sierra, apparently, startled Tamara. *Blythe knows more than she's saying,* she thought. *If there really is a Benning family secret, Blythe knows what it is.*

The subject was dropped. They picked at the food for about ten minutes with very little conversation, then Blythe voiced what they were all thinking and worrying about. "Let's go to bed and do our talking about—" her voice cracked "—the funeral arrangements in the morning."

Tamara was so relieved she immediately got up. Sierra started to pick up the tray, but Blythe stopped her. "I'll take care of this. You two go on to bed. You both look completely done in."

"So do you," Sierra said.

"I'm fine, Sierra, and I'd like to be alone in Mother's kitchen for a while. Go to bed and try to sleep well." Blythe picked up the tray and walked out.

Tamara and Sierra looked at each other. "Well, I guess that's that," Sierra said. "Good night, Tamara."

"Good night," Tamara murmured.

They headed for their respective bedrooms.

The following three days passed in a blur for Tamara. She accepted so many teary condolences from her mother's friends before, during and after the funeral that she couldn't discern one from another. In truth, she didn't even try. Her grief overrode everything else, except for one thing. At some point in the confusion she called Dallas and, since Mr. Grimes was still on vacation, spoke to the director of personnel and explained her situation. "All I can tell you is that I'll be back to work as soon as possible."

The woman was sympathetic and understanding. "Thank you for calling, Tamara."

On Wednesday morning Tamara, Blythe and Sierra dawdled over coffee at the kitchen table after breakfast. They were still emotional, still prone to tear up without warning, but the worst of it—the funeral, the dinner at Myra's church afterward—was behind them and they all felt a modicum of relief.

Blythe brought up the subject of their mother's will. "She left everything to the three of us. There's not much cash in the bank—about forty thousand dollars—but there's an insurance policy for fifty thousand and the house is worth quite a lot. And, of course, someone has to go through…" There was a painful hesitation before Blythe could continue. "…Mother's things." She cleared her throat. "I've given this a great deal of thought, and, Sierra, you have a husband to get back to and Tamara has a relatively new job. I can easily get a leave of absence without jeopardizing my teaching career, so it seems only sensible that I be the one to stay in Coeur d'Alene and handle the estate. What do you think?'' Her gaze went back and forth between her sisters, who, like her, were still in their nightclothes and robes.

Tamara spoke first. ''I think you're very unselfish. Thank you, Blythe.''

Sierra took longer to formulate an answer, but finally said, ''I could stay and help you.''

''And leave Mike alone for heaven knows how long?'' Blythe said. ''Selling this house could take months, Sierra.''

Sierra looked down at the table. ''I couldn't be gone that long. There are things…''

She stopped talking and Blythe quickly stepped in. ''Of course there are. Mike could be the most understanding husband in the world, for all I know, but I doubt if he would want you gone for months.''

Sierra nodded with a sad expression in her lovely dark eyes. Tamara's heart went out to her middle sister. To both sisters, in fact. Why didn't she know them better? Why had none of them made an effort to get closer—if not geographically, then emotionally?

''Did you feel close to Mother?'' she asked abruptly.

''What a strange question,'' Blythe said.

''I can answer it,'' Sierra said. ''Yes, I felt close to Mother.''

''Didn't you, Blythe?'' Tamara persisted.

Blythe lifted her coffee cup for a swallow, and Tamara got the idea that she was stalling for time. Finally Blythe dabbed at her mouth with her napkin and took a deep breath. ''I think you could say we were close, Tamara.''

''Always?'' she couldn't stop herself from pressing the point.

''Goodness,'' Blythe declared with a weak smile. ''We had our ups and downs like any mother and daughter. Didn't you?''

"I think what I'm getting at is if we felt so close to Mother, why didn't we ever feel close to each other?"

"We're all ten years apart in age," Blythe said patiently. "We grew up in three different decades."

"I know that, Blythe. But we're still a family. Do you realize that the three of us are all the family we have now?"

"Sierra has Mike," Blythe said gently. "And you'll marry someday and—"

Tamara interrupted. "I'm talking about blood family." She thought of the child she was carrying and the fact that these two women were going to be aunts. Again it was all she could do not to tell them about her condition and her well-defined plans for herself and the baby.

But if they disapproved, if either of them tensed up and said something even slightly derogatory about her situation, she wouldn't be able to bear it.

"I'm sorry, Tamara," Blythe said softly. "I knew what you meant and I should not have digressed. Maybe things will change. We should stay in touch about the estate, and maybe…well, maybe we'll become closer. Would you like that?"

Tears filled Tamara's eyes. "Very much," she whispered.

All three of them reached for tissues.

After a few emotionally wrenching moments, Blythe wiped her eyes and got up to refill their coffee cups. "Something just occurred to me," she said, returning the pot to the stove and resuming her place at the table. "I mentioned going through Mother's things, and I'll be glad to take care of everything if you two need to get home right away. But it really would be best if you could stay a little longer, just another day or so. Mother's jewelry, for instance. Her will does not designate which of us should have which piece, so we're going to have to choose. Do you see what I'm getting at? And there are other items—the little things around the house she treasured so much, like the family photo albums and her ceramic collection. I don't think any of us are concerned about the monetary value of these things, but their sentimentality is immeasurable. What do you say? Can you stay for at least one more day?''

Sierra nodded. ''I can, and I'm glad you thought of it.''

Tamara felt her sisters' eyes on her. She wanted in the worst way to be a part of this segment of dividing her mother's estate. As Blythe had said, the value of Myra's jewelry and personal treasures wasn't what was important. What did have meaning was possessing some of the things that Myra had loved.

''Yes,'' Tamara said. ''I'd like to be here for that.''

''Then it's settled,'' Blythe said. ''Let's shower, dress and get started.''

They were in agreement and felt a little better because they had a solid plan of action, even though each knew going through Myra's things was going to be traumatic.

But it had to be done, and for Tamara, at least, the idea of spending more time with her sisters, even under these circumstances, seemed wonderful.

''Oh, there's one more thing,'' Blythe said. ''I'd like to return my rental car to the Spokane airport. I can use Mother's car while I'm here, unless either of you object.''

''Makes sense to me,'' Sierra said.

''Absolutely,'' Tamara agreed.

And so it's over, Tamara thought with a sigh as she settled back in her seat for the first leg of her long flight to Dallas. There were plane changes in her schedule and a three-hour layover in Denver. She would not get home until this evening and she would be tired. But it was Saturday and she would have tomorrow to rest up before returning to work on Monday.

Her pulse became erratic as her thoughts turned from the sorrowful events of the past week to all that might happen in the next. New Year's had passed unnoticed and uncelebrated by her and her sisters. Elliot Grimes had undoubtedly read her transfer request by now, and she couldn't help wondering about his reaction to it.

But he really wouldn't mind, would he? Yes, her promotion could be a hurdle. She couldn't imagine Tom Rowland or Mr. Grimes announcing it during her absence, so probably no one in the department knew about it yet. That was a point in her favor, she thought, albeit uneasily.

The uneasiness wouldn't go away. For the first time since she'd turned in her transfer request she felt deep concern over how it would be received. She realized that if she hadn't been handed that promotion she wouldn't be worried at all. She would be just another employee among hundreds, and who would care if she transferred to the Alaska branch?

There would be no promotions in Alaska, would there? In fact, she wasn't sure what she'd be doing there. It was strictly a sales and delivery operation, that much she knew. All manufacturing by Rowland, Inc. was done in the Dallas plants, and what was needed in Alaska was shipped there.

Overwrought, Tamara released a long, deep sigh. She was so tired of worrying, tired of crying, and in a very potent way her troubles were just beginning. She would not be able to afford two apartments and she'd have to give up the one in Dallas when she moved. And the move itself seemed a monumental drain on the energy reserves she had.

But what else could she do? Her plan to leave Dallas was sensible for both her and the baby. There was no one to turn to to help her get through the ensuing year, and what could anyone do to help, anyhow?

What about Sam? a voice in her head asked.

She pursed her lips in anger. *What about him?* Sam was not the sort of man to do the honorable thing. In her opinion Sam Sherard had no honor at all.

No, she would never kid herself about the kind of man he was. She was in this alone, make no mistake.

* * *

Tamara wasn't at her desk ten minutes on Monday morning when Mr. Grimes's secretary called and asked her to come to his office.

With a wildly beating heart and a nervous flutter in her stomach, Tamara went directly to his door and knocked.

"Come in," he called.

Taking a deep breath, she opened the door and stepped in.

Elliot Grimes rose from his desk chair. "Good morning, Tamara. Close the door, please, and come and sit down." He gestured to the chairs in front of his desk.

"Good morning, Mr. Grimes." After shutting the door, she crossed to a chair.

"I was terribly distressed to hear about your mother. Please accept my sincerest condolences."

"Thank you. It was a shock to…all of us."

"By 'all,' you mean the rest of your family."

"I have two older sisters," Tamara murmured, wishing to God her nerves would settle down. She was doing her best to appear calm and collected. It was odd that when she had turned in her transfer request she'd been so certain it would go through without a glitch. But too much time had passed, and her confidence with it, apparently. Now she didn't know what to expect.

Grimes sat down and picked up a piece of paper. Tamara saw it was her request for transfer, and she clasped her hands together in her lap to keep them from shaking.

"So," Mr. Grimes said, "you're getting married."

"Yes, sir."

"Congratulations."

"Thank you."

Grimes looked down at the form. "You wrote here that you met your young man in college."

"Yes," she said weakly. Writing that lie had been much easier than speaking it.

Elliot Grimes dropped the paper and sat back in his chair, his gaze firmly fixed on Tamara. "This is difficult for me to say, Tamara, but I cannot honor your request. We need you here. *I* need you here. Besides, there are no openings in the Alaska branch right now. Even if there were, however, we would not give you a transfer. I understand you'd like to be closer to your husband after you're married, and I empathize. Tom feels the same. But the company comes first, Tamara. It has to."

Mr. Grimes's comments and attitude were not totally unexpected. But Tamara knew that this was undoubtedly her one and only opportunity to change his outlook, and she had better make the most of it.

"There are no openings at all in the Alaska branch? Mr. Grimes, I would take any job," she said, letting her anxiety show.

"Because of your future husband. Tamara, I know how you must be feeling and I'm sorry. But is his career more important than yours? Perhaps he should be the one considering a transfer."

"His—his company has no branches," she blurted, despising herself for lying like this, however much her predicament demanded drastic measures.

Mr. Grimes spoke in a kindly manner. "Tamara, we cannot permit our employees' personal lives to interfere with the operation of this firm. Surely you understand that. You were hired to work in Dallas. You've done an exemplary job and earned a promotion that few of our present employees will ever attain. And you did it in less than a year. You should be enormously proud of yourself. We are. Tom and I are extremely proud of you, and we're also extremely pleased with ourselves for accurately foreseeing your potential. Tamara, there's no chance of us letting you go to Alaska. I sincerely hope you can live with our decision."

It was either live with it or quit working for Rowland altogether, Tamara thought unhappily. She must accept their decision gracefully and act as though it wasn't the end of the world. But what in heaven was she going to do now?

"Very well," she said quietly. "I hope you understand that I had to try."

"Of course I do," Grimes said, smiling and getting to his feet. "We're going to announce your promotion at a departmental meeting this afternoon. A memo will be passed around sometime this morning notifying everyone in sales of the meeting."

Tamara forced herself to her feet and even managed a weak smile. "Thank you."

Mr. Grimes came around his desk and opened the door for her. "I knew you'd take it well. You're an intelligent person, and Tom and I are darned glad you're on our team. We're both looking forward to a long association with you, Tamara. Keep in mind that there's no telling how far you might go in this company. It's really up to you."

She managed another feeble smile. "Yes, sir."

Tamara dragged herself back to her office, sat at her desk and stared at a wall. This couldn't be happening to her, it just couldn't.

She took out a pad and pencil to give the appearance that she was working, and then gave in to the shock and panic overwhelming her. She was too stunned even to cry, or maybe there simply were no more tears left in her system.

She'd had no backup plan in case the first one failed, and that fact was hitting home with cruel clarity.

What *was* she going to do now?

Chapter Nine

Sam's New Year's Eve had been uneventful. He rarely attended parties, and besides, he couldn't think of anywhere he'd rather see in the New Year than on his ranch. Stubby had cooked a good dinner, which they enjoyed eating together, then the older man got himself all slicked up. Wearing the gleeful, anticipatory expression of a mischievous boy, he'd gone off to celebrate the holiday with friends.

Sam had read for a while, then, as midnight approached, he'd turned on the television to watch the revelers in other portions of the country. About 12:20, he switched off the set, put on a denim jacket and went outside. The night was crisply cold and refreshing. He leaned on the corral fence and looked up at the sky. The stars looked like brilliant diamonds against a black velvet sky, an awesome sight that filled his soul with emotion.

The emotion expanded as he rejoiced again over owning this ranch. He had started with nothing and accomplished something worthwhile, and there were moments, like this one, where pride in what he had done with his life was almost a religious experience.

Sam always took the month of January off, although he never thought of it as a vacation. He spent the time on the ranch, working hard to implement plans to improve the place that kept formulating in his mind throughout the other eleven months of the year. This January he was going to replace the ancient fences around the perimeter of Sherard land. It was a big job and would undoubtedly take most of the month to complete. But he was excited about it, and enjoyed the thought of sturdy new fencing protecting his livestock.

Of course, there were regular customers who would call him when they needed something for their operation, and he would take care of their requests by faxing their orders to the company. But everything could be handled by telephone. This was the month he looked forward to all year. He would not be on the road, staying in motels ranging from west Texas to upper Oklahoma, or eating greasy food in greasy restaurants; he'd be here.

"Thirty great days," he said under his breath. It was the way he felt every New Year's Eve. Thirty days he could call his own.

A yawn and a stretch told him it was bedtime. After tonight he wouldn't be staying up so late. He'd be up at dawn and in bed before nine; the hours in between would be spent working his tail off on that fencing.

He could hardly wait to get started.

The next few days were agonizing for Tamara. Along with her promotion and a raise in salary, she was given a larger office, located much closer to Elliot Grimes's, and she tried very hard to be happy about it. But underlying every smile and comment was bone-jarring worry, the kind of worry that gnawed at a person's vitals and never receded for so much as a second. She had no answers for the question constantly harping in the back of her mind: *what in heaven's name am I going to do?*

Her first major assignment was to revamp the company catalog. She studied recent catalogs and could find nothing wrong with them. But Tom Rowland had decided the company had used the present format long enough, and he wanted something fresh and special. Tamara had the advertising department to assist her in this endeavor, but it was her responsibility. Unfortunately, with so much else on her mind, she couldn't seem to concentrate on something she found quite dull to begin with.

On Friday she left work early to keep her appointment with an obstetrician. She had deliberately chosen a woman doctor, and immediately liked Dr. Charmaine Edmon, who was around fifty years old and possessed a million-dollar smile. After a physical examination and a few tests, Dr. Edmon told her to get dressed and then go to her office, where they would talk.

Tamara hurried into her clothes, left the examining room and rounded the corner to the doctor's private office. She sat in one of the comfortable chairs at the front of the desk and waited.

Dr. Edmon came in and sat at her desk. For a few moments she read from Tamara's file. Raising her eyes, she said, "You're not married."

Tamara had decided to be totally honest with her answers on the form she'd been asked to fill out, and had written "Miss" before her name on the designated line.

"No, I'm not," she said with a quake in her voice.

"Did you make a conscious decision to have a child?" Dr. Edmon asked.

"No," Tamara whispered.

"What does the father have to say about all of this?" Dr. Edmon asked.

"He doesn't have anything to say about it. He doesn't even know."

Dr. Edmon's left eyebrow rose.

"He wouldn't care," Tamara blurted out. She suddenly had to tell it all. "I was a fool one weekend in early November, Dr. Edmon. I thought there was something important between us, and there wasn't."

"Oh, dear," Dr. Edmon murmured. "Tamara, sometimes life hands us more than we think we can handle. But the human spirit is very resilient. Try to look at your problems realistically. What do you think would help in this situation?"

"Well, obviously, a husband would help a lot," Tamara said. "I'm going to start showing very soon now, and people *are* going to know."

Tamara looked at the doctor as a plan started to form. What she needed was a marriage of convenience. And Sam would be the perfect partner. She was silent for a long moment, but during that time her nerves began to calm down and the tears in her eyes dried up. Finally she spoke again. "A marriage of convenience," she said under her breath, as though talking to herself.

"You need to do some thinking about what is best." Dr. Edmon glanced down at her notes. "Well, the good news is that you're a healthy young woman. Using the date of conception you gave me, your baby should be born on June 29, give or take a day or two. I recommend having an ultrasound within the first few weeks of your second trimester, but if you develop any problems at all, call me and I may up that timing. I'm giving you some pamphlets regarding proper diet, recommended weight gain, exercise and such. Please read them." Dr. Edmon rose to her feet and smiled. "The receptionist will arrange your next appointment on your way out. I'll see you then."

The phrase kept repeating in Tamara's mind: *a marriage of convenience.* Would she be afraid to broach Sam with that idea? "Not on a bet," she muttered. She despised the man, but she wasn't afraid of him or anything he might say. In fact, there was a whole slew of things she wouldn't mind saying to him. Dr. Edmon was right to bring up the subject of her baby's father. It was Tamara's nature to accept full responsibility for her own behavior, but she hadn't made this baby alone and half of the responsibility should be dumped squarely on Sam's broad shoulders.

Instead of going home from the appointment, Tamara returned to the Rowland building and her office. Without taking off her coat, she sat at her desk. For some reason she still had the field reps' files in her bottom drawer, and she flipped through them until she came to Sam's. All she wanted was his telephone number and address, which she jotted on a piece of note paper.

Determinedly she closed the file. Despite the vague rural address, she would find Sam's ranch some way, somehow. She was going to pay Mr. Sam Stoneface Sherard a visit tomorrow morning. If he wasn't home, she would leave a message with Mr. Draco to have Sam contact her immediately.

The reason she wouldn't call first was because whether Sam was there or not, she wanted to see where he lived.

Who had a better right to intrude on his safe, guarded little world? she thought with a bitter thrust of her chin.

Sam and Stubby were dirty and sweaty from putting in new fence posts all morning. At noon they went to the house, washed up and made some lunch, which they were eating at the kitchen table when they heard a car. Since the driveway was a long one, there was no question someone was coming to the house.

Stubby got up and peered out the window. "It's a woman. Stranger to me."

Frowning, Sam left his chair and looked through the window. "I don't believe this," he mumbled. But then, unexpectedly, something came alive inside of him and he grinned. "I'll be damned."

Stubby stepped back. "You must know her."

"You bet I know her. I'll go out and escort her in."

Sam hurried through the back door and reached Tamara's car just as she was getting out of it.

"This is a surprise," he said with an honest-to-gosh twinkle in his eyes. *A real nice surprise,* he was thinking, and it sure wasn't one he could ever have dreamed up.

Tamara faced him squarely. There was fire in her eyes, Sam saw. His good mood faded and a nameless, uneasy premonition suddenly cramped his gut. "I'm sure it is," she said coldly.

The twinkle vanished entirely from his eyes as he regarded her suspiciously. However, he spoke cordially. "How'd you find me?"

"It wasn't hard, believe me," she drawled derisively.

Her whole attitude was a challenge, and he felt himself sinking deeper into that dark mood. Okay, he thought. He might as well get to the bottom of this right now. "You're mad about something. You've *been* mad about something. Is that why you're here—to give me hell over something I don't even know I did?"

Tamara put on a saccharine smile. "Now, isn't that just like a woman, to get mad over nothing?" Her smile vanished. "Listen, you conceited jerk, I wouldn't lower myself to look you up if I had any other way to go."

Sam's eyes narrowed on her. "What's wrong? Don't beat around the bush," he drawled with some sarcasm of his own. "Tell me straight out."

"I fully intend to." Tamara inhaled deeply. "I'm pregnant, the baby is yours and I want you to marry me."

Sam took a step back, leaned his hips against the front fender of her car and stared off into the distance. To give him time to digest what she'd just told him, Tamara leaned against the *back* fender of the car, folded her arms across her chest and waited. She felt hard inside, not a bit sympathetic toward Sam.

Without looking at her Sam said, "How do I know it's my baby?"

Tamara's head jerked around so she could glare at him. "Because I said it is, and I'm not a liar!"

Sam realized that Tamara Benning could tell the tallest tales in Texas and he wouldn't know it. But she could also be telling the truth. He hadn't used protection the first time they'd made love that weekend, and once was all it took if a woman was in the fertile part of her cycle.

It was beginning to sink in—Tamara's militant attitude, the idea of a shotgun wedding, the loss of his freedom and contented way of life. He cast her a sidelong glance. "Why don't you stop throwing attitude all over the place? I think I have the right to ask a few questions."

"You have no rights at all," she snapped. "I want nothing from you but your name. I've humiliated myself by coming here, but I do need a short-term husband. What's yours will remain yours, what I have will remain mine. You have heard of a prenuptial agreement, haven't you?" she finished with scathing sarcasm.

Sam pushed away from the car. "That's enough! I'm willing to talk, but I don't have to put up with any snide remarks." He started walking. "Come on, we'll talk in the house."

Sam's sudden evolution from mouse to man was daunting enough to cut Tamara's temper by half. She followed him, and for the first time took a good look at his house. It wasn't a mansion by any means, although it seemed to be in good repair and the yard was clean. There was a modest patch of lawn and several enormous old trees, barren of leaves at the present but nicely situated to shade the house's pleasant front porch during hot weather.

Some distance behind the house was a large barn, several smaller buildings and a corral. Sam's Jeep and a white pickup were parked near the barn. Farther out Tamara could see cattle and horses. *His precious ranch,* she thought with rancor as she followed him into the house through the back door.

They walked into the kitchen. "Stubby, Tamara," Sam said, in the shortest possible version of an introduction.

For a moment Stubby looked startled at Sam's terseness, but then he got up from the table and smiled warmly at Tamara. "It's a pleasure meeting you, ma'am."

Tamara could not be rude to this kindly older man, not even if her success with Sam depended on it. She'd wondered who Stubby Draco was, and now she knew. "Nice meeting you, Stubby," she said, meaning it. Sam sent her a pointed look, which she didn't miss but ignored. If he hoped she was going to be that nice to *him*, he had another thought coming.

"I'll be getting back to work now," Stubby said to Sam, proving himself a tactful man. "Goodbye, Tamara."

"Bye," she murmured. There was food on the table and it was obvious she had interrupted their lunch. She hadn't planned to arrive at noon, but the roads had been unfamiliar and it had taken her longer to get here than she'd thought.

"Are you hungry?" Sam asked. "There are plenty of sandwich fixings."

"No, thank you," she said frostily.

With a grim expression, Sam began transferring cold meat and cheese from the table to the refrigerator. "We'll do our talking in the living room. Go on in. It's through that doorway."

Holding her head high, Tamara walked out of the kitchen and into the living room. There were colors in here that she would never have put together, but every chair looked comfortable, as did the sofa. There was a table with a telephone on it, and a tall bookcase crammed with all sorts of books and magazines. One wall contained a stone fireplace with a sturdy wood mantel. Dead center of the mantel was an interesting clock. Tamara went over for a closer look. "Hmm," she said, realizing that it was a good piece and probably worth more than everything else in the room combined.

But she wasn't here to compute Sam's financial status, and she moved to the sofa and sat down to wait for him. Almost immediately a black-and-white cat ambled into the room and jumped up on the sofa to sniff her.

"Well, hello there," she said quietly. "Want to make friends?" He settled down next to her and began purring. "Guess so," she said. She was petting the cat when Sam came in. "Nice cat. What's his name?" she asked.

"Jo-jo." Sam leaned his shoulder against the mantel and watched her petting the cat. Unquestionably, Tamara was one of the prettiest women he'd ever known, but as he'd thought many times before, there was more to her than her looks. He thought a moment and figured out what was special about her: she seemed to light up the room. He'd never seen her dressed like this before, in jeans, a plain blue sweater and loafers, and he liked the way she looked in casual clothes.

"Jo-jo's very friendly," Tamara said.

"Not always."

"I'm surprised you have a cat."

"I don't. He belongs to Stubby." Sam moved from the fireplace to a chair and sat down. "Have you seen a doctor?"

Apparently the small talk was over. Tamara put the cat out of her mind and answered curtly, "Of course I saw a doctor. Do you think I would drive clear out here without knowing for sure?" She was looking directly at Sam and unconsciously registering his soiled gray T-shirt, ancient jeans and dusty boots. Even with his hair tousled and wearing dirty clothes he was the best-looking man she'd ever seen. It infuriated her that she would notice.

"How would I know what you might do?" Sam retorted.

"Oh, that's right," she snapped. "We only spent one weekend together, didn't we?"

A lightbulb came on in his head. "So *that's* your big

gripe. The phone lines run both ways, you know. If you wanted to see me again, why didn't you call?''

"Me call a disinterested man? Not on a bet." Tamara leaned forward. "And I'd like you to know that I wouldn't be here today if my plans had worked out."

"What plans?"

Her chin came up defiantly. "I asked for a transfer to the Alaska branch. If they had given it to me, you never would have known about the baby."

Sam felt as though someone had just punched him in the gut. How dare she say something like that to him? If she was carrying his baby, she should have come to him the minute she knew about it. "How long have *you* known?" His eyes were hard as nails.

"Since just before Christmas."

"Not very damned long," he muttered. Then it dawned on him how snippy she'd been at the Christmas party. "Did you know the day of the party?"

She didn't like the way he was grilling her. In truth, with all that had happened in the past few weeks, it was difficult for her to accurately pinpoint dates and events. "Let's get on a different tack here, okay? I *am* pregnant and the baby *is* yours. I'm not talking about a lifelong arrangement between us. I'm doing well with my job, and I'm not asking for one red cent from you. I tried the transfer idea—"

"Yeah, let's talk about *that*. How would a transfer to Alaska have changed the situation?"

Tamara took an impatient breath. "I was going to arrive in Alaska as a married woman—improvised, of course—stay there until the baby was three or four months old, then request a transfer back to Dallas—as a divorced woman."

"Good God," Sam groaned. "What a manipulative mind."

Tamara's eyes shot angry sparks. "You might be a little manipulative, too, if you found yourself pregnant and unmarried. I believe I have a spotless reputation with the company, and I would do almost anything to maintain it.''

"You're worried about gossip.''

"Is that a crime in your book?''

Sam had never given gossip much thought. He didn't listen to it, nor pass on any he happened to stumble across accidentally. But there were things in his own life he wouldn't want discussed and snickered over among the people he worked with, so he understood Tamara's dread of it.

"No, it's not a crime," he said.

Tamara was suddenly weary of this whole encounter. He hadn't said yes, he hadn't said no and it was time he gave her a definite answer. But before she pressed him for one, she should explain her plans in more detail.

"I said I didn't want anything but your name and that's the truth. Other than going through the ceremony and then announcing our marriage, our lives would not change. You would continue living here, I would keep my apartment. After a month or so, I'll tell people I'm pregnant. Some might add up dates, but I can live with that. My medical insurance would pay the bills and I earn enough to support the baby after it's born. You needn't even see it. We could get a divorce shortly after the baby's birth, and I'll pay for that, too. I'd like to wait about six months before the divorce, but…''

Her voice trailed off as Sam jumped up, walked over to her and glared down at her with his hands on his hips. "You think you've got it all figured out, don't you? Well, think again, sweetheart. I *will* marry you, but don't count on me staying away from my son or daughter.''

Tamara's jaw dropped. "But…but—''

"No 'buts.' Take it or leave it," Sam growled.

Tamara felt just as trapped as she had before coming here, but in a much different way. It had never once occurred to her that Sam would demand parental rights. She didn't want him involved in their baby's upbringing, but dare she "leave it," as he'd so crudely put it?

"I don't have a choice, do I?" she snapped furiously.

"You might not like it, but yes, you have a choice," Sam snapped back.

She slid to the edge of the sofa cushion, grabbed her purse and got to her feet. "I despise the ground you walk on."

"I'm not overly fond of you right now, either," he returned. "So, what's it going to be?"

She spat the words out as though they were poisonous. "We'll get married."

"When?" His query lashed the air.

When? *Oh God,* she silently moaned. Was this really the answer, or was she digging herself a deeper pit?

"The sooner the better, I would think," Sam said. "Tell you what. You go home and pack an overnight case. I'll make plane reservations and pick you up in a few hours."

Her eyes narrowed suspiciously. "Plane reservations to where?"

"To Las Vegas, Nevada. It's the shotgun-wedding capital of the world, honey. Didn't you know that?"

Chapter Ten

When Tamara was finally on the plane, she didn't know whether to laugh, cry or stand on her head. Her life wasn't merely chaotic anymore, it was totally upside down. For four hours she had moved with the speed of light getting ready for this flight—except for the drive from Sam's ranch back to Dallas, of course. That had been a most disturbing, nerve-racking trip as she had tried to maintain the speed limit, concentrate on the road, debate the wisdom of such a hurry-up wedding and wonder what she should take with her, all at the same time.

She stole a glance at Sam, in the seat next to her. He was clean, nicely dressed and, unlike her, seemingly unruffled. Since picking her up at the apartment, he had been neither friendly nor unfriendly, except for one moment. She'd asked him how he had obtained confirmed flight reservations on such short notice, and his answer had been a brief, bordering on cynical, "Just lucky, I guess." So even though he appeared calm, Tamara suspected that what he really was doing was taking his medicine like a good little boy.

It was bitter medicine for both of them, she thought without a whole lot of pity for Sam. This sort of wedding was a slap in the face for her, and the death of a longtime dream of wearing a gorgeous, flowing white dress when she married a man she adored and who adored her. Instead, she would participate in an impersonal, loveless ceremony wearing a pale blue sheath and matching jacket, chosen because it was made of a fabric that didn't wrinkle in a suitcase.

At her apartment Sam had laid out his plan. They would arrive in Las Vegas at 10:15 p.m., check into their hotel, where she could change clothes if she wished, then go to the wedding chapel and get married. It was a simple process in Las Vegas, he had added. At that point Tamara had almost called the whole thing off. Nothing about their situation was simple, and Sam putting that label on what was undoubtedly going to be an event with neither taste nor warmth was almost more than she could take.

But she had no acceptable option, so she'd clamped her lips together and kept her resentful feelings to herself.

The plane took off, the steward served drinks—they both ordered colas—and they sat there next to each other without talking. Tamara truly felt like the bottom had dropped out of her world during the past weeks, and she couldn't stop tears from forming in her eyes. She dug in her purse for a tissue, and to her chagrin Sam picked that moment to look at her.

"Are you crying?" he asked.

"No, I'm laughing myself to death."

"Getting married like this isn't the end of the world, you know." *Oh, yeah?* he thought. Didn't he feel a little bit like crying himself?

"I'm not crying about *our* situation," Tamara said sharply. "My mother died less than two weeks ago, and I was thinking of her."

Sam looked stunned. "Tamara, I'm really sorry. I didn't know."

"Just forget it. It's not something I want to talk about right now." The reason she'd given to Sam for her teary eyes was true and it wasn't. She *had* been thinking of her mother, but only as part of the overall pain she had lived with since that foolish weekend in November.

"Fine," Sam said stiffly, and turned his face away from her. The truth was he had a lot to think about and wasn't all that thrilled with conversation on any subject. Laying his head back, he closed his eyes. It was hard to believe he was going to be married. *You don't have to do this,* he told himself. *Is there any proof the baby is yours?*

That was the strange part of this whole affair. He believed Tamara and didn't know why. He still had to question why she hadn't come to him the second she'd suspected her condition, and it made him angry as hell that she had instead plotted a transfer to Alaska rather than tell him what was going on. If Rowland had given her the green light on that nefarious scheme, he would never have known of his son or daughter.

The muscles in his jaw clenched every time he thought of that. If Tamara still thought he was going to stay uninvolved in his child's life, she was in for one very big surprise. But deep down he knew that was what she was hoping for, even though he'd already told her differently. She was really one for the books, and he suspected their marriage, short-lived as it was going to be—and probably their relationship on into the future because of the baby— would involve a string of stormy confrontations. At this point he'd bet anything that their ideas about how best to raise a child were miles apart.

He opened his eyes just enough to take a peek at Tamara without her knowledge. She was wearing taupe slacks and a matching blouse, with a darker jacket. Her lush, thick, honey blond hair was a tangle of curls, and she was the prettiest little thing he'd ever seen, even with that harsh, unhappy expression on her face. His heart softened toward her. No man would ever know what a woman felt during pregnancy, especially when she found herself pregnant and alone. It didn't bother all of them, of course. Some women wanted a baby without a husband. Tamara, obviously, had more traditional expectations. Maybe that was the reason he believed her. He sensed that she was moral, and truthful, even though he didn't know her all that well.

He frowned slightly. If Tamara's morals were so high, how come she had spent that wild weekend with him? A sudden possibility occurred to him. What if she had really felt something for him? Was that the reason for her angry remarks about his not calling?

Sam's stomach sank. At the time he had honestly believed it was just a weekend fling for both of them. If it had been more for Tamara, she must have felt kicked in the teeth by his silence afterward.

He sighed quietly and told himself that things would work out. At this point, what else could he do?

Regardless of Tamara's blue mood, she couldn't help feeling excitement when the plane descended for its landing at McCarran International Airport in Las Vegas. She had never seen so many lights in her life, and as the plane dropped lower, she could pick out specific hotels glowing like brilliantly colored jewels, fabulous to see, especially for a first-time visitor. Her face was practically glued to the window as one marvel after another appeared.

"Beautiful, isn't it?"

She'd all but forgotten Sam was there. "It's unbelievable," she said with awe in her voice. "Have you been here before?"

"A couple of times. A night landing is much more impressive than a daylight landing. I'm glad we came in after dark so you could see it."

Tamara stiffened. He was being nice, and she didn't *want* him to be nice to her. They weren't friends and never would be. Their marriage was going to be a farce, a facade to protect her reputation and their child's legitimacy, and in no way was she going to pretend otherwise.

She sat back, as though the scene below was of no consequence whatsoever. Sam got the message loud and clear, and faced front with a grim expression.

A steward announced the impending landing and instructed the passengers to fasten their seat belts and put their seat backs in an upright position. Tamara tightened her belt and realized she felt queasy. In a few hours she would be a married woman. Oh Lord, she thought, what was she doing? Panic almost choked her. She gripped the ends of the armrests so tightly that her hands ached.

Sam noticed and asked, ''Are you all right?''

''What do you think?'' she said through lips that felt almost numb. It was an effort to move at all, but she managed to turn her head and look at him. ''Are *you* all right? I doubt it. Well, just multiply what you're feeling by ten and that might give you an idea of how trapped *I'm* feeling.''

Sam's lips thinned. ''Okay, so we're both trapped. But why not make the best of it?''

''You know, I was expecting to hear that pearl of wisdom come out of your mouth sooner or later. Let's keep this honest, Sam. Neither of us is happy about what we're doing, so let's cut all the phony-baloney, okay?''

''Asking if you're all right is phony-baloney?'' Sam said scornfully. ''Lady, do you know that you've got a real attitude problem?''

''And you think I should be ashamed of it? Think again, Sam.'' She turned away to look out the window again. The plane set down in a smooth landing. The engines reversed and it slowed down and began taxiing to the terminal.

We're here. This is it, Tamara thought despondently. *You danced to the music, and now it's time to pay the piper.* A feeling of remorse hit her. It was as though she were blaming the baby for being conceived!

Sam was right: her attitude *was* horrible. He was also right about trying to make the best of things. Maybe he wasn't so bad. He was here, wasn't he?

She took a breath and looked at him just as the plane stopped at the gate. "I—I've been a terrible grouch. I'm sorry," she said.

Sam stared in surprise for a moment, then nodded. "Let's both forget it and start from here."

She nodded, too. In the next instant people were getting up from their seats and crowding into the aisle. The two of them waited for a break in the stream of passengers, then Sam got up and retrieved their overnight cases from the overhead storage.

Together they left the plane and entered the terminal. Tamara's mouth dropped open. "There are slot machines in the airport!"

Sam laughed. "They're everywhere, Tamara." He took her arm and she let him steer her through the throng leaving the gate.

The airport reeked of excitement, Tamara noticed at once. Arriving in Las Vegas was not like reaching any other destination to which she'd flown. Deplaning passengers laughed and joked while making their way through the immense terminal to the baggage department, obviously thrilled to be here and anxious to get to the gaming tables and machines.

There was so much to see that Tamara continued to let Sam hold her arm and do the driving, so to speak. Glitzy signs advertising hotels and the stars appearing in various showrooms caught her eye. There were tall, beautifully sculpted palm trees made of some kind of metallic material decorating certain areas, and so many shops and restaurants that Tamara couldn't take it all in. The walk through the airport accomplished one positive thing: she stopped feeling sorry for herself.

By the time they reached the door marked Taxis and Limousines, she was smiling from the heady rush of adrenaline in her system.

"What a place," she exclaimed as they went outside.

"There's only one Las Vegas," Sam agreed, heading her toward a line of taxis. After they were settled in the back seat of one and Sam had told the driver where to go, he apologized to Tamara. "I'm sorry we won't be staying at one of the big hotels, but it's Saturday night, the busiest night of the week, and I was lucky to find a vacant room at all."

"Oh, anywhere will do." Tamara was craning her neck, trying to see everything as the taxi sped toward the Strip. Then Sam's "vacant room" comment sank in. But surely he'd meant to say "vacant rooms," she told herself. After all, he couldn't possibly expect them to share a room.

Twenty minutes later she found out differently. A bellboy had shown them to a room in a nicely appointed hotel, Sam had tipped him, the young man had gone and Tamara was standing with her arms folded, tapping her toe while glaring at Sam.

"One room?" she said angrily.

"And lucky to get it," Sam retorted. "I told you in the taxi—"

"This is a huge city. Do you actually expect me to believe there was only one vacant room in the entire place when you called for reservations?"

Sam took an impatient breath. "There's the telephone. Find out for yourself."

"I'll do *exactly* that," she said, and walked over to the bed and sat down to peruse the phone book.

"Before you get too hoity-toity," Sam drawled, "remember that there are some areas of Vegas you wouldn't stay in on a bet, just like any other city."

She sent him a dirty look, then started calling the hotels with the biggest ads. Some she recognized because of national fame, but whether familiar or not, every answer was the same. "Sorry, we have no vacancies tonight."

Giving up, she stood and went to the window. Sam had disappeared into the bathroom with his overnight case, so she was quite alone to ponder her fate, sigh with utter hopelessness and again feel sorry for herself. Even the nighttime brilliance of Las Vegas couldn't lift her spirits this time. How easy it was to shatter one's entire way of life, she thought despairingly. One moment of carelessness was all it took, just one.

Sam came out of the bathroom and saw her standing at the window. "It's time to go to the chapel," he said quietly.

Tamara turned around. Sam had changed his casual shirt and windbreaker for a white shirt, a tie and a jacket that matched his trousers. He looked clean, crisply put together and devastatingly handsome. Her mood turned bitter. It was his good looks that had gotten her into this mess, and damned if she was going to be taken in again, even if they did have to share a room tonight. She'd sleep on the floor if she had to, or on a chair. She was not going to get into that bed with Sam if she had to lean against a wall all night!

"I'll get changed," she said coldly, reaching for her overnighter and swinging past him into the bathroom.

The door slammed behind her and Sam shook his head. Obviously she'd had no luck in finding a hotel with two rooms to rent tonight, which he'd known would be the case as he'd gone through the same exercise—via long distance—that she had just wasted time on.

He took her place at the window and stared out. This was not one of the grand hotels, but it wasn't a dump, either. It had a nice-sized casino downstairs and several restaurants. He'd done the best he could, given the circumstances, and he was getting tired of Tamara's thankless attitude. What in hell did she expect from him? He was going to marry her. They weren't the first couple who'd found themselves in this situation and they for damned certain weren't going to be the last.

Turning, he looked at the bed. It was king-size and big enough for both of them to use without ever getting near each other. He was in no more of a romantic mood than Tamara was, and she didn't have to worry about him trying anything.

Tamara sailed out of the bathroom. "I'm ready," she announced while picking up her purse.

She looked beautiful, and he would have told her so if he'd thought she would have accepted a compliment without some derogatory comeback.

"Let's go then," he said without inflection.

They rode the elevator down to the first floor without speaking one single word.

"By the authority invested in me by the state of Nevada, I now pronounce you man and wife."

Tamara turned away at once. There was not going to be a wedding kiss, and she didn't care what anyone thought of it, either. The inexpensive ring on her finger, which Sam had purchased at the chapel, felt like a shackle, and she hated it.

Sam thanked the minister, smiled weakly and followed his bride to the door and out to the parking lot, where their cab waited. He opened the back door for Tamara and then climbed in himself.

"Would you like to take a drive and see the Strip?" he asked her.

"No, thank you," she said frostily. Her excitement over Las Vegas had vanished entirely. The only thing worse than her wedding had been her mother's funeral, and she felt the imminent threat of a tearful breakdown. What was galling was that because Sam would be in the room with her, she would not have the privacy she so desperately needed. She had to try to keep her badly bruised emotions in check and didn't know if she could.

Sam told the cabdriver to take them back to their hotel, then leaned back with tension stiffening his spine. In the lobby, on their way to the elevators, he said, "Let's have something to eat before going up."

"You do whatever you wish. I'm not hungry."

Her curt reply was the final straw. Sam pressed his lips together. He escorted Tamara to the door of their room, unlocked it and pushed it open. Then he looked her right in the eye. "You are, without a doubt, the rudest person I've ever had the misfortune of knowing. Good night."

Wide-eyed and startled, she watched him striding back to the elevators. Anger developed swiftly, but not fast enough. "Go to hell," she yelled, but Sam was already in an elevator with the doors closing, and she doubted that he'd heard her. "Jerk," she muttered.

Feeling totally bereft and alone, she went into the room and closed the door. Falling across the bed, she sobbed her heart out.

Sam decided he'd hang out downstairs all night and leave the room to Tamara. He ate dinner in the hotel's excellent steak house, wandered among the throngs of gamblers in the casino for an hour or so and finally decided to play a little blackjack. He was in a to-hell-with-everything mood and even drank a couple of beers. But by 3:00 a.m., he could barely keep his eyes open and there was no place to go but to the room. He got in the elevator and exhaustedly leaned against a wall for the ride up.

Approaching the room, he spotted a tray of dirty dishes on the floor by the door and was glad Tamara had unbent enough to order something from room service. Not eating would not be good for the baby. So what if she wasn't happy. Was he? Hell, he thought cynically, was anyone?

Entering the room without a sound, he silently shut the door behind him. The bathroom door was ajar a few inches, and light filtered through the crack into the bedroom. Tamara was in bed and appeared to be sound asleep.

It was hard to tell for sure in the dim light, but her night-gown seemed to be pink. One of her arms was thrown over her head. Her hair fanned out on the pillow beneath her head. Looking at her, Sam didn't let himself think any-thing remotely personal about his bride, especially not that old bromide regarding conjugal rights. Tamara had done her best to let him know how much she resented him, and he'd done his best to let *her* know he was willing to at least be civil to her. Apparently civility was out of the question for her, and he wasn't a man to beg for favors, so things weren't apt to change between them. There was a sad sort of finality to that conclusion, and Sam wondered if Tamara had also reached it. Could be, he thought, since the blankets were twisted around her legs as though she'd done some rolling and tossing before falling asleep.

Well, he was beat, he thought with a quietly stifled yawn. That bed was big enough that she would never know he was there. Tiptoeing to the opposite side, he noiselessly shed his clothes down to his briefs, draped the garments over a chair, cautiously drew back the blankets and lay down, being especially careful not to jostle the mattress.

He was asleep two seconds after his head hit the pillow.

In that twilight world between sleep and wakefulness, Tamara got out of bed and went into the bathroom. Since her pregnancy began she'd had to get up at least once every night to use the commode. Functioning on automatic pilot, she washed her hands and, with her eyes still half-closed, returned to the bedroom.

About to climb back into bed, she froze. Her eyes opened wide as she stared at Sam's bulk on the other side. His back—bare and broad—was to her, and he seemed to be in such a deep sleep that he was barely breathing.

Her first thought was *how dare he!* But a modicum of reason created a second: *where else would he sleep?*

Unnerved, she slipped on her robe and sat on a chair to watch Sam with a brooding expression. When had he returned to the room? She'd heard nothing, so he must have come in very quietly. She turned the ring on her finger around and around and felt an unwelcome onslaught of emotion. This had to be one of the most pathetic wedding nights in the history of the institution. Was it a forerunner of their relationship from this day forward?

That thought was surprisingly disturbing. It was her fault they hadn't at least eaten dinner together. He'd tried to be nice and she'd cut his every effort to ribbons. Was she going to continue being a shrew? *Why* had she been so nasty to Sam all day? Because he hadn't tried to see her again after their weekend together?

It hurt terribly to remember that weekend—the wonder of their lovemaking, Sam's touch on her body, his kisses. Biting her lip, she recalled her foolish fantasies of falling in love, and how anxiously she had waited for him to bring up their next meeting. He'd never even considered a next meeting, she thought sadly. She'd been a weekend affair for him, nothing more, while she...

She bit her lip harder as tears stung her eyes. She could still love Sam, couldn't she? What kind of fool was she? But no other man had ever made her skin tingle the way Sam had, or kissed her into such mindless abandonment. How did a woman forget things like that? How would she, especially now that they were married?

Her heart suddenly skipped a beat. Was it possible to make theirs a real marriage? If she crawled into bed and snuggled against him, what would he do? Make love to her and then forget it, as he had before? Or would he hold her as a loving husband held his bride, and talk, really talk to her, about the birth of their child, about a future together as a family? What a lovely picture that made in her mind. But it didn't linger for long.

"Oh, stop with the silly ideas," she disgustedly mumbled under her breath. Sam might have married her, but he was still the same guarded, self-centered egotist he'd been before she'd cornered him on his own ranch. Yes, he'd probably make love to her, but if she ever permitted that to happen again, she had better remember how little it meant to Sam.

Too tired to sit there any longer, Tamara got up, slipped out of her robe, left it on the chair and returned to bed. She lay down, got as comfortable as she could under the circumstances and closed her eyes.

It took awhile, but she finally went to sleep.

Sam awoke to the sound of the shower running. He checked the time—7:10 a.m.—then stretched and yawned. Four hours' sleep wasn't enough, but he could catch up on the plane ride home. Thoughtfully he stared at the ceiling. Tamara had to have seen him in bed with her when she woke. If she came out of the bathroom upset and angry, it wouldn't surprise him.

But so be it, he thought. If she intended living the rest of her life mad at him, there was little he could do about it.

Hearing the shower stop, he got out of bed and pulled on his pants. Waiting for Tamara to appear, he stared out the window and thought about being a married man. It didn't seem to matter that his wasn't a real marriage; he still felt different than he had yesterday morning. Maybe it was because of the baby, he mused.

Getting down to the real truth, though, hadn't he felt different from the moment he'd met Tamara? Damned right, he thought. Maybe he'd wanted her on sight and just hadn't let himself admit it, but whatever, something unusual had happened that day. Well, they were both in for it now. Tamara, he and their child—boy or girl—were bonded for years to come.

Thoughts of the future made Sam frown. He didn't want his son or daughter brought up helter-skelter, as he'd been. It was only by the grace of God that he'd escaped the destructive negligence of his parents. The two most important things parents could give a child were love and stability. How could he provide those crucial components if he lived on the ranch and Tamara and their child lived in the city?

With Tamara's attitude toward this liaison, however, he would be lucky to see the baby a few times a month. It was far from acceptable, but what could he do about it?

Sam narrowed his eyes as he contemplated the heart-rending scenario. The birth of the baby was still a long way off, however. If he truly wanted to be an important part of his child's upbringing, maybe there *was* something he could do about it. Eliminating Tamara's resentment of him wouldn't be easy, but he had little to lose by trying.

Sam's downcast mood began evolving into hope. Yes, he thought, a slender thread of excitement running through his system, why *not* try to turn this thing with him and Tamara around? She'd liked him once or she never would have invited him into her home that weekend, and with the right factors in play, she just might like him again.

He didn't even think of the word *love*. He'd lived his entire life without love, so why would he worry about it now? The only thing that really mattered was giving his child a real home. On the ranch, of course.

He drew a satisfied breath; his mind was made up. He was going to dedicate himself to convincing Tamara that a child should be raised with both parents.

He would do whatever it took to accomplish that goal.

Chapter Eleven

Tamara listened in shock to Sam merrily telling a flight attendant that they were newlyweds. The young woman smiled warmly and congratulated them. A searing flush heated Tamara's cheeks, and the second the woman walked away, she asked, "For crying out loud, why did you do that?"

Sam smiled, slow and easy. "It's the truth, isn't it?"

"Yes, but you sounded…you actually sounded *proud!*"

"Would my being proud of our marriage offend you?"

"It would probably knock me off my feet," Tamara retorted.

"Not a bad idea," Sam said in a soft, low voice reeking of sexual innuendo. "Tamara, do you realize what kind of a wedding night we *could* have had?"

She turned red again and said angrily, "I am *not* going to be a part of this conversation."

"Chicken," he said with a teasing grin.

"Just stop it!" Tamara turned her face to the window.

What was wrong with him today? He'd smiled over nothing all during breakfast, making her intensely uncomfortable, as Sam was not a smiler. At least, to her knowledge he wasn't. No, it wasn't just *her* knowledge confirming that fact; he wasn't called Stoneface around the office for no reason.

Tamara's stomach sank at the thought of work. Tomorrow she would have to announce her marriage. Natalie would probably pass out when Tamara told her *who* she had married. And not just Nat. There were going to be some very surprised faces when people heard that Tamara Benning and Sam Sherard had gotten married.

But she couldn't procrastinate on that announcement, not when she had the one about the baby to deal with at the first sensible moment. Tamara groaned inwardly. That was going to be a tough one. People were bound to calculate dates. She'd be facing *some* gossip, no doubt about it. All she could do was hold her head high and ignore it. At least it would be nothing like what would have been discussed if she *wasn't* married. Sam had saved her from that, thank God.

Why had Sam saved her? she wondered with a frown. And why was he acting happy about it today, going so far as to boast of their newlywed status to a stranger?

Sam suddenly leaned toward her. "What are you doing now?" she demanded.

"Taking a look out the window. It's a beautiful day, isn't it? The sky is so blue it's dazzling."

She didn't like the quickening of her pulse just because he was so near. "You've had your look, so please stop crowding me."

Instead of moving away, he gazed into her eyes. "I can't stop regretting last night," he said softly. "It could have been so great, and we let it slip away."

She licked her suddenly dry lips. "Sam, you have to stop thinking like that. Nothing's going to happen between us."

"Not ever?" he whispered. "How can you be so positive?"

What was she seeing in those eyes of his, which were certainly every bit as dazzling as the blue sky outside of the plane? His scent was assailing her senses, and she was beginning to feel addled. *Just like that weekend,* she realized, and tore her gaze from his.

"I'm *very* positive," she said stonily. "If you don't want an elbow in the ribs, get back in your own seat."

Sam couldn't help chuckling at her threat, but he moved over. He'd almost gotten her going, he thought, feeling good at this first effort to break through her defenses.

It would happen, he thought. Sooner or later, it would happen.

Sam insisted on carrying in Tamara's overnight case after their drive from the airport to her apartment. Trailing behind him, she mumbled under her breath, "Hell's bells, I've been toting that thing for two days. What's wrong with that man?"

She knew she was not imagining Sam's differences. For some reason he had developed a silly smile and was acting as though she had suddenly become the love of his life. Of course, that whole idea was totally unbelievable, so Tamara didn't waste any time on that explanation and kept trying to come up with one that made sense.

Sam bent over to set the case down in her living room. Standing tall and straight again, he said, "I'm sure I mentioned my taking January off from the job, so—"

Tamara cut in abruptly. "Sorry, but you didn't."

"Oh. Well, I always take January off." He flashed a smile as open and wide as the all outdoors. "Mostly to get caught up on the work at the ranch. Anyhow, that's where I'll be if you need me for anything. My phone number is—"

Tamara broke in again. "I have your phone number."

"You do? Oh, fine. No problem then. Call anytime. Or drop in, if you feel like it."

Tamara couldn't take another minute of his new attitude. With a glare, she put her hands on her hips. "For pity's sake, what is going on with you?"

Sam's expression became the epitome of babelike innocence. "I don't know what you mean."

"You do, too, you big phony! You're no happier about this marriage than I am, so stop acting like everything is wonderful."

"*I* happen to be making the best of things," Sam said, conveying an almost haughty pride in his behavior today. "You might give it a try, too. We *are* going to have a baby, you know."

Tamara's heart sank. Just as she'd worried about last night, Sam fully intended to play father to their baby. She had to discourage that idea, she thought with a rising panic. The thought of Sam in and out of her life for years and years made her legs go weak.

"I—I told you my plan," she said, striving to speak firmly. "A quickie marriage, a quickie divorce when the time is right. You agreed."

"Anything I agreed to yesterday is null and void," Sam said calmly. "I was in a state of shock."

"You're reneging on our deal!" she shrieked.

"That's one way of putting it, I suppose." He paused for a moment. "You know, I never thought I'd have a wife. I never thought I'd have children. This whole thing was one very big surprise, but I'm getting used to it, and I take responsibility seriously, which is something you'll eventually understand about me."

"I am not your responsibility!"

"Tamara, calm down. Think of the baby. Is all that yelling good for him?"

"I'll yell all I want!" Too agitated to stand still, she began pacing the room. "I knew you were without one dram of honor," she fumed through clenched teeth. "Your word isn't worth two cents. You made an agreement with me, and now you're backing out of it.''

"I've lived up to it so far," Sam said mildly. "We're married, aren't we?"

"Much to my regret," she snapped. The only thing she'd accomplished by going to Sam was to trade one set of problems for another. Granted, her immediate concern had been eliminated by his marrying her, but the future looked pretty damned ominous right now.

"Have it annulled," Sam suggested. "It won't change anything as far as the baby goes, but if you don't want to be married, that's easy enough to fix. Just get an annulment. You've got grounds. We never consummated our marriage, you know."

Tamara put her hands over her ears. "Oh, just shut up! And leave! Get out of my home!"

Sam grinned. "Sure, anything you say, sweetheart."

Tamara followed him to the door, because she wanted to tell him to never come back and then slam it off its hinges. She had never been angrier in her life. She was so angry, in fact, that her guard was down, and before Sam went through the door, he moved swiftly, clasped the back of her head and planted a hard kiss right on her lips. She was so stunned she stood there like a ninny and let him kiss her! It was the sexual explosion in the pit of her stomach that brought her back to life. She would *not* feel anything for Sam, damn him. She wouldn't!

Enraged, she pushed against his chest. "How dare you?"

"I'm a daring guy," he said with a maddening grin. "See ya, wife." He opened the door and skipped down her front steps.

Tamara slammed the door so hard the windows rattled, but it wasn't nearly as satisfying as she'd thought it would be. She didn't have the upper hand, Sam did. Tears flooded her eyes and she walked the floor and cried until she was sick to her stomach, all the while thinking of the vile names she should have called him. He'd hear them the next time he tried anything funny with her, that was for sure.

Oh, God, why did she keep making such horrible mistakes?

At eight that evening Tamara dialed Sierra's home number in San Francisco. She had showered and was wearing her nightgown and robe. Her emotional state was calmer, although she suspected nothing would rid her of that black cloud of depression hanging over her head. But she had to tell her sisters of her marriage, and she had to present the news in a way that they believed she was ecstatically happy about it. It was going to take some award-winning acting to do this, but she was pretty sure she could pull it off.

A maid answered the phone, and a minute or so later Sierra came on the line. "Tamara, what a nice surprise. How are you?"

Tamara frowned. Her sister's voice was dull, thick and stuffy, as though she'd been crying for a long time. "I'm holding up," Tamara answered. "What about you?"

"I'm all right. I—I have a bit of a cold, nothing serious."

A cold, my eye, Tamara thought. All was not well in Sierra's world. Tamara had suspected something was wrong, but Sierra had never offered any information and Tamara hadn't pried. But then, they were really just getting to know each other, and besides, the trauma of their mother's death had put all three sisters through hell.

Tamara wanted to pry now. She felt such a powerful urge to ask questions—*Is it your marriage? Are you and Mike having problems? What is it, Sierra? Tell me what's bothering you, please*—that she had to force herself to change the subject entirely.

"I called to tell you something," Tamara said, amazed

that she could sound giddy with joy when she felt so far down in the dumps. "I'm married."

After a few seconds of silence, Sierra said, "Oh, Tamara, you are?"

Tamara had never heard anyone speak as sadly as her sister just had. To heck with standing on ceremony! She was going to get to the bottom of Sierra's despondency right now, she thought with a burst of determination. But before she could get a word out of her mouth, Sierra's voice changed from sad to elated. "That's wonderful, Tamara. Who's the lucky man? When were you married? Oh, tell me everything. I'm very happy for you."

Yeah, right, Tamara thought. Sierra was a darned good actress, too, wasn't she? What was wrong with the Benning sisters that they couldn't talk openly and honestly to each other? In her case, why not tell Sierra the truth about her farce of a marriage?

Instead, she heard herself saying, "His name is Sam Sherard. He works for the same company I do, which is how we met. Neither of us could take the time off for a big wedding right now, so we slipped away for the weekend."

"Slipped away where?"

Tamara cleared her throat. "To Las Vegas."

A heavy silence preceded Sierra's response. "I see. So you really haven't had a honeymoon."

"No, and we're not sure just when our schedules will coincide so we can. Sierra, I hope your feelings aren't hurt because you weren't invited to the wedding. We decided to do it so quickly there really wasn't time to let anyone know."

"Don't give it a thought. You and Sam had every right to marry however and wherever you wished. Have you told Blythe yet?"

"I'm going to call her next."

"Well, little sister, you have my blessing and very best

wishes. I hope you and Sam remain as happy as you are right now for the rest of your lives.''

''Thank you, Sierra. Tell Mike hello for me, okay?''

''Uh, yes. Yes, of course.''

After saying goodbye and hanging up the phone, Tamara felt as though that black cloud of despair she'd been battling was about to engulf her. Sierra wasn't happy, she herself was miserable and they had just lied to each other something awful. Now she had to do the same with Blythe. At least Blythe had nothing to hide, Tamara thought, and maybe talking to her oldest sister would make her feel a little better.

Tamara dialed her mother's number in Coeur d'Alene with a grievous sigh. In an effort to keep at bay the tears that threatened every time she thought of Myra, Tamara comforted herself with the fact that she wouldn't have to lie about her marriage to her, at least.

After the third ring, Blythe answered with a drowsy, ''Hello?''

''Goodness, are you already in bed?'' Tamara asked.

''Oh, hi, Tamara. No, I was dozing in front of the TV. I hate when I do that because then it's difficult to fall asleep when I do go to bed. How are you? I'm so glad you called.''

''I'm fine. I've thought of you often, being there alone in Mother's house. Are you making it all right?''

''I like being here, Tamara.''

''But don't you miss Connecticut?''

''I feel that Idaho is my home, not Connecticut. I've always felt that way, Tamara.''

''I—I don't understand.''

''I know you don't. Maybe I'll tell you about it someday.''

Tamara's shoulders slumped. Sierra obviously had a secret of some sort, *she* certainly did and now Blythe was sounding as though she did, too. *And so did Mother,* Tamara thought sadly. Myra had taken hers to the grave.

Would Sierra and Blythe be so determinedly close-mouthed? Tamara's own secret could be easily figured out by her sisters when her baby was born, if either of them cared enough to add two and two, that is.

Dejected by it all, Tamara spoke listlessly. "Blythe, I called to tell you I'm married."

"You're married! Since when?"

"Since last night."

"Then you're on your honeymoon."

"I'm home in my apartment. My husband's name is Sam Sherard…" Tamara recited the same story she'd told Sierra—about Sam working for Rowland, Inc., and about schedules that prevented a honeymoon.

"Well, put your husband on the phone. I'd like to say hello to him," Blythe said when Tamara wound down.

She nearly choked. "Uh, he—he isn't here right now, Blythe." She thought fast. "We…I…we sort of ran out of groceries, and Sam went to the supermarket." She breathed a silent sigh of relief over that quick-thinking fabrication.

"Oh, too bad. Another time. Tamara, is he wonderful? Are you madly in love?"

"Of course." *That* lie made Tamara sick to her stomach. She could not go on with this conversation. "Oh, Blythe, I'm sorry, but I have another call coming in. I'll call again."

"All right, Tamara. Tell Sam I said hello and welcome to the family."

"I will. Bye." She hung up and fell back in her chair with tears streaming down her cheeks. What a mess she'd made of her life, and now she was telling terrible lies to the only two women she truly cared about. Someday she wanted them all to be close, but how could that happen when each of them kept her personal life so private?

Stubby switched off the television set when Sam walked in. "Did you do it?" Stubby asked.

Sam dropped his overnight case to the floor and plopped down into a chair. "Signed, sealed and delivered," he remarked wryly.

"Well, heck, Sam, it won't be so bad. She's a mighty pretty little gal."

"She's a mighty pretty little gal who wants to use me for a year and then wave bye-bye," Sam retorted. "I'm talking about the baby, too. She thinks she's going to convince me to stay out of my child's life." Sam shook his head. "Fat chance. In fact, what's really going to happen is that *I'm* going to convince *her* of exactly the opposite."

Stubby was frowning. "I see trouble brewing, Sam."

"Could be," he said calmly.

"Could come to a legal battle," Stubby said.

"It's possible, but there are a few tricks up my sleeve to try before our opposition gets that far."

"Is she as stubborn as you are?"

Sam grinned. "Heck, Stubby, I'm not stubborn."

"And dogs don't have fleas, either. Sam, you're my best friend. Could be you're the best friend I've ever had. But you are a stubborn cuss, and if Tamara is only half as mule headed, there's going to be a lot of butting of heads in the next year. Sure would hate to see you have to go through that."

Sam sobered. "It's that or forget my baby, Stubby. Which would you do?"

To Sam's surprise, Stubby's eyes misted over. "Never talk about it much, but I had a son. He was killed in the Vietnam War. If he'd lived he'd be almost fifty years old now. Hard to believe." Stubby wiped his eyes. "His name's on that wall in Washington, D.C. I went to see it some years back. Anyhow, Jimmy hadn't ever married, so that was the end of the Dracos. What would I do if I were you? The same thing you're going to do—fight for my son or daughter."

Moved by Stubby's story, Sam spoke quietly. "That's

what I thought you'd say. I'm sorry you lost Jimmy, Stubby.''

"Me too, Sam, me too. Well, guess it's time to hit the hay.'' Stubby got up. "'Night, Sam. See you in the morning.''

"Good night, Stubby.'' Sam sat there thinking. He was not going to lose his child before it was even born. True, trouble could be brewing, as Stubby had said. But that baby was becoming more real to Sam by the hour. The shock Tamara had delivered yesterday—God, was it only yesterday?—had worn off, but it had changed his life permanently. The old Sam was gone. Long live the new one, he thought cynically.

And there was one more thing he was positive of, however much trouble it might cause. His child was not going to be raised by the scruff of the neck, as he'd been. In that respect, Tamara could like it or lump it.

Getting ready for work the next morning, Tamara began worrying about the details of her impending announcement. She knew exactly how people—women, in particular—reacted to surprise engagements or weddings. The first thing she would hear was, "Oh, let me see your ring!"

Well, she wasn't proud of the plain gold ring on her left hand. Maybe if it had been put on her finger with love she would feel differently about it, but it hadn't been, and she honestly couldn't see herself holding out her hand for her co-workers' inspection.

An idea struck her, and she quickly went to her closet and pulled down a shoe box from the top shelf. It contained a pair of her best pumps, but there was also a small tissue-wrapped packet tucked in the toe of one of the shoes. When she, Sierra and Blythe had divided their mother's jewelry and other personal items, they had done so very democratically. "It's the only fair way to do it,'' Blythe had stated, and they had drawn numbers to see which of them would have the first choice in each cate-

gory. Blythe had drawn number one for the jewelry and
had taken Myra's wedding set. Tamara had second choice,
and she had picked a gold ring inlaid with tiny diamonds
and rubies. Myra had owned quite a lot of lovely jewelry,
so each sister had ended up with four items, but it was that
ruby-and-diamond ring that most interested Tamara at the
moment. She'd intended on renting a safety deposit box
for these things as soon as she got home from Coeur
d'Alene, but with so much going on in Dallas, she hadn't
yet gotten around to the task.

This morning she was glad she hadn't. Removing Sam's
ring from her finger, she slipped on her mother's. It fit
well enough and was very beautiful. Tamara held her hand
up and admired the ring, then got very sentimental and
weepy because of the times she had seen it on Myra's
hand.

But time was passing, and she could dawdle no longer
if she wanted to get to her desk on time. Running to the
bathroom, she dabbed at her eyes and checked her makeup.
Then she dashed from the apartment to the garage and left
for work.

Sam worked hard on the fencing all week, but at the
same time wondered how Tamara was faring. He especially wondered what story she'd told the folks at Rowland, Inc. about their marriage. About midweek he realized
that his curiosity was tinged with worry, and by Saturday
afternoon he couldn't bear the suspense any longer. A
phone call would not do; he had to see Tamara's face when
he asked how she had handled it.

He called it quits for the day around three, and he and
Stubby put away their tools and tramped to the house to
clean up. After taking showers and donning clean clothes,
Stubby mentioned supper.

"I'm driving to Dallas to drop in on Tamara, and I'll
grab a bite on the road," Sam said.

Stubby nodded, and Sam ignored the twinkle in his old

friend's eyes. From the sly little remarks Stubby had made all week, Sam knew he believed there was a lot more going on between him and Tamara than was the case. Sam had told Stubby the facts of their relationship, but apparently the old man had formed some romantic notions that overrode anything Sam had said.

Well, who really knew? he thought as he got in his Jeep and drove away. He would romance Tamara in a split second if it would smooth things over after the baby came. As he drove, that concept became more logical. But he had never "romanced" a woman in his life, and when he'd thought of breaking through Tamara's guard in Las Vegas and during the flight home, it had been all about sex. What if he forgot the sex angle and concentrated on romance? Would that work with Tamara?

Hell, how did a man forget about sex? he disgustedly asked himself. And what constituted romance?

He should have asked Stubby, who had more lady friends than most men half his age. He had to know something Sam didn't.

Spotting a phone booth next to a convenience store, Sam put on the brakes and pulled into the parking lot. But then he just sat there. Asking Stubby how to romance a woman could be damned embarrassing. Sam waffled on the subject for about ten minutes, then, with a grim set to his lips, got out of the Jeep and went over to the telephone. Using his telephone credit card, he called the ranch. Stubby answered on the second ring.

"This is Sam. I need to ask you something."

"Go ahead," Stubby said.

"Promise you won't laugh," Sam said brusquely.

"What if it's funny?"

"Stubby, dammit, I'm serious!"

"All right, all right, I was only teasing. What do you want to ask?"

Sam cleared his throat. "Uh, how does a man, uh, romance a woman? I'm not talking about sweet-talking her into bed, I mean…'' Sam's voice trailed off. He looked around in case someone was standing nearby and listening, which would humiliate him beyond words. No one was around, and he focused his thoughts again. "Do you know what I'm getting at?"

"Yep, sure do. Sam, it's the easiest thing in the world. Bring Tamara some flowers. Tell her she's pretty. Talk to her. Ask how her day went. Ask how she's feeling. Write an affectionate little note on something and leave it behind when you go. She'll find it and think you're a silly, wonderful guy. If she feeds you, compliment every dish. Smile a lot. Tell her jokes if you know any. *Clean* jokes. Not too many females appreciate smut. If she says anything remotely amusing, laugh to kill yourself. And say nothing, not one word, that you suspect ahead of time might upset her. That's romance, Sam. All that stuff makes a woman feel special."

"Good Lord," Sam muttered.

"Hey, do it once and it comes natural as breathing after that."

"Once is all I could stomach," Sam retorted.

Stubby chuckled. "You just might change your mind about that, Sam. Good luck, boy. Enjoy the evening."

"You, too, Stubby, and thanks."

Sam drove the rest of the way to Dallas worrying. He had never done any of the things Stubby had recited, and wouldn't he feel like a jerk trying them now? Besides, weren't priorities all screwed up where he and Tamara were concerned? Romancing one's wife seemed a lot like closing the barn door after the horse had already escaped. Romance should come *before* marriage—even he knew that much. Tamara would probably think he'd lost his mind if he started fawning all over her.

But what if it worked? he thought with a reflective frown. What if he could get Tamara to like him enough that she *wanted* him involved in their baby's future? Wasn't that possibility worth going out on a limb for?

Hell, he could try it once, he decided. If Tamara laughed him out of the apartment, it might hurt his pride, but he really wouldn't be any worse off than he already was. He just didn't want to be on the outside looking in when the baby was born.

Truth was, he admitted again—this time with choking emotion—he would try almost anything to be a real part of his child's life.

Chapter Twelve

Tamara was clearing away her dinner dishes when the doorbell rang. She had worked on the new catalog all morning at Rowland, shopped for groceries on the way home, then changed clothes and given the apartment a good cleaning. Just before preparing something to eat, she had showered and gotten into her nightclothes. Her plan for the evening was a movie on TV that started at eight and bedtime after that.

The doorbell startled her. She couldn't imagine who would be coming by on a Saturday night. On any night, for that matter. Her social life was pathetic, she thought disgustedly as she strode from the kitchen to the front door, and it wasn't apt to improve now that she had advertised her marriage.

Peering through the peephole, she took a step back. *Sam!* What on earth was *he* doing here? At the same time that that question took shape in her mind, a peculiar fluttering began in her chest. Her hands rose to her hair, which was still damp from her shower and shampoo. She should have done something with it, she thought nervously. Along with a head of messy hair, she wasn't wearing any makeup.

Well, he would have to take her as she was, she decided, irritated that he would just drop in without the courtesy of a phone call first.

She undid the locks and yanked the door open, all set to tell him a thing or two about courtesy, when she saw the huge bouquet of flowers he was holding. Her gaze moved from the flowers to his face, and the warmth in his eyes took the wind completely out of her sails.

"Um, hello," she mumbled.

"Hi. Here, these are for you." Sam held out the bouquet.

She took the flowers because she didn't know what else to do. "Thank you." The roses in the bouquet were too beautiful to ignore, and she raised the flowers to her face to smell them. But Sam bringing her flowers was one very big surprise, and she started wondering what he was up to.

"May I come in?" Sam asked. She looked at him over the flowers—studied him, really—and Sam began to get nervous. "You look very pretty tonight," he said.

Tamara frowned at such obvious nonsense, but now her curiosity over Sam's visit was too piqued to let him leave without unearthing his reason for bringing her flowers and saying she looked pretty when she didn't. She moved back from the door. "Come in."

"Thank you," he said with another warm, friendly smile, which earned him a second intense look of scrutiny from Tamara.

Who is this guy tonight? she thought as the strongest urge to giggle suddenly welled up within her. Maintaining a straight face through supreme effort, she led Sam into the living room. "Sit down, if you'd like," she said without looking at him. "I'm going to put these in water." She hurried off to the kitchen, where she nearly collapsed with spasms of giggles that she could barely keep muted. Why was Sam acting so weird? Telling her how pretty she was when she couldn't look worse if she'd tried, bringing her a hundred-dollar bouquet of flowers, saying thank you and smiling to kill himself. He wasn't *wooing* her, was he?

The giggles stopped abruptly as that idea took root. Edgy suddenly, Tamara quickly found a vase, put some water in it and then the flowers. It was truly the largest, most beautiful bouquet of cut flowers anyone had ever given her, and she took a moment to admire it. Her stomach turned over at the thought of returning to the living room and Sam. Maybe she *didn't* want to know what he was up to, she thought, while hastily finishing the job of clearing the table that his arrival had interrupted. She should not have invited him in, flowers or no flowers. He was much more clever than she'd given him credit for, showing up with flowers and a smile that would charm any woman, she decided grimly.

Well, *this* woman was on to him, and he'd better not try anything! Carrying the vase, Tamara walked into the living room. Sam jumped up from the sofa. "You arranged them, uh, beautifully."

"I put them in a vase," Tamara said.

Sam's stomach clenched nervously. *Change the subject. What do you know about flower arranging? Compliment her on something else.* "You know, I was looking at your living room, and you have a real talent for decoration."

"You think so?" Tamara set the vase of flowers on a table and sat down in a chair. "You know, if there's one thing I could never have imagined, it's you noticing how a room was decorated."

"Uh, I don't...usually." *Oh, hell, this isn't going to work. I'm making a complete ass of myself.* But he was here, and he hadn't yet tried simple conversation. Maybe he'd have a go at that before calling it quits on Stubby's advice. Sam resumed his seat on the sofa and did his best to appear relaxed. "So, how's the job going?"

"Sam, do you honestly expect me to believe you care?"

"I care about a lot of things, Tamara. I don't always show it, but I care."

"I know what you care about, the *only* thing you care about."

"You're talking about the baby, and yes, you bet I care about him. But he's not the only thing."

"*He* could be a she, you know."

"Just a figure of speech." Sam looked at his wife and something happened inside of him, something potent and painful, something he didn't totally understand but recognized as important. He was married—he'd *never* thought it would happen to him—and he wanted to *stay* married. Flowers were fine, and so were compliments, but his best tool was honesty.

He took a breath. "I think you're a fair person. Am I wrong?"

Tamara became very cautious. "What are you getting at?"

Sam looked everywhere but at her. Tamara watched him doing it and knew he was having a hard time saying what was on his mind. He would *always* have a hard time with that. Had he ever told a woman he loved her, for instance? She doubted it, unless it was something that just happened to come out of his mouth while making love.

She winced inside. They had made love how many times that weekend? He was an ardent, tireless lover, and not once had he made the mistake of whispering "I love you" while in the throes of passion.

So why was he here tonight? What was he having such a difficult time saying?

She became impatient. "Spit it out, Sam," she finally said. "Sticks and stones may break my bones, but words will never harm me."

His head jerked around. "Don't tell me you think I'm searching for a way to harm you!"

"The harm's already been done, Sam. I think I came

up with a sensible solution to a complex problem, with which you agreed, I might add. You unilaterally voided that agreement, so now I don't know what to think about you.'' She paused briefly. ''I really don't know what you're capable of doing, do I? Why the flowers, Sam? Why come here and flatter me? Do you think I'm blind? The minute I saw that bouquet in your hands I suspected something was on your mind.''

''Then why did you invite me in?'' Sam's voice was harsh.

She faltered a moment, then said, ''I don't have all the answers. Maybe I should have slammed the door in your face. Would that have worked for you?'' She could tell from the look on his face that he was still undergoing an internal battle.

Tamara was right about that, as Sam was wondering if he should give up, get up and leave or stay where he was and fight it out.

Her attitude suddenly softened. She'd vowed to be more civil and here she was sniping at him again. ''Look, Sam,'' she said with a sigh of resignation, ''the cards were dealt and neither of us got a winning hand. What can we do but accept it?''

''Isn't that what we've been doing?''

''To a point, yes.''

Sam got up and moved around the room. Tamara kept an eye on him. His agitation was obvious. Something was on his mind that he still hadn't revealed. She decided not to press him, as it just might be something she'd rather not hear.

He turned abruptly, facing her from about three feet away. ''I want a chance, Tamara.''

Her whole system went on red alert. ''A chance to do what?'' she asked suspiciously.

''A chance with you.'' Before she could do more than stare in surprise, Sam stepped closer and knelt beside her chair. ''Tamara, I'm not going to con you by saying I'm madly in love with you. Hell, I don't even know what love is. But we're married, we're going to have a baby, and shouldn't we at least try and make it work?''

The sincere plea in his eyes touched Tamara, but his past attitude toward her had been devastating to her pride. ''You're not suggesting we live together, are you?'' she asked in a decidedly chilly manner.

They stared into each other's eyes. Sam's discomfiture was as obvious as the nose on his face, but Tamara held her gaze steady, refusing to look away first.

''Would that be so terrible?'' Sam finally asked. ''Look, I'm not saying we should share the same bed. You have a guest room, don't you? Tamara, if I felt free to come here, we could get to know each other. I know you're not going to drive out to the ranch, but I'm in Dallas a lot and if I was staying here we could do things together.''

''Like what?''

''Like seeing a movie, going out to dinner, spending time together. Maybe...'' Sam paused for an uneasy breath ''...maybe by the time the baby is born we wouldn't want a divorce.''

Tamara was weakening, and she wasn't sure she should. The things Sam said they could do together were much too reminiscent of the fantasies she had dreamed up during that infamous weekend. And then he'd left and her fantasies had turned to ashes. It would be so easy to be taken in again, to make another mistake with Sam. She was still foolishly gaga over his good looks, and he was near enough to remind her traitorous body of the bliss of making love with him. She'd been so close to falling in love with him, and what if she really did and he *never* did?

Sam could tell she was vacillating back and forth about his idea. But she hadn't said an immediate and adamant no, and that gave him hope. He took her hands in his and put all the emotion he could into his eyes.

''Tamara, please,'' he murmured. ''If you can't do it for us, do it for the baby. He deserves to be raised with both a mother and a father, and if there's any chance this might work, we should give it our best shot.''

Tamara recalled her own thoughts in Las Vegas about the three of them becoming a real family. She also remembered deeming that idea preposterous and discarding it almost as quickly as it had arisen. But she hadn't had Sam's passionate sincerity influencing her that night as she did now, and she could feel herself falling under his spell.

''I…don't know, Sam,'' she said in a near whisper. ''What if it *doesn't* work?''

''Would we be any worse off than we are right now?''

''We might be, yes.'' *I might be. If I let myself fall in love with you and it doesn't work out, I would be a lot worse off.*

Sam brought her hands to his chest. ''I won't hurt you again, Tamara. I know now that I hurt you before, and I swear it won't happen again. I'll spend all my free time with you. I have to finish the fencing at the ranch, but while that's being completed, I could drive in a few nights a week for dinner together. And Stubby and I usually don't work on Sundays. I could be here every Sunday. We'd do whatever you want, I swear it.''

Tamara frowned. ''You really mean this, don't you?''

''If I'm not a thousand percent sincere, may God strike me dead. Tamara, I would give it my all.''

''And you would use the guest room.''

Sam nodded. ''I'd do anything you say.'' His fingers were twining with hers, and he felt the wedding ring on her left hand.

But it wasn't a plain, smooth band he was feeling, and he looked down at their hands. The diamond-and-ruby ring on Tamara's finger was such a shock, he actually reeled. His eyes flew up to probe Tamara's. ''What's this?''

The most searing embarrassment of her life hit Tamara. ''It was my mother's ring,'' she said in a thin little voice.

''You haven't been wearing the one I put on your finger when we got married?'' Sam's voice was hard suddenly.

"Have you been wearing this one to work? You have, haven't you? Are you ashamed of the one I gave you?"

Her embarrassment was turning to anger. "We had a sordid wedding and that ring has no value of any kind!"

"You mean it didn't cost enough to meet your standards?" His eyes narrowed. "Did you tell the people at work we're married?"

"Of course I did."

"And you let them think I gave you *this* ring?"

"Yes! At least this one means something to me!"

Sam's eyes darkened. It was all he could do not to explode, but outright fury right now would cancel every gain he'd made with Tamara tonight.

"Okay, the ring isn't important," he said gruffly. "What we do about the future is. Are we going to try and make a go of our marriage or not? You know how I feel about it, so it's all up to you. What do you say? Is it yes or no?"

Tears were stinging the back of Tamara's eyes. She should have remembered the ring and taken it off when he arrived. She recognized hurt when she saw it, and her exchange of rings had cut Sam to the quick.

"I—I'll give it a try," she said in an unsteady voice. She knew she was agreeing because of the pain she'd just inflicted on Sam, but she couldn't help feeling bad about it. And maybe there *was* a chance for them. If she refused to at least try, she might regret it for the rest of her life.

Sam looked slightly stunned. "You will?" Deep down he really hadn't believed he would be able to talk her into it, and her acquiescence was nothing short of a miracle.

"I said so, didn't I?"

"And you really mean it."

She nodded and stammered, "I—I'm sorry about the ring."

"Forget the ring. Wear any damned one you want." There was an elation in Sam he'd never felt before. This beautiful lady was his wife. His *wife!* Desire suddenly streaked through his body. He thought of her passion that weekend, how she looked naked, how she *felt* naked.

Abruptly he let go of her hands and got to his feet. It was either that or do something foolish. They were going to be using separate bedrooms in their quest for a durable marriage, and grabbing Tamara at her first show of friendliness would not be at all wise. Maybe they'd work up to sleeping in the same bed, maybe not, but he couldn't sense anything in Tamara tonight that suggested she would be receptive to a pass.

Tamara rose, as well. "Would you like to have a key to the apartment?"

"I guess it makes sense, doesn't it?"

"Yes, it does. Wait here, and I'll go and get it."

In her bedroom, Tamara closed the door, then leaned breathlessly against it. She was positive Sam had been thinking of kissing her. If he had tried, she knew darned well she would have responded. She didn't trust herself with Sam, and if they were together as often as he claimed was going to be the case, she knew exactly what was going to happen.

This was a dangerous game for her to be playing. Not because she was bound to end up in bed with Sam again, but because she had only a fifty-fifty chance of their experiment ending well. It was the same odds Sam would be living with, but he wasn't nearly as apt to fall in love as she was.

"God help me," she moaned. If Sam walked off again and left her with a permanently broken heart, she would have only herself to blame.

Gathering her wits, she took the extra door key from the small box on her dresser and returned to the living room. Sam held out his hand and she dropped the key into it.

"I probably should be going now," he said. He waited a second for her to tell him to stay longer, then added, "How about dinner and a movie on Tuesday evening?"

Tamara swallowed nervously. "Sure…yes…that would be great."

Sam walked to the door, turned and smiled. "Well…see you then. Good night."

"Good night." She shut and locked the door behind him, then fell onto the sofa, feeling utterly drained. If this was another mistake, she would despise herself for the rest of her days.

All she could do at this point was bolster her courage and hope.

Telling her co-workers of her marriage had not been as traumatic as Tamara had feared. She had started with Elliot Grimes. He'd been surprised, of course, but no more than she'd expected. "You married Sam Sherard? *Our* Sam Sherard?"

"Yes, sir," she'd answered. "One and the same."

"Um, correct me if I'm wrong, but weren't you engaged to someone else?"

Tamara had also expected some sort of comment about the man she'd met in college and was going to marry, that fictitious person she'd dreamed up and given as her reason for requesting that transfer to Alaska, so she was well prepared for Mr. Grimes's curiosity.

"I was, yes, but Sam came along and…" she had deliberately smiled with charming helplessness, as though the winds of romance had simply swept her away "…everything changed."

Grimes had returned her smile and said, "Well, you and Sam both have my very best wishes."

Natalie was the second person Tamara had told. "You what?" Nat had exclaimed with a stunned expression.

"I married Sam Sherard this weekend," Tamara had repeated calmly.

"But…have you two been dating? Why didn't you say something?"

"Because I didn't know it was going to get so serious so quickly."

Natalie had looked terribly uncomfortable. "And all this time I've been calling him Stoneface."

Tamara had forced a laugh. "Sam deserved it, so don't you dare be embarrassed."

"Oh, let me see your ring!" Tamara had held out her left hand, and Nat's mouth had dropped open. "Tamara, it's gorgeous!"

"Yes, isn't it?"

From that point on, the word had spread around the office without further effort on Tamara's part. Every time she ran into someone, he or she admired her ring and offered congratulations. By day's end, Tamara had been a bundle of nerves, but she'd accomplished her goal, and felt that everyone's interest would rapidly wane. She'd been right. The next day and the rest of the week had been normal.

Tamara worried all day Sunday about her agreement with Sam. She especially worried about having given him a key to her apartment. She could have tried his idea without going that far, and the fact that he could now just walk into her home whenever he chose haunted her. By Tuesday afternoon she had decided to ask him to return the key. How she was going to do that without arousing his anger or resentment she didn't know, but for her own peace of mind it had to be done.

Dallas was going through a cold spell, so when Tamara got home from work on Tuesday, she changed from her business suit into a pair of charcoal-colored wool slacks, a cream-colored, cotton turtleneck and a charcoal-and-cream-plaid jacket. She was as jumpy as a drop of water on a hot griddle about the upcoming evening, but it wasn't because she regretted accepting Sam's invitation. The truth was that she really wanted their first date to go well, and her nervousness was mostly caused by anticipation, although concern was part of it, too. The diamond-and-ruby ring on her finger, for instance. Should she wear the one Sam had given her when they were together?

Tamara took the thin gold band from her costume jewelry box on the dresser and looked at it. It had not been put on her finger with love, and for her it signified nothing beyond a reminder of her awful wedding ceremony in that gaudy little chapel in Las Vegas. If she and Sam actually made a go of it, it wouldn't be because of a ring. With a heavy sigh, she returned it to the jewelry box.

Sam was on his way to Dallas, driving with an overfast heartbeat and what felt like butterflies in his stomach. He'd never before been nervous about a date with a woman and knew he was floundering in unfamiliar territory. What really bothered him was how much he wanted Tamara to like him. He hadn't gone so far as to actually think *love him,* but he felt those two words floating on the fringes of his subconscious and he wished he knew why. Was it possible that he loved her?

He gulped hard and tried to conquer the dryness of his mouth by licking his lips. What *was* love, anyway? he asked himself. If it was what had held his bickering, drunken parents together for so many years, he wanted no part of it.

But there must be more to it than that, he thought uneasily. He wasn't an avid reader, but he'd read enough through the years to know that there were very few books with a plot that didn't include at least one couple falling in love. And movies were the same. He'd heard the phrase "Love makes the world go round" more than once and had let it go in one ear and out the other because it hadn't meant anything to him. Did it mean something to him now?

The "new" Sam wasn't doing so well, was he? he thought wryly. The more he saw of Tamara, the more confused he became. Hell, just thinking of her seemed to turn his brain to mush, and he'd done a whole lot of thinking about her since Saturday night. Especially when he'd gone to bed at night. Instead of falling immediately to sleep, as he was used to doing, he'd lain there wide awake, thinking about Tamara. Was *that* love?

"Don't mistake insomnia for love," he muttered over his wayward thoughts.

But he'd never been an insomniac, and something was causing the affliction.

"It's anxiety," he mumbled. "Just plain old anxiety. You want your kid, and the only way to get him on a permanent basis is to get Tamara on your team."

Yeah, that's all it was. The sleeplessness, the raw nerves, the butterflies in his stomach were nothing but anxiety.

"It's a hell of a life if you don't weaken," he muttered, and turned the Jeep into Tamara's driveway. Switching off the ignition, he drew in a massive breath, opened the door and got out.

Tamara heard Sam arrive, and her physical reaction startled her. A tingling excitement seemed to permeate her entire body, and she suddenly couldn't breathe very well. *Oh, this will never do,* she thought rather frantically. *Calm yourself. Why are you feeling all giddy and girlish, anyhow?*

But she knew why, though she would rather walk on hot coals than admit it to anyone, especially to Sam. This boded no good and she hadn't expected it. If Sam ever caught on that he possessed such power over her senses, he would take full advantage and manipulate her into doing everything his way. Tamara stood in the center of her living room and nervously pondered that concept. Was Sam really capable of such devious behavior, or was she judging everything he did now by the unpleasantness of the past? He'd had his fun that weekend and then walked out and forgotten her. If that wasn't proof of a selfish and insensitive attitude toward women, what was?

Tamara heaved a long-suffering sigh. She'd made her bed and must lie in it. Sam wouldn't be here or even know about the baby if she hadn't forced him to marry her. He had to resent her for changing his life so drastically, and yes, he was capable of manipulating her. She must watch her step every minute they were together, and above all she must not permit any sort of physical intimacy between them.

It was all very clear in her mind now. Their marriage would endure under one condition, and only one: that Sam fell in love with her. She would not remain married to a man who didn't love her, however she might feel about him. If this experiment they were trying resulted in heartache for her, so be it. Far better to be aching alone than with a man who would rather be someplace else, or with someone else.

Hearing footsteps outside, Tamara hurried to the front door and peered through the peephole, waiting for Sam to come into view. Surely he wouldn't use the key she'd so recklessly given him and was determined to get back. He had more sense than that, she hoped.

Sam stepped up onto Tamara's front stoop, and to her surprise just stood there. Though his image was somewhat distorted through the tiny peephole, she was certain she saw tension on his face. She frowned. Was he as unnerved by this date as she was? Was it even possible that his thoughts rambled through the same anxious territory as hers?

She was relieved when he finally pushed the doorbell. Waiting a few moments so he wouldn't know she'd been all but glued to the door, she put on a smile and reached for the knob.

Chapter Thirteen

In Tamara's estimation, the evening went well. Sam took her to a pleasant little restaurant with good food. After dinner they went to a theater with first-run movies and laughed through a marvelous comedy.

Although they didn't discuss it, Sam shared Tamara's opinion of their first date. He noticed, however, that as funny as the film was, the two main characters fell in love. He watched the progress of their developing feelings very closely, and realized how many ups and downs the writer had instilled in the story so that the man and woman didn't acknowledge their love for each other until the very end.

The plot was nothing like his and Tamara's unstable relationship, and yet there were similarities—a step forward in the characters' affection for each other, two steps back, a giant step forward, and so on. *Maybe falling in love never runs smoothly,* he mused as they left the theater and walked to his Jeep.

"That was a great movie," Tamara said, huddling deeper into her overcoat against the cold.

"Yes, it was. I like comedies." *But I like you better. Sitting in that dark theater, what would you have done if I'd put my arm around you? I wanted to, very much.*

"So do I. Actually, the only films I avoid are horror pictures. I really don't understand why people would want to scare themselves to death by watching that sort of movie. I don't even read books of that nature."

Sam unlocked the passenger door and held it open for Tamara. "What kind of books do you read?"

"Oh, I have a long list of favorite authors." Seated in the Jeep, she looked at him. "Don't you?" She realized her heart was suddenly in her throat. *Do you have to be so damned handsome? You're ten times better-looking than the star of that movie we just saw. Is it any wonder I fell so hard that weekend?*

"Never thought about it, but I suppose I do." The bottom of Tamara's long overcoat was hanging over the edge of the seat, and he tucked it inside the vehicle before shutting the door. During those few seconds leaning toward Tamara, he inhaled her subtle perfume and felt its impact shoot through his system like a ricocheting bullet. Although he'd truly enjoyed the movie, he had also undergone bouts with that perfumed bullet every so often and suspected, grimly, that it was going to be one more thing to keep him awake nights.

Tamara noticed the taut lines of his face as he rounded the front of the Jeep, and narrowed her eyes speculatively. He'd been nice tonight, even talking to her during dinner. True, their conversation had been focused on his ranch, but at least they hadn't eaten in awkward silence. She had enjoyed the evening and thought he had, as well. Now, considering his dark expression, she wondered if it had been a trial for him and he'd merely put on a darn good act.

He got in and started the engine. "How about stopping

somewhere for a cup of coffee before I take you home?''
he asked, all smiles again.

Confusion beset Tamara. If being Mr. Nice Guy for four
hours had been a pain in the neck for him, wouldn't he
rush her home now instead of prolonging the agony?

''Do you really want coffee?'' she asked with a hint of
a frown. *Or are you thinking that suggesting a cup of
coffee is something you should do?*

''I'd like some, yes. If you'd rather just go home, I
could get some on my way out of the city. It's a long drive
to the ranch and coffee helps keep me alert.''

Tamara felt a little ashamed of herself. She was much
too quick to misconstrue Sam's conduct. That taut facial
expression she'd thought she'd seen, for example, could
have been nothing more than a trick of the dim lighting
on this dark night.

To quiet her own conscience more than anything else,
she said, ''If you want coffee, I'll make a pot at the apartment.''

Sam had not expected to be invited in after driving her
home, so her suggestion came as a surprise. His brain was
suddenly buzzing with memories of the first time she had
asked him in, but he spoke calmly as he pulled the Jeep
into the traffic. ''That would be great, thanks.''

''You're welcome.'' *You haven't mentioned the key yet.
You should have done it during dinner.* Tamara chewed
on her inner lip while pondering the best approach to what
was a rather delicate subject. After all, he hadn't asked for
a key to her apartment, she'd offered it. She sighed, wishing ardently that she hadn't acted so hastily. How many
times had she told herself to watch her step with Sam, and
how many mistakes was she going to make before heeding
that advice?

Goodness! she thought in sudden alarm. She had just
made another one by inviting Sam in!

But how could she reverse herself now without looking
silly?

Well, all she could do was to make that coffee as fast as possible, give him one cup and pour the rest in a thermos that he could take with him. He shouldn't be in the apartment more than fifteen minutes.

But during that fifteen minutes she had to ask him to return her extra key.

Tamara felt the start of a tension headache and harshly chided herself for constantly getting into uncomfortable situations with Sam. Why had she rushed to give him a key? Had she lost her ability to reason, for pity's sake?

"Let him keep it," she mumbled under her breath.

"Pardon?" Sam said.

"I was just talking to myself," she replied lamely. "About nothing important." *Yeah, right. You'll worry every day and night about Sam using that key.*

Of course, he hadn't just walked in tonight, she rationalized, so maybe he would only use the key if he came by and she wasn't home. She sighed again, not finding that idea particularly comforting.

"Do you often talk to yourself?" Sam asked, speaking with friendly amusement.

"I don't think so. Maybe. I'm not sure."

"Probably most people do, don't you think?"

Tamara turned her head to look at him. "I can't picture you doing it."

"You can't? I wonder why."

"It's because you seem so self-controlled."

"With that observation, should I assume you're *not* self-controlled?"

"I never had any trouble with self-control until I met you," Tamara said.

Sam drove silently for a few moments, then murmured quietly, "*That's* definitely food for thought."

"Yes, isn't it?" Tamara muttered.

"Know what I think?" Sam said after a reflective pause. "I think you're blaming me for that weekend we spent together."

"Should I blame the mailman?" Tamara retorted.

"You *are* blaming me," Sam said with amazement. "You're looking at that weekend as a loss of self-control. That puzzles me. Correct me if my memory is faulty, but I seem to recall your total and complete cooperation. You seemed to be in full control of your faculties, and never once did you appear to be *out* of control."

"Oh, good grief," Tamara said disgustedly. "We were *both* out of control. We were strangers, and strangers with any decency at all do not behave the way we did."

"What do you mean, we were strangers? We'd met before that weekend."

"Just barely. Sam, in most ways we're still strangers."

"The hell we are! Strangers don't get married. Tamara, you have some mighty peculiar ideas."

"And I suppose all of *your* ideas are—"

"Wait! Please don't say it. We're working up to a knock-down, drag-out here, and I despise marital bickering."

"Marital bickering, did you say?" Tamara's eyes were wide with astonishment. "Do you honestly believe we're going to stay married?"

Sam's lips thinned. "You agreed to try."

"Which is the only reason I'm in your Jeep this very minute. But I don't have a whole lot of faith in this—this experiment, and you might as well know how I feel about it."

They were almost to Tamara's apartment complex. Sam turned the Jeep onto her street, wondering miserably what had started this rift. Oh, yes, he thought, it was his noticing her mumbling under her breath and then being stupid enough to say something about it. He'd broken one of Stubby's most important rules for romancing a woman: never, never say or do anything to upset her.

But was their relationship really so fragile that a remark he considered genuinely innocent could cause Tamara to lose all interest in making their marriage work? He had to do something to change her mind again.

He pulled into her driveway and sent her the warmest smile he could drum up. "Well, here we are, safe and sound." Before she could renege on her coffee invitation, he got out and rushed around the Jeep to open her door.

Feeling as though the weight of the world rested on her shoulders, Tamara got out of the vehicle and preceded Sam to her front door, unlocked it and went in. They took off their coats, and she hung them in the foyer closet. "I'll go make the coffee," she said listlessly, and vanished into the kitchen.

Sam checked his watch. It was almost eleven and they both had to get up early in the morning. He wouldn't stay long, but he couldn't leave without at least trying to pull Tamara out of the doldrums she'd sunk into.

He walked into the kitchen and sat at the table. Tamara glanced at him and went on preparing the coffeepot.

"How have you been feeling?" Sam asked.

"I'm fine," she said dully.

"Tamara, I'm talking about, uh, your condition. Are you healthy? Is the baby?"

She switched on the pot and turned around. "When I saw her, my doctor said I was fine."

"When do you see her again?"

"I'll be seeing her every month until the final six weeks. Then she recommends weekly appointments."

"I read something about natural childbirth, where the parents take classes together. Are we going to do that?"

"You're talking about Lamaze classes. I don't know, Sam."

"I'd like to be a part of our child's birth," he said quietly. "With your approval, of course."

Tamara regarded him for a long time. He looked back, and that's all there seemed to be in that kitchen, other than the gurgling of the coffeepot—the two of them looking at each other. Their situation suddenly felt to Tamara like the saddest that could ever befall a couple, and her eyes began spilling tears.

Sam got up so fast he nearly knocked over the chair. Before he could reach her she had turned around again, as she didn't want him to see her crying. He put his hands on her shoulders. "Tamara, don't turn away. Tell me why you're crying."

A sob shook her body. "No…please," she whispered.

"You can talk to me, Tamara. Anytime and about anything. Don't shut me out."

Tamara couldn't believe those words had actually come out of Sam's mouth. In fact, they startled her so much, she turned and faced him, teary face and all.

"Did I hear you right?"

Sam looked perplexed. "Did I say something unusual?"

"For you, yes. You're the most closemouthed individual I've ever known, and now you're telling me I can talk to you about anything? Since the moment we met I've walked on eggs so I wouldn't say the wrong thing. Your demeanor does not invite confidences, Sam—not even normal conversation, to be brutally honest. Why would I open up with you when every word I hear from you has to be dragged out?"

"Tamara, that's not true." Sam looked first stunned, then worried. "Is it?"

"You tell me. Think about it. Are you a naturally friendly person?"

"I have friends," he said defensively.

"I never would have guessed it," Tamara retorted. "Certainly not from what *I've* seen."

They were on the verge of another argument, Sam realized. It happened so fast with them, and he could come up with only one reason why Tamara took offense at everything he said.

"You really don't like me, do you?" he said quietly. "It isn't going to matter how many times I talk you into seeing me, I'm not going to be able to make you like me."

"Sam, it's *you* who doesn't like *me!*"

"That's ridiculous," he snorted. "If I didn't like you, I wouldn't be here."

"Do you think you'd be here if *I* didn't like *you?*"

Their eyes met and held. Tamara swore she would not look away first, but so did Sam. Something was happening here, and each was determined to see where it led.

Without breaking eye contact, Sam finally said softly, "So I'm to believe you do like me?"

Tamara lifted her chin a bit. Her heart was beating a mile a minute. But even though she knew they were behaving like adolescents, she couldn't stop it. "And I should believe that you like me?" she said challengingly.

"As I already said, if I didn't like you I wouldn't be here."

"Oh, we're going to go around again. Let me see. I believe I asked you if you thought you'd be here if I didn't like you." She was suddenly weary of the game. "Can't you just say it? 'Tamara, I like you'?"

Sam sucked in a breath. "I can say it. Can you?"

"Oh, give me strength," she groaned. She *was* the one to look away first, because she tried to duck around him. Sam clasped her shoulders again and stopped her. "What?" she asked belligerently, her eyes laden with suspicion.

"I like you," Sam said flatly.

Again their gazes locked. Tamara licked her dry lips as her heart began pounding unmercifully hard. Now she should say, "And I like you," but instead she heard herself asking, "Why should I believe you?"

Sam's eyes darkened with anger. "You little witch, *this* is why." Yanking her against himself, he pressed his mouth to hers in a hard kiss.

It took Tamara so by surprise that she tried to push him away. But then his lips gentled on hers, and the kiss became warm and loving, the kind of kiss she had dreamed of receiving from him. It wasn't lustful, as his kisses had been that weekend. It was tender and emotional and so sweet it brought tears to her eyes.

She parted her lips in total surrender and permitted his tongue to slide into her mouth. She could tell the tenor of the kiss was changing again; Sam was becoming aroused.

But so was she. No man had ever affected her as Sam had that weekend, and it was happening again. She had vowed it wouldn't, not ever, but she was discovering that making that sort of self-promise had been much easier than keeping it. His mouth left hers, and she heard him take a labored breath as his lips moved over her face.

"Do you believe me now?" he whispered raggedly, a mere second before mating their mouths again.

She wanted to, more than she'd ever wanted anything. But even while she was kissing him with unbridled passion, there was a nagging doubt in the back of her mind. He wanted them to stay married so he could have his child full-time. He seemed like the kind of man who got what he wanted, whatever it took. Dare she trust him? Maybe she'd already given him too much ammunition by telling him he wouldn't be here if she didn't like him. Dare she present him with more?

Her knees were wilting, she realized. She was becoming weaker and more pliable by the moment as his hands caressed her. Sam had a power over her senses that no one else had ever attained. If she let this go on they would end up in bed again, and that would be going too far.

She tore her mouth from his and gasped, "Sam...no."

He raised his head and looked at her through glazed eyes. "Why not? Tamara, I want you so much, and you want me, too. Don't you think I can tell?"

"I—I can't do it, Sam," she whispered.

He hesitated. "Because of the baby?"

Tamara blinked. He knew so little about pregnancy that she could easily con him right now into believing her doctor had told her sex was off-limits during her pregnancy.

But she preferred that he know the truth. "It's not because of the baby,'' she said in an unsteady voice. ''But we're just now getting on the right track. If we're going to make this work, that is. I need some time to digest what might be happening, and so do you. Let's go…slower, all right?''

Sam was in an agony of desire. ''Tamara,'' he breathed pleadingly, trying to kiss her again.

She eluded him by turning her head, and his lips landed in her hair near her ear. ''Please,'' he whispered. ''You're my wife. We'd be doing nothing wrong.''

That argument turned Tamara cold. Had he worried about right and wrong before this? No way. She'd been exactly on the money when thinking that he would do whatever it took to get what he wanted.

''No, Sam,'' she said, speaking in a firm, unshakable tone. At the same time she escaped from his arms and put some space between them. ''Look, you said I could talk to you and that's what I'm going to do. We had a nice evening together. I enjoyed going out with you and I hope we do it again. But we're not going to make love, Sam, not tonight and not the next time we're together. And please don't insult my intelligence again by telling me we'd be doing nothing wrong because we're married. I didn't think we were doing anything wrong the weekend we made this baby, and we weren't married then. But the baby changed everything for me, Sam, everything.''

Tamara laid her hand on her chest. ''I feel different inside, Sam. I *am* different. So much has happened—finding myself pregnant, losing my mother, forcing you to marry me. And starting to get to know my sisters. Did I tell you about my sisters, Sam?''

''Not much,'' he mumbled thickly.

''Well, I'd like to do that. Not tonight, but maybe the next time we're together.'' Tamara paused for a moment. ''Is there going to be a next time, Sam?'' she asked.

He cleared his throat. ''Why don't you tell me?''

Tamara shook her head sadly. "You see, you give nothing of yourself."

Sam muttered a curse. "Look, I'm trying to do everything your way, and you keep saying things like that. What part of me do you want, Tamara?"

"Your honesty, dammit!"

"I've never been anything but honest with you!"

"Obviously your definition of honesty and mine are very different."

Sam had to forcibly beat down the frustrated anger he was feeling. He took in a long, slow breath. "Okay, let's go back to where you asked if there was going to be a next time. Yes, Tamara, there is, if you agree. Is that better?"

"Sam, I'm not *trying* to make you angry. Yes, that was much better, and I do agree."

"Fine," he said stiffly. "Is Saturday all right?"

"I'll be working Saturday morning, but any time after that would be fine."

"I'll get my coat." Sam started from the kitchen.

"Wait! What about the coffee?"

"It's late. I'd better be going."

"All right. You get your coat and I'll fill a thermos you can take with you."

In a few minutes they were at the front door. Tamara put the thermos in his hand. "Drive safely."

Sam forced a little half smile. "See you on Saturday. Probably late afternoon."

Tamara nodded. "Good night." When he was gone, she locked the door and then leaned her back against it. After a moment she sighed and headed for her bedroom, turning off lights as she went.

Were they making any genuine headway, or was it all a big farce?

How would she ever know?

Sam drove out of the city with a relentless knot in his stomach, a grim expression on his face and mass confusion in his brain. The more he saw of Tamara, the more he wanted her. Wanted her to remain his wife. Wanted her to let go with him and laugh and be the woman she'd been that weekend. Oh, yes, he remembered it all very well. She'd been so open and carefree, so giving, so adorable. He'd been the one to hold his feelings in check, not Tamara. Now everything was reversed. *He* had dropped his guard and *she* had erected one.

He had misjudged that entire weekend, wholeheartedly believing that the desire to which he and Tamara had succumbed had been nothing more than fun and games. Obviously Tamara had felt differently. He knew now that she wasn't the type of woman to fall into bed with a man on a whim, but would she ever forgive him for not knowing it then? For not calling afterward?

And then she'd discovered her pregnancy and done everything she could to get her life straightened out without revealing to anyone the cardinal sin she had committed. If the powers-that-be at Rowland had consented to that transfer, she would be in Alaska right now. Coming to Sam as a last resort must have been a monumental blow to her pride. He grimaced. How in hell did a man atone for mistakes he hadn't even been aware of committing?

There was another aspect of the situation to think about, as well. He'd always been a loner, and why was he so driven to alter that status? Before meeting Tamara he'd been a contented man. He could drop the whole thing and return to his single life. It had been Tamara's plan to do exactly that, after all. A brief marriage to save face, a quickie divorce down the road, end of story. Why couldn't he just forget her and the baby? She'd been going to forget him, hadn't she?

Sam realized he didn't know himself anymore. His confidence had taken a beating, as well as his ego. At the same time his stubborn side had gained momentum. One thing he'd always had was determination, which was the trait that had probably saved him from the self-destructive pattern of life into which his parents had fallen. Even as a very young boy he'd hated the drinking and fighting, the unkempt hovels they'd lived in, the constant moving from place to place, and he'd sworn to get away from it all as soon as he was old enough, and to make something of himself. Determination was the reason he'd succeeded.

But with all that running through his mind, the most startling thing to contemplate was how he was beginning to feel about Tamara. He was *not* going to forget her or his child, even if that might be the most sensible course for a man of his nature to take. But that decision aside, there was something both painful and joyous inside of him when he thought of Tamara, something he had never before felt about anyone.

He had pondered the subject of falling in love before this—only since his marriage, of course—but tonight it seemed to have an especially stinging impact. Maybe it was because of that incident in Tamara's kitchen. He had wanted her so badly he still ached from it, but the discomfort wasn't all in his groin. It was in his heart, his soul, in every cell of his body, and its strength shook him. As hard as it was to face, he knew it wasn't going to suddenly disappear, or even gradually dissipate. He was a man doomed to a life of misery if he didn't keep his family.

"My God," Sam whispered, shocked to his soul. "That's it." He'd been thinking of Tamara and the baby as *his family!* What he'd grown up with wasn't family, not anything like he'd seen in other people's homes. That was what he so desperately wanted now, a real family—Tamara, the baby and himself.

He gritted his teeth as determination filled him. He *was* going to have his family, by damn, or die trying.

Chapter Fourteen

On Wednesday Tamara received a large package from Sierra. The accompanying note read:

Tamara, you always liked this painting, so please accept it as a wedding present. I hope Sam likes it, too.

Love and best wishes,

Sierra

Thrilled at the gift, Tamara tore the wrapping from the large oil painting. It was one of Sierra's early efforts, a depiction of three girls on a beach, and though Tamara had been very young when Sierra had finished the piece, she had loved it on sight.

She leaned it against the television set, stepped back and studied it. The painting glowed with sunlight and Tamara could almost feel the sea breezes. The girls were wearing pastel dresses and walking down the beach—away from the viewer. Two of them had blond hair, one had almost black hair, and they were of varying heights, the tallest appearing to be full-grown, the smallest hardly more than a toddler.

"Why, it's us," she said in amazement. "Sierra, Blythe and me." Maybe she'd been too young at the time to fully appreciate what her sister had created, but now she understood it and was so deeply touched that her eyes filled with tears.

On Thursday she received another package, this one from Blythe. It was a genuine Tiffany lamp, carefully packed, and Tamara again got teary-eyed. Blythe's card read:

My dearest Tamara and Sam, I wanted to give you something that was especially meaningful to me. This lamp was one of my own wedding gifts, and I have treasured it through the years. I had the lady watching my home in Connecticut ship it to me so I could send it to you. Enjoy it with my blessings and every wish for a bright and happy future together.

Love, Blythe

Tamara immediately wrote her sisters warm letters of thanks. She mentioned Sam only once in each: "Sam sends his regards, and his thanks for your thoughtful gift."

On Friday morning Tamara's heart sank when she buttoned the waistband of her skirt and noticed how snug it was. She hurried to the full-length mirror in the corner of her bedroom to give herself a thorough inspection. Rather frantically turning this way and that, she checked her figure. She'd already had to buy some larger bras, but she had not expected her waistline to start expanding so soon.

Leaning closer to the mirror, she examined her face. Were her cheeks plumper? "Oh, Lord," she whispered, and ran for the bathroom scale. She had gained five pounds, seemingly overnight! And today, of all days, she did not need the additional burden of worrying about how she might look to her co-workers. She had finally come up with an idea for the new catalog and was going to present it to the sales department's decision makers at a ten o'clock meeting, which was a nerve-racking enough prospect. If she thought that everyone was assessing her measurements during that presentation, it couldn't possibly go well.

Quickly she changed from the slim, fitted skirt to a long dress made from fabric that had been tinted a rainbow of muted grays, mauves and greens. A matching vest reached her hips. Comfortable and in vogue, it was an outfit she never got tired of wearing to the office. The mirror confirmed her choice: no one would see a dram of difference in her figure today.

But how much longer would she be able to camouflage her condition? Sighing heavily, Tamara put on a little more makeup than she usually wore, patted the classic roll of hair at her nape and decided she was ready to leave for work.

Traffic was moderate at this early hour and she made good time, arriving at the Rowland Building at six-fifteen. She was normally at her desk around seven, but this morning she wanted to go over her presentation again and make sure everything was in perfect order.

At five minutes to ten, she gathered her material, calmed her speeding pulse with a deep breath and headed for the conference room. At ten sharp everyone was seated around the large table and Elliot Grimes began speaking.

"We have a few items on the agenda, and then we're going to hear from Tamara." Every eye turned to her, and she could feel a flush creeping up her neck. She smiled and received smiles in return. Feeling a bit more relaxed, she took part in discussing the firm's current sales figures and several new products.

Then Elliot Grimes introduced her. "Now we'll hear what Tamara has to tell us. Tamara, you have the floor."

She got up from her chair. "Thank you, Mr. Grimes." She looked around the table. "I was asked to design a new catalog, which I'm sure you all know. In fact, several of you have worked with me on this project, for which I thank you. I must confess that coming up with any improvements had me stymied for a while. I studied copies of catalogs that went back to the 1930s—when Rowland began issuing them—looking for some obvious flaw, something that had been overlooked for sixty years. Of course there was nothing. Every catalog depicted Rowland's excellent products in a timely, easily understandable way, just as our present catalog does."

She paused and again let her glance sweep around the table. "About a week ago there was a glossy insert in a Dallas newspaper advertising hard hats. Did any of you see it?"

There were several nods and some murmured no's.

Tamara continued, "The advertisement wasn't extraordinary. What was interesting was that the company manufactures and sells hard hats in almost every color of the rainbow. A photo of a bright pink one caught my eye and got me thinking. I came to work that day and began researching our client list. Do any of you know the statistics regarding the gender of our buyers? It surprised me, but nearly twenty percent of our client companies are run by women. I dug deeper, poring over human resource statistics, and learned that there are almost as many women working at one job or another in the oil business as there are men."

Tamara paused to let that information sink in, then said quietly, "Never once, in any of the catalogs I studied, did I see a photo, an article or anything else giving recognition to our female buyers, or *potential* buyers." From the bottom of her stack of material, she pulled a large rectangle of white cardboard. Holding it against her chest, she said,

"This is what I would like to run on the cover of our next catalog." She turned over the cardboard for all to see. It was a drawing, a rendering of a confident-looking woman in work clothes and a bright pink hard hat.

The table began buzzing as comments were made. Tamara looked at Elliot Grimes and saw that he was smiling. Confident herself now, she went on. "We would have to find the perfect model, naturally—someone who projects authority and intelligence. Or better still, I'd like to use a woman who is actually in the oil business. If we can find one who would agree, of course. I have another drawing...." She reached into her stack and brought it out. This one depicted the woman in the pink hard hat standing near a pump-jack, with wording to the side that read I wouldn't use anything but Rowland equipment in my operation.

"This idea needs expansion, of course," Tamara said. "What I've shown you is strictly preliminary. For instance, I feel it's crucial that the woman we use is attractive but not provocative in any way. We're not putting out a girlie calendar. Our catalogs are serious publications, and our model must reflect that. But we could photograph her checking out a drilling rig or overseeing the unloading of a truckload of pipe. The possibilities are endless, but always she would be wearing that pink hard hat. It would be her trademark.

"My second suggestion is that we personalize the catalog by dedicating one page to people in the oil business. Call it a newsletter for now. We could incorporate current oil prices, the opening of a new field, even permissible anecdotes. Imagine if our clients reached for our catalog as soon as they got it to read that one page, then thumbed through the other pages to follow our lady in the pink hard hat's adventures in the oil business. I believe this could become a very solid connecting point between the company and its buyers." Tamara paused and smiled. "I think that's it for now. Thank you for listening." She sat down.

Beaming from ear to ear, Elliot Grimes rose from his

chair. "Well, I have one word to say—brilliant! Tamara, I am sincerely impressed, as I believe everyone else at this table must be. I'd like Tom Rowland to see your work as soon as possible. I'll talk to him about a meeting for the three of us and let you know. Hopefully he has some free time this afternoon."

His smile took in everyone around the table. "I believe that concludes our business for today."

Many of the people filed past Tamara on their way out and congratulated her on a job well done. Elliot Grimes approached her. "Leave your material, Tamara. I'd like to take a closer look at it."

"Certainly," she said.

"I'll be talking to you very soon."

"Thank you." She left the conference room empty-handed and feeling as though she was walking on air. She was doing so incredibly well with her job; why couldn't she do as well in her private life?

That question brought her back down to earth with a thud.

Tom Rowland was pleased with Tamara's ideas and dumped the entire project in her lap. "I particularly like the idea of using a woman who's actually in the business for our model. Find her," he instructed. "You'll need some help with this, Tamara. Pick and choose your assistants from our present personnel, as you please." Rowland looked her straight in the eye. "But you are to head the project."

"Yes, sir," she replied, both proud and uneasy. Where to begin? she thought. Oh, where to begin?

After leaving the two o'clock meeting she decided that particular question was probably going to be the one most easily solved in this complex project. She spent the remaining hours of the workday talking to sales reps and assistants, picking their brains. Somewhere within the ranks of their many female buyers had to be a woman suited to the task, and did the reps and assistants have any suggestions? Tamara jotted down names, addresses and phone numbers, all the while wondering how on earth she would actually *see* these women. They lived all over Texas, Louisiana and Oklahoma, and it would take weeks of travel to call on them.

Driving home that evening, she realized that she wasn't all that thrilled with her meteoric rise in the firm. If her job was the only thing on her mind, she would feel much differently, but her personal problems were too weighty to shove aside just because she wished she could.

She spent an absolutely miserable evening wondering if she should talk to Tom Rowland again and ask him to assign the project to someone else. She could blame her ambiguity on her pregnancy, which, of course, would entail a full-scale explanation of her situation, and could she do that? Sit across a desk from that portly, dignified man and bare her soul?

No, she didn't think so.

She was once again caught in a trap of her own making.

Since Sam's revolutionary thoughts about family, his family, he'd been grouchy as a bear with a thorn in its paw. Stubby let him growl, snap and snarl without comment until Saturday morning, when he leaned on his shovel and gave Sam a disgusted look.

"If you're mad at me about something, get it off your chest and let's get back to normal. If it's something else, you should *still* get it off your chest. You've been a royal pain in the butt most of the week, and I'm getting a little tired of being on the receiving end of your bad humor."

The temperature was hovering in the sixties, the sun was bright and Sam was sweating. He'd pushed both Stubby and himself hard to finish the fencing job, and there were only a few more posts to go, a few more yards of new wire to string. He knew he'd been ill-tempered and impatient lately, so Stubby's dressing-down was no surprise.

Removing the leather glove from his right hand, he pulled his handkerchief from the back pocket of his jeans and wiped his forehead. "You're right," he said, looking down the line of new fencing with a grim twist to his lips he couldn't seem to eradicate, however "right" Stubby was.

"Well?" Stubby said.

Sam scowled at his elderly friend. "Well, what?"

"You gonna keep what's bothering you bottled up till you explode? Don't think it won't happen, 'cause it will. Sam, in case you've forgotten, I'm still a good listener. Let's clear up one thing right away. Am I the problem? Something I did or said?"

"No," Sam said brusquely. "Forget that notion."

"Then it has to be your wife."

Your wife. Sam's nerves twanged like a plucked, untuned guitar string. "Yeah," he said gruffly, "it's my wife."

Stubby stood there a moment, obviously thinking. Then he said, "You two aren't communicating, right?"

"We talk, but never about the same thing."

"That's what I mean—you're not communicating. Sam, I have to be honest with you. You and I get along, but even with me you always seem to hold back the best part of yourself. Do you follow what I'm saying?"

"You're saying I'm probably doing the same thing with Tamara."

"Are you?"

"Stubby, it's easy to think I'm going to do this or that the next time I'm with Tamara, but it takes two to make a conversation. She finds something wrong with everything I say."

"Gets upset, huh?"

"An understatement," Sam grumbled. "I don't understand women. I especially don't understand Tamara."

"She's a sweet little flower, Sam."

Sam looked thunderstruck. He'd heard Stubby pin that label on women before, but Tamara? Stubby had talked to

Tamara once, for about three minutes. "How in hell did you come up with that idea? She's about as sweet as vinegar."

"That's your fault. Sam, think of the fairer sex as gentle creatures. Think of their softness, their scent. Believe me, the good Lord knew exactly what he was doing when he created women."

"Sometimes I think he created women to torment men," Sam said dryly.

"No, no, you've got it all wrong. Sam, do you resent Tamara for getting pregnant and forcing you to marry her? You know, you could have said no. You could have told her to get lost, or to tell her troubles to someone else. Instead, you snapped to and married her. Have you asked yourself why?"

Sam's already scowling face got darker. "I did it for the baby."

Stubby sighed. "You're a tough nut to crack, Sam. It's easy to see why Tamara gets upset with you. Open up, man! Heck, you can't even do it with me."

"What in hell do you want me to say?" Sam nearly shouted.

Stubby held up his hands in a sign of defeat. "Sorry I stuck my nose in your business, Sam. Guess you'll have to figure it out for yourself." Stubby went back to work. "We'll be finished with the fence in about another hour. We got it done a lot sooner than we figured, didn't we?"

Sam took a calming breath. "Yeah, we did." He'd never yelled at Stubby before, and he felt bad about doing it now. But what *had* the older man expected him to say?

Stubby was tamping dirt around a post and didn't look at Sam. "That's good. Now you'll have the rest of the month to spend with your wife."

Sam shook his head in frustration. *He* wasn't the only royal pain around here. Working the leather glove back onto his right hand, he moved to the next rotted post and started digging it out of the ground.

Stubby's attitude toward women stayed in Sam's mind as though embedded in cement. His friend was right about him not opening up with anyone. Sam could have told him that he was in love with his wife, that he ached for her, that he wanted his family so much he was in agony over it. There was so much he could have said and hadn't. What was wrong with him that he couldn't speak his mind when it came to personal matters?

Maybe it would be different this evening, he told himself hopefully. Stubby had said it was Sam's fault that Tamara wasn't sweet, and maybe the old guy was right. Sam felt wedged between a rock and a hard place, without knowing how to loosen the vise. His longtime habits, routines and way of life hadn't prepared him for a serious relationship.

He remembered vowing at one point after the wedding to change, going so far as to think of himself as a new man. Well, he *wasn't* a new man, and he didn't know how to become one. For the first time he envied men like Stubby—men with a gift of gab, men who could babble silly nothings to a woman and get her to laugh, men who could flirt outrageously and then be labeled charming for behaving like an idiot.

Sam's entire love life had been no more than a string of one-night stands, he thought dourly. And now, when he longed—with a desperation he'd never before experienced—for just one woman, he didn't know how to incite her interest, to make her want him as he wanted her.

Sam thoughtfully narrowed his eyes as he recalled that feverish kissing session in Tamara's kitchen the last time he'd seen her. She had pushed him away before it had gotten out of hand, but there was no way he could have misinterpreted her initial response. *And think of her uninhibited participation during that weekend,* he told himself. It was probably the one advantage he had in their relationship—the power of sex—and instead of using it, he'd been tearing himself apart trying to become someone else, someone he could never be.

Sam's pulse began beating faster. Maybe it would work, maybe it wouldn't, but at least he had a new idea of how to approach Tamara tonight. That alone was enough to elevate his spirits.

Tamara spent the afternoon in a beauty parlor, after which her hair was six inches shorter and her fingernails beautifully manicured and polished. The second she arrived home, she hurried to the bathroom mirror to inspect her new hairstyle. Her natural curls stopped at her jawline and gave her face a whole new look. She stole a nervous breath. This was a startling change, and one moment she liked it, the next she didn't. Using a hand mirror, she checked the back of her hair. "It's really quite beautiful in back," she murmured, then turned to worry again about how it looked in front.

She touched it, patting it here and there, and remembered how the stylist had gone into raptures over her unusually thick hair. "And this color is your own? You don't have it streaked?" the woman had asked.

"It's all mine," Tamara had exclaimed.

"The curls, too?"

"Born with them," Tamara had said.

"Well, you are one very fortunate young woman," the stylist had stated with a sigh.

Tamara had thought of that remark while six inches of her hair fell to the floor. In many ways she *was* fortunate. It was terribly sad to lose a parent, but that happened to everyone sooner or later. But she had a good education and a good job. She had her health and even she had to admit her looks were above average. And dare she forget that she had two sisters whom she was beginning to think of as wonderful, caring women?

Okay, those were the pluses. On the minus side of the ledger was her personal situation. Even that might not be so problematic if Sam had let her be after their marriage. Why was he so damned stubborn? Her plan had been very simple. Never in a million years could she have foreseen his persistent determination to be a part of their baby's future. Which, of course, meant her future, as well.

What did he want from her? He couldn't possibly expect her to stay married to a man who didn't love her. That thought created an ache in her heart. She'd been so close to falling in love with Sam that weekend. Nothing else could have made her behave as she had. Loss of control? You bet she'd lost control.

And she had almost done it again in her kitchen on Tuesday night.

Seated in that stylist's chair, she'd drawn a deep breath. Maybe part of her would always love Sam a little, but what about the part that remembered the humiliation of the aftermath of that weekend? Not one phone call, not *any* form of contact. It was as though Sam had driven out of her apartment complex that Sunday and vanished from the face of the earth.

But she'd known he hadn't vanished. He had gone about his business without one single thought of her. The reality of their relationship was that it had existed in her own mind, and to be so easily forgotten was a wound she didn't foresee healing for a long time to come. Didn't Sam understand that? Didn't he grasp her point of view at all?

Okay, if you're so certain your marriage has no chance, why are you permitting Sam to come around?

That question arose again while Tamara studied her new hairdo, and with it arose a feeling of utter hopelessness. Sighing heavily, she put down the hand mirror and began undressing for a shower. Sam hadn't given her a specific time for their Saturday date, but if he arrived before she was ready, he would just have to bide his time until she was.

Since she'd had a shampoo at the beauty parlor before the stylist cut her hair, she pulled on a shower cap and then stepped into the stall.

Chapter Fifteen

Sam rang Tamara's doorbell and waited. Her front stoop was near the living room window, and he could see lights filtering through the drapes. There wasn't a peep from inside, and he shifted his weight from one foot to the other and pushed the doorbell button again. After a minute or so he took his keys from his jacket pocket, located the one Tamara had given him and then stood there, undecided about using it.

But why would she have offered her key if she hadn't expected him to use it? He didn't think she was very far away, maybe at one of her neighbor's units. Or possibly she'd made a quick run to the store. He couldn't see into her garage, and she could have taken her car somewhere, leaving the lights on inside the apartment so he would know she'd be right back.

Yeah, that was probably it, Sam reasoned, inserting the key in the lock and opening the door. To bolster his rationale, he called, "Tamara?" before going in. There was no response, and he stepped across the threshold and closed the door. That was when he heard the shower. An image of Tamara naked and wet hit him instantaneously and with a walloping impact.

Was this an opportunity he should do something about? They had showered together during that weekend, or rather, they'd made burning hot love under a spray of warm water. Sam's eyes narrowed as he tried to remember if that had happened more than once.

It was possible, he decided, and it was also possible that Tamara might throw him out on his ear if he invaded her privacy tonight without invitation. This was one opportunity he had better skip. His first order of business should be to check out Tamara's mood.

Taking off his jacket, he hung it in the foyer closet, went into the living room and sat on the sofa.

In the bathroom, Tamara turned off the water, stepped out of the stall and reached for a towel. After drying herself, she pulled the plastic cap from her head and shook her hair free. It fell into place, and looking at herself in the mirror, she decided that she did like it. She'd left the bathroom door open, so the air wasn't steamy, nor was the mirror.

Yes, she thought, fluffing the curls around her face, she liked her new look very much. Would Sam? She became very still and stared into her own eyes; she shouldn't care what Sam thought about anything. But she did care, didn't she? She cared and he didn't. Oh, he was acting as though she meant something to him, or was trying to, but why should she trust anything he said or did?

Oh, stop! she told herself sharply, not wanting to go through that painful progression of thoughts again. Sam was coming to Dallas this evening, she was permitting it and she was weary of whining about their relationship, if only to herself.

Tossing her curls again, she realized that she was thirsty.

Deciding to get one of the small bottles of water from the refrigerator to drink while she got ready for the evening, she wrapped a dry towel around herself, securing it over her breasts with a twisted fold, and padded barefoot from the bathroom to the kitchen.

Sam did a double take. Tamara had passed through the dining part of the L-shaped room and hadn't even glanced his way. *She's so incredibly beautiful,* he thought while getting to his feet. The adrenaline rush in his body caused even his fingertips to tingle. Every intimacy of their weekend in this apartment suddenly flashed through his mind— they'd done the shower scene *twice*—creating an almost torturous quickening of his blood. She'd made him think of that weekend before this, but not with such clarity, nor with the sort of cataclysmic reaction that he felt now.

Tamara, his wife, the mother of his unborn child. Sentimentality mingled with the desire racking Sam's body, and a whole new feeling gripped him. He wasn't sure if it was a newly found wisdom or merely the facts of life that were so stunningly clear in his mind, but the words *I love her* seemed emblazoned with stars, stripes and spinning pinwheels. *I love her!* he thought again with utter amazement.

He stumbled across the carpet to the kitchen doorway. Tamara was standing at the counter with her back to him. He couldn't deny himself the pleasure of looking at her in that towel. It covered her from the middle of her back to just below her knees. And she'd done something to her hair. It was different, shorter.

Should he tell her now? he wondered anxiously. Just walk up to her and say, "Tamara, I love you. I've been thinking about it off and on for a while, but I know for sure now. I love you." Sam frowned. And then what would she say? What would she *do?* If she laughed he wouldn't be able to take it. He shouldn't rush this, should he? There was too much at stake. Far better that he wait until he sensed positive feelings from her. That day would come; he just had to be patient.

Tamara turned with a plastic bottle of water in her right hand, saw him and let out a shriek of terror. The bottle fell to the floor as she frantically sought escape.

Sam rushed forward. "Tamara, it's me!" He managed to catch her by the shoulders.

The wildness in her eyes subsided a little. "Sam, you scared me to death," she gasped.

"I'm sorry. Oh, honey, please forgive me." He pulled her against his chest and felt the trembling of her body. "You didn't recognize me right away?"

"All I saw was a man." A shudder went through her. Sam was stroking her back, and gradually she began to calm down.

But with calmness came the ability to think. He'd used the key! He'd walked in, probably while she was in the shower. She should let him know how she felt about that. She should, this very second, ask him to return her key, and if he had the gall to question her attitude, she could plead temporary insanity for giving it to him.

Knowing what she should do and actually doing it were two different things, however. For instance, she knew that she should put some space between them. Only his arms around her felt so good, and he smelled clean, manly and wonderful. Her pulse was all aflutter, and the fluttering in the pit of her stomach was even more pronounced.

"I wouldn't deliberately frighten you for anything in the world," Sam murmured. "I hope you know that." The smell of her hair was clouding his brain, and it was all he could do to hang on to a sensible thought. "I rang the doorbell before I came in."

Her voice came out very low and husky. "I was in the shower." Sam's hands had glided down her back to cup her buttocks and bring her closer. Instead of verbally objecting or pushing him away, she slid her hands around his waist and locked them together at the small of his back.

Each had similar thoughts, the gist of which was *Is this really happening?* Tamara felt blissful, while Sam's imagination took wing. He *did* love her, so much that it felt as though something solid and glowingly beautiful had taken residence in his chest. Never had he thought it would happen to him, but then, had he predicted a shotgun wedding? Tamara had changed his life. She'd changed *him*. If only he dared say what was in his heart. Caution still reigned, however. If she took it wrong, or didn't believe him... No, he couldn't chance it. Not yet.

"Tamara," Sam whispered, and brought one hand from behind her to take her chin and tip up her face. Their gazes met and melded. Sam saw female softness in Tamara's eyes, and she saw hunger in his. Desire for her body. But there was something else, as well. Dare she interpret it as affection?

"What are you thinking?" she whispered huskily, hoping madly that he would give her a believable answer.

"That I want you more right this minute than I've ever wanted anything."

Well, it's believable, anyway, she thought with a wistful sigh.

"What are *you* thinking?" Sam asked, hoping against hope that they were approaching the point of talking about feelings.

Tamara had not expected Sam to turn the tables on her, and his question caught her totally unprepared. "That...uh, I..." she stammered. Self-disgust ran through her. She was no better than Sam. But it was his fault, dammit! He was the only person she knew that she had trouble talking to. And it wasn't her doing, it was his. She'd already known he wanted her; why couldn't he have said something romantic? Yes, some genuine romance in her life was exactly what she needed. She'd gone through hell in the last few months. She'd survived, of course, but not happily.

Sam was positive he understood her plight. She wanted him, too, and just couldn't say so. But in her way she'd given him the green light, he believed, and he moved his hand from her chin to run his fingers through the curls at the back of her head. "I like your hair this way," he whispered, a mere second before he pressed his lips to hers.

Tamara knew she wasn't going to push him away as she'd done on Tuesday night when he'd kissed her. There was something very potent between them, even if it wasn't love, and for some reason she felt especially alone tonight. Sam's brand of comfort, probably what *he* thought of as romance, was entirely sexual and came in spurts, but it was far better than none.

Besides, no other man had ever kissed her the way Sam did. His kisses had been her undoing that weekend, undoubtedly the reason she'd lost her mind and let him lead her into the most sensual two days and nights of her life.

It was what she wanted tonight, she realized dizzily—another taste of that delicious forbidden fruit. Only it wasn't quite as forbidden now as it had been then, was it? They were married and had every right to make love.

To hell with it, she thought boldly. Tonight she needed Sam, and if she was sorry tomorrow, she'd live through it, the same as she'd managed to do with every other misery-causing event of the past few months.

She stood on tiptoe and slid her hands up around his neck. Sam's mouth was warm and mobile on hers. His tongue was an active participant in kisses that melted one into another. They breathed when they could, a trivial matter in the face of so much passion.

Sam became so excited because *she* was excited that he thought he might burst. She was the Tamara of that weekend again, without inhibitions, lush in his arms and as eager to give pleasure to him as to feel it herself.

While her fingers struggled to unbutton his shirt, he yanked the towel from her body, placed it on the counter and then lifted her to sit on it. Then he couldn't stop himself from just looking at her. Tenderly he held her breast. "You're fuller," he said softly.

"Yes," she whispered, actually thrilled that he hadn't *totally* forgotten her the second he'd driven away that weekend.

He used both hands to trace the contours of her body. His throat was clogged with…well, the only word he could think of to describe his feelings at this moment was *adoration*. She was so utterly beautiful without clothes, more beautiful than he remembered. One hand skimmed down her belly, and his heart swelled with emotion when he thought of the baby growing inside her. *His* baby.

She was raptly watching his face while his eyes devoured her body. She was just starting to ask herself what she was seeing in his expression when he spread her legs and then pulled her closer to the edge of the counter. Her heart leaped into her throat. He was going to make love to her right here, right now. His shirt was partially unbuttoned, but he was certainly still dressed.

Avidly interested in just how he was going to go about it, she remained intent on his every move. Without the slightest show of modesty, he opened his jeans and shoved them and his briefs down just enough. In the very next heartbeat he had wedged himself between her legs. His arms went around her and he kissed her with complete abandonment, kissed her until she was dazed and straining against him.

"Please, Sam," she whimpered, desperately needing him to take the final step. His hot arousal pressing against the very core of her desire was pure torture.

His hands skimmed down her back. "Put your legs around me," he whispered raggedly. When she did, he grasped her hips and moved into her at the same time.

"Oh, Sam," she moaned, burying her face in that special little nook where his throat curved into his shoulder.

I love you, I love you. Being inside Tamara was heaven on earth. Sam shut his eyes, held her close and gritted his teeth. His movements were deliberate and languorously sensual. He knew if he let himself go it would be all over in two minutes, maybe even less, and he couldn't do that to Tamara. Her pleasure had to come first, and he thought of ice-cold showers to keep his blood pressure down.

With every thrust of his manhood, Tamara felt the tide rising a little higher. She nibbled on his throat and made little gasping sounds. Her hands went under his shirt to caress his bare back. His skin was hot and smooth, exactly as she remembered. She also recalled that nothing had ever been so good as making love with Sam. It was the same this time. In this they were a perfect match. What an incredible marriage two people would have if they were this compatible in all aspects of their lives.

Tears sprang to Tamara's eyes. She and Sam were such different types. Even though she hadn't made a lot of friends in Dallas, she liked people. Sam didn't. What chance did they have?

All thought suddenly stopped when Sam pulled back her head and kissed her mouth. Simultaneously he slithered a hand in between them and began gently rubbing the most sensitive area of her body. In five seconds she couldn't sit still, and was moaning and straining into him.

"My own true love," he mouthed against her lips.

She jerked her head back and stared at him through glassy eyes. "What did you say?"

His answer was another kiss, this one rougher and more needful than the others. He began moving faster, taking her with him on that final climb to the pinnacle. They reached it together, just as Sam had planned. Their cries of supreme pleasure resounded for a moment, then everything stopped.

Sam's legs were trembling, he was breathing so hard he could hear himself and he had to cling to Tamara for support. She felt totally wilted, and collapsed against his chest. It took some time, but gradually their breathing slowed and their pulse rates returned to normal.

Tamara stirred and raised her head. Sam looked into her

eyes. "Hi," he said with a little half smile. "Everything okay?"

She took in a long breath. "Why don't you tell me? Is everything okay, Sam?"

"Seems like it to me. I'm happy. Are you?"

"I'm sexually satisfied. Is that happiness?"

"I'd say so."

Their gazes were still locked. "You're an incredible lover, but I'm sure you know that. Lots of experience, right?"

After a brief hesitation, Sam quietly asked, "Is lots of experience what made *you* an incredible lover?"

Tamara flushed. "I do *not* have a lot of experience!"

"But I do?"

"Do you expect me to believe you don't?"

Sam studied her closely, probing the depths of her beautiful hazel eyes. "All right, I'll tell you the truth. Yes, I've had experience. Does it please you to hear me say that? I'll tell you something else, Tamara. Every woman in my past has no face. They meant nothing to me."

Tamara's jaw dropped. "I wouldn't be so quick to boast about that, if I were you. If I hadn't gotten pregnant, *I* wouldn't have a face, either!" She pushed on his chest. "Please move away so I can get down from here."

"Dammit, don't you dare get mad! You asked me a question and I gave you an honest answer. Would you rather hear lies?" He grasped the back of her neck and held her head still. "Don't look away from me!"

Her eyes jerked up to meet his again. "And don't you order me around as if I were some kind of moron! Granted, I've acted like one with you, but—"

"Tamara, stop. I know you're not a moron. You're probably the brightest, most intelligent woman I've ever known."

"Even though none of them have a face," she said, disgusted. Her expression changed as she muttered, "Who gives a damn? Move so I can get down!"

Sam's eyes narrowed. ''You're mad because we made love.''

''Sam, if you knew half as much as you think you do, they'd be calling you Einstein instead of Stoneface!''

Sam heaved a sigh. ''So you've heard my nickname around the office.'' She looked startled. ''Good Lord,'' he exclaimed, ''did you think I didn't know about it?''

She felt so embarrassed she didn't know where to look. How could she have said such a thing to him? It occurred to her that no one had referred to Sam as Stoneface in her presence since she'd announced their marriage, but she would bet anything people in the office were still using it behind her back.

She forced herself to look at Sam again. ''I did think you didn't know,'' she said. ''I apologize for even bringing it up. I don't know why I did that.''

''To hurt me,'' Sam said quietly. ''To alleviate your conscience for making love with me. Tamara, how can you make love with a man you don't like?''

She sighed wearily. ''Oh, please, let's not get into that liking thing again. Sam, please move so I can get down.''

This time he nodded, took a small step back to untangle their bodies, then clasped her by the waist and lifted her down from the counter. Without looking at him, she grabbed the towel and fled from the kitchen.

Chapter Sixteen

Tamara reappeared fifteen minutes later wearing a gray sweat suit and a pair of house slippers. When she walked into the living room, Sam got up from the sofa, eyeing her curiously. As adorable as she looked in those baggy sweats, she wasn't exactly dressed for an evening out.

She got right to the point. "I don't feel like going anywhere now, if you don't mind."

"And if I do?"

"Please don't be difficult."

"Tamara, you have to eat dinner. We could go somewhere casual, maybe a pizza house."

"No, I don't think so. I'll have a sandwich—or something—later on. Don't worry about it."

"In other words, our date is over and it's time for me to go." Instead of doing so, Sam sat down again. "I'm not ready to leave," he stated calmly.

Tamara started as though struck. "This happens to be *my* apartment," she said with asperity.

"And *you* happen to be my wife," Sam retorted. He looked stubborn. "I'll leave when I'm good and ready."

Tamara stared, he stared and a heavy silence hung between them. A list of options ran through her mind, but every one of them would only bring on an argument. She finally sat in a chair, folded her arms across her chest and sent Sam the dirtiest look she could muster.

"I can sit here *much* longer than you can," she said icily.

"A challenge if ever I've heard one," Sam retorted. "Do you like challenging me, Tamara? You're constantly doing it, so you must."

"Don't try to analyze me, Sam. Believe me, you don't have the credentials."

"Insult number one. I'm not educated and you are. Take your next shot, Tamara. Tonight I'm up to it."

Why, he was *trying* to pick a fight! Tamara eyed him suspiciously. "What's going on, Sam?"

He sat back and laid his arm along the top of the sofa. "I'll tell you what's going on, sweetheart. You've run the show long enough. Now it's my turn."

"What on earth are you talking about?" she snapped.

"Before we get into that, let's talk about something else. Let's talk about making love on the kitchen counter. Let's talk about how much you liked it, how much we *both* liked it and how we both know it's going to happen again."

Tamara's face colored, but she kept her chin high. "After this annoying and completely unnecessary standoff, I would recommend you rethink that idea," she said stiffly.

"No need. You see, I *know* I can make you want me. Anytime, anywhere."

"Don't let your massive ego get in the way of good sense, Sam," she said with crisply stated sarcasm. "I might be weak and witless *once* in a while, but certainly not anytime, anywhere."

"Massive ego, huh? Insult number two. Tamara, I could make you want me again right now."

She scoffed. "Don't be ridiculous."

"I'd be happy to prove it," Sam said.

She had never seen that sort of intriguing expression on his face before, and it eased some of her tension. "Now who's challenging who?" she drawled.

Sam laughed, surprising Tamara again. "Guess it's me challenging you this time," he said. "Do you accept?"

"Accept what?"

"My challenge."

"Oh, that," she said scornfully. "There's nothing you could do to make me play the fool again tonight. Once was more than enough, believe me."

"Once sure wasn't enough that weekend, if I remember correctly."

"Don't remind me," she said.

Sam smiled. "Getting back to the subject at hand, you're certain that there's nothing I could do to make you want me again tonight. Do I have it right?"

"Absolutely."

"Okay, challenge issued and accepted. Shall we get started?" He got up from the sofa and walked over to her.

Wide-eyed and startled, she stared up at him. "Sam, I'm not playing your game. Go back and sit down or get your coat and go home."

"No, Tamara. I have something to prove to you, and I can't leave until I do it." He knelt in front of her and laid his hands on her thighs.

She slapped at his hands. "Stop that! I told you I wasn't playing your silly game, and I meant it."

"Your bluster is a cover-up, sweetheart. You know I can do what I said, and you don't want to admit it."

"You most certainly can not!"

He slid his hands from her thighs up to her waist and leaned his torso against her knees. "You're so afraid I'm right that you're quaking in those cute little fuzzy slippers."

"Afraid of you? Never!"

"You're not afraid of me, honey, you're afraid of yourself."

"You are the most absurd man I've ever known!"

"And just possibly the sexiest?"

"There's a laugh."

"But you're not laughing, are you?" He bent forward, putting his face very close to hers. "I can tell you're already feeling it. You know, all soft and squishy inside?"

"You make me sound like a glob of mud."

He chuckled softly. "I was thinking more along the line of warm, melting chocolate."

She cocked an eyebrow. "A sunstruck candy bar? Really, Sam," she said disdainfully. But bandying words with him was not preventing the internal combustion going on within her. He was right, damn him. He had the power to get her juices flowing just by touching her. She could admit it and put an end to this game of his, but did she want to give him that satisfaction? He was already conceited enough. He was acting as if he *knew* she had no resistance against his physical charms, but he couldn't possibly tell that much about her. He was guessing, maybe hoping, but no, he couldn't know for sure.

And she would bite off her own tongue before admitting anything to him.

"I'm really feeling nothing but crowded," she said in the coolest voice she could manage. "And I don't understand why you're doing this."

Sam was beginning to wonder if he understood why himself. Hadn't he already proved their mutual attraction in the kitchen? What did he want from her—some sign, a word, a gesture, indicating his superiority? Did he want her weak and whimpering because he was just too, too irresistible?

No, definitely not, he thought, while boldly studying the lovely contours of her face. He liked her strength and independence, her courage. It had taken guts for her to find him at his ranch and demand marriage.

What he wanted most from Tamara was her love. If he said it now, *I love you, Tamara,* would everything fall into place, or would she get all righteous and indignant? Thus far in their extremely unusual relationship they had connected in only one area of human interaction: sex. *That* was why he was on his knees in front of her, he thought, recalling his vow to use whatever advantage he had to get her to cross that invisible line she'd drawn between them. If it took a little game playing, so be it.

"I really wish you'd stop staring," Tamara said sharply. "And I wish you would stop crowding me. Go back to the sofa, for heaven's sake. Honestly, Sam, don't you feel just a little bit foolish leaning on me like this?"

Sam ignored her wishes *and* her question. "You know what Stubby said about you? He said you were a sweet little flower. What do you think of that?"

An urge to giggle rose in Tamara's throat. Sweet little flower? Good grief. On the other hand, even though she had talked to Stubby just that one time, he had seemed to be the sort of courtly old gentleman who would say something of that nature.

"What a delightful compliment," she said, holding back that giggle through sheer willpower. "Tell Stubby I said thank you."

Sam hadn't expected that sort of warm reaction, and his face showed his surprise. "You *like* Stubby's comment?"

Tamara truly enjoyed replying, "From that alone I can tell Stubby knows how to treat a lady."

Sam's eyes narrowed slightly. "Meaning I don't."

"If the shoe fits..." Tamara felt she was holding her own in this nonsensical battle of wits, but in the back of her mind she realized there was more to this little drama than the obvious. For one thing, Sam was talking to her. It might be no more than foolish patter, but it *was* conversation. And was it possible he was merely teasing her about proving himself too sexually appealing for her to resist? There was something he was hoping to accomplish with this uncharacteristic horseplay, and it could only be one thing—her giving up completely and telling him she wouldn't get a divorce after the baby came—which she simply could not do.

But then she made an almost fatal mistake. She looked directly into his heavenly blue eyes, and the result was a jolt of electricity that made the fine hairs on her body stand on end. She'd told Sam he didn't have the credentials to analyze her behavior, but did she have the knowledge to assess *his* conduct? Especially when his hands were on her and he was so close she could see the minute silver and black flecks within the deep blue of his eyes?

Sudden breathlessness stole over her, growing more pronounced when he produced a slow-burning smile. Her lips parted to take in some much needed air, and her voice actually came out a squeak when she attempted to regain her previous footing in this game by asking, ''*Does* the shoe fit?''

''No,'' Sam whispered, adjusting his position again and dipping his head so close to hers that she could feel his breath on her lips. She tried to avoid what she just knew was coming next, but there was only so much room in that chair, and the back of her head was already pressed against it. Instead of the kiss she expected, however, Sam said, ''Your eyes are as big as saucers. Do you concede?''

She swallowed a bit nervously, but stubbornness would not permit concession. Not with Sam, for heaven's sake. Concession would mean handing him her freedom, her right to make decisions for herself—one decision in particular, the one that was causing both of them a lot of sleepless nights. Oh yes, she was certain Sam wasn't sleeping any better than she was. Maybe she didn't know every facet of his life and personality, but she knew in her heart that he was a man who took what he wanted and to hell with the rest of the world. His disdain for the human race had backfired in her case, and if he was getting a full quota of sleep every night, she would be eternally surprised.

"I concede nothing," she said with a defiant gleam in her eyes. She watched a flush creep up Sam's neck to his face.

"You're driving me crazy," he muttered.

She didn't doubt it, but she was not going to concede that point, either. She was about to tell him that he would never win this war when he kissed her. Taken by surprise, Tamara swore to feel nothing, but it wasn't three seconds before she was kissing him back. Her hands wound around his neck, and his went under the top of her sweat suit and found her breasts. It was the beginning of the end, and both knew it.

To Sam's credit, he didn't gloat. He might have if he wasn't so deluged with emotion. This incredibly sensual woman was his wife, and he loved her so much that tears stung his eyes. At that moment he didn't care if Tamara saw them or not. He got to his feet, picked her up out of that chair and headed for her bedroom.

Tamara didn't see Sam's tears, but she certainly felt her own.

He had just proved that he *could* make her want him, hadn't he?

How terribly sad to be in love with a man who merely wanted to maintain the upper hand.

Tamara opened her eyes and realized she must have fallen asleep. Her first glance was at the bedside clock; she had dozed for about an hour. Turning her head on her pillow, she looked at Sam. He'd bunched his pillow to put his head higher than hers, and he was wide-awake and watching her. Instantly she wished she had extinguished the lamp by the bed, which Sam had insisted be left burning while they made love. A heated flush turned her face pink and warm as she thought of their abandoned foreplay.

"Uh, you didn't sleep?" she asked uneasily.

"I was thinking."

"Oh." They were intimately tangled. Her knee was

wedged between his thighs, and she could feel the softly rounded contours of his most personal assets against her skin. His left hand was burrowed under the pillow beneath his head, and his right rested on her waist. A sheet and blanket covered them. She tried to make light of what was really a very discomfiting situation by asking playfully, "Did I snore?"

Sam smiled. "Only a little."

"Really?" Goodness, *had* she snored? How embarrassing.

"No, of course not. I was only kidding."

She hadn't known Sam was capable of kidding and almost said so. But he seemed to be in a lovely, mellow mood, and she didn't want to say something to destroy it. She *would* like to move her knee, however, only she wanted to do it in such a way that he couldn't possibly be affronted.

"I need to get up," she murmured, deliberately sounding reluctant. At the same time she wondered why she wanted to maintain the mellowness of spirit between them. Maybe because it was so uncharacteristic of Sam, and of herself *around* Sam. Was something important happening here? He seemed so loose and relaxed. Was he on the verge of opening that tightly locked door to his private self and inviting her in?

"Hurry back," Sam said quietly.

"I will." Sliding over to the edge of the bed, she took a quick look around for something to put on. The room seemed as though it had been hit by a small tornado. Her clothes—and Sam's—were scattered as if tossed by a high wind.

Well, why in heaven's name would she worry about him seeing her naked now? she asked herself wryly. No intimacy was off-limits for Sam, and she'd been swept along in the maelstrom of his passion. *Her* passion, she quickly amended. She didn't have the gall to blame Sam for the things *she'd* done.

Leaving the bed, she felt Sam's eyes on her backside as she went to the closet for a robe. "It's chilly in here," she explained while slipping into it. Sam merely smiled.

After she'd gone, he stretched out full-length and locked his hands behind his head to stare at the ceiling. If he died this very second, he thought, that same smile firmly fixed on his lips, he would go to the great beyond a happy man. In his whole life he'd never felt like he did right now. What a woman he'd married! A wildcat in bed and a lady out of it, Tamara was the perfect combination of sexuality and intelligence. No man could ask for more in the woman he wed.

Of course, at this stage all he could do was hope that Tamara felt the same about him. As crazy, wild and wonderful as their lovemaking had gotten, neither of them had said a word about love. Sam's reason for holding back those special words was that he really felt as though he was making headway with Tamara and was afraid of scaring her off. Was it possible that she had the same misgivings about him? Wouldn't it be ironic if they were *both* biting their tongue to keep from talking about love and permanency?

But it would be a lot worse than ironic if he said "I love you" and Tamara bolted!

He'd best play it cool for a while longer, he decided. He definitely had her attention in the sex department; he could be patient about the rest of it. He did have something to talk to her about, however, which he would do when she returned.

Refreshing herself in the bathroom, Tamara would have been stunned if she'd known how similar her thoughts were to Sam's. If she marched back into her bedroom and announced "I've fallen in love with you," what would be Sam's reaction? She winced at the image that came to her mind—of him jumping out of bed, grabbing his clothes and making a hasty getaway. Sam didn't want love from her, he wanted his child. Oh, he also wanted sex from her, but probably only because she was the handiest female around.

Tamara took her time in the bathroom, as she wasn't in any hurry to get back to Sam. How much longer was he going to stay? Surely he didn't expect to stay all night, but knowing Sam—she was beginning to—he could decide to do almost anything.

She fiddled with her hair in front of the mirror, pushing curls this way and that, and decided that she should have had her hair cut and styled a long time ago. Goodness, the hours she'd wasted on all that long hair, rolling it, twisting it, attempting dignified hairdos for work. Now all she'd have to do was shampoo it in the shower, towel dry it and shake out the curls. For the first time in a very long time, she was grateful for so much natural curl. And this new style made her look much more mature, she thought with a final pat. Not older than her twenty-three years, but capable and mature.

Sighing, she turned from the mirror. She might *look* capable and mature, but given her behavior with Sam, she had to wonder. If she even had some idea of what he might pull next, she might feel better about the whole thing. For all she knew he could have taken the notion to vanish into the night, and was already dressed and waiting at the front door to say goodbye.

The idea embedded itself so deeply in her mind that she peered around the bedroom door before entering. Sam wasn't dressed and, in fact, looked as though he'd barely moved at all since she'd left. *That* picture gave her pause. Did she want him staying the night?

Sam saw her. "What're you doing?"

She walked in. "To tell you the truth, I was looking at you."

He grinned. "You were? How come?"

"Because I wasn't sure you'd still be here."

Sam's grin faded. "I'll leave if you want me to, but first

I'd like to talk to you about something." He patted the bed. "Come and sit down."

A discomfiting wariness developed within Tamara. Why would he suddenly become intent on a serious discussion? It could only be about one thing, of course—their shaky, unstable marriage. Did she want to hear his opinion on that subject again?

Still, she sat on the edge of the bed and waited for him to begin.

Sam noticed that she'd sat as far from him as was possible. Obviously this discussion was not going to be influenced by anything physical. Just as obvious, she was suspicious of what he might be planning to say. It was funny how clearly he read her some of the time and how muddy the waters were at other times.

He took a breath and looked her in the eye. "Tamara, do you like working?"

She blinked, surprised by his question, which had nothing at all to do with their marriage. Not very long ago she would have started gushing over her job and how well she was doing in it. Now she wasn't so sure. The project she herself had conceived and received such kudos for—the new catalog—was going to be terribly time-consuming. Plus, she was going to have to do a lot of traveling to find the perfect woman to use as the model, and Tamara's present frame of mind was not at all conducive to traipsing all over several states.

"It's not a matter of liking to work, Sam. I *have* to work."

"No," he said quietly, "you don't."

She gave a sharp, disbelieving laugh. "I don't? And who would support me, you?"

"Yes, me."

She stared for a long moment, then gave another sharp laugh. "Let me get this straight. You're offering to pay the rent on this apartment and—"

Sam cut in. "I didn't say that. You'd be giving up the apartment."

Her eyes narrowed suspiciously. "And living where?"

"At the ranch."

"The ranch! Sam, have you lost your ever-loving mind? You're suggesting I quit my job, give up this apartment, change my entire way of life and move to your ranch?"

"Yes, that's exactly what I'm suggesting. But I'm *not* suggesting you make a decision right now. Just think about it, that's all I'm asking."

She spoke incredulously, bluntly. "What on earth makes you think I would even consider such a thing?"

"The baby. Tamara, how much maternity leave will you have?"

"Six weeks."

"And then what?"

"I'll go back to work, of course."

"And who will be raising our baby while you're at work?"

She thought of the long days she put in at her desk and became very still. She thought of Natalie Cross, who was so guilt-ridden over leaving her children every workday morning that she very rarely went anywhere in the evening or on weekends. Tamara thought of how much she already loved the small life in her womb, and one final thought hit her very hard: how was she going to manage it all? Juggling motherhood with a career could not be easy. Other women did it—*many* other women—but could she? Her own mother had always been there when she got home from school. Wasn't that what she wanted for her child?

Sam was offering an alternate plan. It was not something she would have ever thought of herself, and she resented him for giving her another decision to make. Besides, his idea was motivated strictly by selfishness. He wanted his child so much that he would even have her living under his roof. Yet his idea did have merit.

She was so torn over this discussion that she felt the

painful start of a tension headache. Rubbing her temples, she got to her feet and walked around the room. Sam watched her with an ache in his heart. He'd known his idea would unsettle her, but he'd had to present it. For him it was the perfect solution. For him and the baby, that is. It could be perfect for Tamara, as well, if she would let it be.

But that was why he'd started this conversation by asking if she liked working. To his way of thinking her choice was a career or a family. Oh sure, she could probably manage both, but why should she? The ranch was too far away for a daily commute and nothing much would change if she maintained her apartment, which she would have to do if she kept her job.

Sam frowned over the way she was pacing the carpet. Obviously he had confused her. Realizing that she needed to think about his idea from all angles, he got out of bed and began dressing.

It took a few moments, but she finally noticed. "Are you leaving?"

He nodded and shoved the tail of his shirt into his jeans. "You need some time alone. How about if I come back tomorrow afternoon?"

Tamara thought about it. She wasn't going to solve this problem in one day. "Give me a week, Sam. Come back next weekend."

Her forlorn expression tore at his heartstrings. He walked over to her and put his arms around her. With a heavy sigh she laid her head on his chest.

"It would work, Tamara," he said softly. "I'm not a wealthy man. I probably never will be. But I swear you would never go without, nor would our child, and he'd be raised by the people who love him, his parents."

Sam always referred to the baby as male. She'd told him before that the baby might be a girl, and she considered doing it again.

But the thought was fleeting. She had too many serious things on her mind to worry about trivialities.

Sam tipped up her chin and looked into her eyes. "Do you really need a whole week?" He knew he would worry and fret every minute of every day and night until he saw her again.

"At the very least."

"I'm going back to work on Monday," Sam said.

"You're not waiting until the first of February? I thought you said something about always taking the month of January off."

"February's not that far off, and I want to start making money again." He smiled gently. "I have a family to support now."

"Sam, I haven't said I would do it."

"I know, but I'm hoping with all my heart. Tamara..."

She waited a second, then asked, "What?"

"Nothing, sweetheart."

"Sam, you were going to say something. What was it?"

"It'll keep. May I kiss you?"

"Now you're asking?"

He chuckled softly, bent his head and tenderly kissed her on the mouth. Tamara thought her heart would split wide open. Could a man be so tender with a woman if he didn't have very deep feelings for her? Oh, if only he could say what he really felt.

Sam moved away from her, sat on the bed and yanked on his boots. Tamara saw him to the front door, and he kissed her again.

"Eat something before you go to bed," he said, while gently brushing a curl from her cheek. "I'll see you next Saturday. Try to have a good week, sweetheart." He went through the door, closing it behind him.

"I don't think that's possible," she whispered.

Chapter Seventeen

By Sunday evening Tamara felt she had come to a decision. Moving in with Sam would be pure heartache and she already had more than enough of that to deal with. She had an exceptionally good job that paid a good salary, and if her work seemed a bit difficult at the present, it was because she was permitting personal problems to block her concentration. Millions of mothers worked, and as soon as she announced her pregnancy to the world, she would also begin the task of finding a reliable child-care facility.

So her answer to Sam next Saturday was going to be no. She was not going to live at the ranch with him; he was not going to be her financial support. She knew he wasn't going to like her decision, but it was something with which he would just have to live.

Tamara went to bed around ten and slept fairly well. She got up at five and, as was her habit on workdays, immediately took her shower. After drying off, she stepped on the bathroom scale. "What?" she cried when the dial indicated another weight gain. She was gaining a pound every other day, an almost unbelievable occurrence.

She was careful about what she ate, and she had bought a treadmill—installed in her extra bedroom—for daily exercise. Already she had gained almost all of the poundage recommended by Dr. Edmon for a healthy term, and she was only three months along! How was that possible?

Panicking, she rushed to the phone and dialed Dr. Edmon's number. Naturally, she got the physician's answering service, which she would have foreseen if she'd stopped to think of the time. Regardless, she told the voice on the other end of the phone line that she *must* speak to Dr. Edmon.

"Is this an emergency, ma'am?"

"It is to me," Tamara exclaimed. "Please have Dr. Edmon call Tamara Benning at her first opportunity." Tamara passed on her phone number. "Thank you."

At six-fifteen Tamara's phone rang. She was about to leave for work, but she felt certain the caller was Dr. Edmon, and she grabbed the phone as though it were some sort of lifeline.

"Tamara? This is Dr. Edmon. What's wrong?"

"I'll tell you what's wrong, Doctor. I'm gaining weight at an alarming rate—lately a pound every other day—and I shouldn't be. I'm doing everything you said to do—watching my fat and sugar intake, exercising..."

"How much weight are we talking about?"

"Twelve pounds since I last saw you."

"Yes, that's too much too fast. Tamara, I'm going to order an ultrasound examination. When I get it arranged, I'll call you with the appointment information."

"Call me at work, Doctor. Rowland's number is 555-6611, and my extension is 732."

"Very well. Tamara, you sound frantic. You must calm yourself."

"I *am* frantic! Why would I be gaining so rapidly?"

"It could be for any number of reasons. I'm not going

to go into them now. Let's see what the ultrasound shows, and then we'll talk. I believe I'll order a blood workup, also. You'll be hearing from my office sometime this morning. Goodbye, Tamara."

"Goodbye, Doctor, and thank you for calling so soon." Tamara hung up, gathered her purse and briefcase and hurried to the garage.

The minute she walked into her office, her phone rang. She dropped her things on the desk and, still wearing her coat, picked up the phone. "Extension 732, Tamara speaking."

"Good morning, Tamara." It was Elliot Grimes. "I have a rather urgent request. Yesterday my wife and I dined at Tom Rowland's home, along with his two sisters and their families. We had an impromptu business meeting after dinner, and they're all quite taken with your innovative concept for the new catalog. However, they would like more information about it. What I need is a written report, an in-depth procedural outline of your ideas, to pass on to them. I would like to have it in my hands before closing today. Is that possible?"

Tamara's heart sank, but she kept her voice businesslike. "Yes, sir. I'll get to work on it immediately."

"Thank you, Tamara. I knew I could count on you." The phone went dead.

Tamara suffered her second panic attack of the day, then shook her head to clear it. She had no time to stand around and worry. Taking off her coat, she hung it in the small closet in her office. Then she returned to her desk and began placing in-house calls to the people working with her on the catalog project. Annie Campbell in advertising answered at once, and Tamara told her about Mr. Grimes's request. "We need to get together and finalize our plans before I put them down on paper, Annie. Can you come to my office in about an hour?"

Annie said yes and Tamara placed her second call. Hal Delaney, a top salesman, had been very helpful with names and suggestions regarding female clients who might fill the requirements for the catalog's model, and Tamara wanted him to sit in on this meeting.

But Hal didn't answer his phone. Frowning, Tamara dialed reception. Natalie answered, her voice sounding thick and clogged.

"Hi, Nat, this is Tamara. Do you have a cold?"

"No." Natalie began crying in Tamara's ear.

"Nat, what's wrong?"

"It's nothing you can do anything about, Tamara. Hold on while I blow my nose." In a few seconds, Natalie came back on the line. "I'm sorry. What can I do for you?"

"I need to talk to Hal Delaney. Apparently he's not at his desk, and I wanted you to track him down. He could be anywhere in the building."

"I can do that."

"Nat, why were you crying?"

"Because... Oh, Tamara, you have no idea. No one could who doesn't have kids. But my son has the flu, and he couldn't go to school. I'm fit to be tied, because I had to leave him alone today. There's no one with him, Tamara, and he's sick and only eight years old, and..." She broke down and wept again.

"Natalie, for crying out loud, go home!"

"I can't. Ruth called in sick and I'm the only one on the phones," Natalie wailed.

Ruth was the other receptionist. One person could handle reception and the phones if she worked like crazy. The whole company would fall apart if no one was there to take incoming calls, however.

"Natalie, listen to me. I'm going to find someone to do your job today so you can go home."

"Everyone has their own job to do," Natalie said, sniffling.

"I am going to find someone, so stop worrying. In the meantime, try to locate Hal."

"All right."

Tamara put the phone down. Contacting a temporary help agency would be the answer if she didn't need someone right this minute. That would work for tomorrow if both Natalie's son and Ruth were still ill, or possibly even this afternoon, but Nat needed to be home *now!*

It struck Tamara that she herself could be in Natalie's shoes in less than a year from today. A sick child, a demanding job? Oh, yes, she could easily find herself in Natalie's present dilemma at some point in her child's life, and she undoubtedly would. It was something that most working mothers probably had to deal with more than once.

Well, standing there and fretting over her own future problems wasn't helping Natalie, she thought with a heavy sigh. Leaving her office, she went directly to the clerical supervisor and explained the situation.

At first the woman was unsympathetic. "My people are extremely busy, Mrs. Sherard."

"I'm sure they are," Tamara replied. "But this is an emergency. Natalie Cross *has* to go home, and someone *has* to man the phones. I'm only trying to help, Mrs. Layton."

Tamara didn't let up until the woman relented. "I'll send someone to work reception, but only for today, Mrs. Sherard. I suggest you have personnel call for a temp if this problem goes beyond today."

"I'll do that, Mrs. Layton, and thank you so much for your consideration."

Tamara left, mumbling to herself, and headed into the personnel department, where she again explained the situation. Of course a temp could be arranged for tomorrow, the woman in charge told her. She would take care of it immediately.

Tamara hurried to reception. "Get ready to leave," she told Natalie. "Mrs. Layton is sending someone from clerical to take your place for today. And tomorrow a temp will do the job. Stay home with your son for as long as he's ill.''

Natalie was amazed. ''How did you do it so quickly?''

''I guess I just bullied my way through it. Oh, did you manage to locate Hal?''

''Yes, he was down in the inventory department. He said to tell you he'd be back at his desk in ten minutes. I'm sure he's there by now. Tamara, thank you so much.''

''You're very welcome. Talk to you later.'' Tamara returned to her own office, sat at her desk and gritted her teeth to keep from bawling. This was not a good day, not a good day at all.

Two hours later Hal, Annie and Tamara were still tossing ideas back and forth when the phone rang. Tamara picked it up. ''Extension 732, Tamara speaking.''

''This is Dr. Edmon's secretary, Mrs. Sherard. You have an appointment with the Dallas Diagnostic Center tomorrow morning at ten. It's just next door to the building we're in, suite 306.''

Tamara drew a quick breath. ''Thank you, I'll be there.'' Putting down the phone, she looked at Hal and Annie. ''Sorry about that. Where were we?''

Tamara left the Rowland building that evening around eight, totally exhausted. The report had been delivered to Mr. Grimes, and she could hardly believe she had actually gotten it done in one day. Hal and Annie had helped, of course, but only with finalizing the ideas. It was Tamara who had coordinated everything and put it all down on paper.

When she finally got home, incredibly relieved that the traumatic day was over, she ate a bowl of soup, changed into pajamas and fell into bed. She was asleep in minutes.

Tamara had never had an ultrasound before. After changing into a gown, she was brought to a small, dimly-lit room and instructed to lie on the table. A machine with a monitor screen sat nearby. Tamara was alone only a few minutes before a technician walked in.

"Mrs. Sherard, I'm David Helm. I'm going to do your ultrasound test. Are you comfortable?"

"I'm fine, thank you."

The young man sat on a stool in front of the machine and turned dials and flipped switches for a moment. Then he opened Tamara's gown so that just her lower abdomen was uncovered, and squirted gel onto her skin.

"Ever had an ultrasound before?" he asked.

"No."

"Well, what I'm going to do is take a look at your baby. I'll also be taking photos of the images as we go."

Tamara craned her neck but couldn't see the screen. "You'll actually be able to see the baby?" she asked.

"Yes, ma'am. Ready?"

"Ready."

He had what to Tamara's untrained eye looked like a computer mouse in his hand, and he placed it on her abdomen and began moving it over the gelled area. Tamara watched his face as he watched the screen.

"Whoa," he said with a startled expression.

"What?" she exclaimed, fearing that he'd just seen something terrible.

"There's more than one heartbeat."

"Oh my God!" Did her child have two hearts? Tamara suddenly felt faint.

"Hey, don't get alarmed. There's more than one baby in there."

"Twins?" she asked anxiously. Were there twins in her or Sam's family tree? She couldn't remember any on her side, but what did she know of Sam's family? Very darned little, she thought, resenting his reticence again.

David Helm stared hard at the screen and kept moving

the gadget in his hand. He finally drew a long breath and said, "Mrs. Sherard, you're going to have triplets."

Tamara was too stunned to speak. She lay there benumbed while David Helm worked that thing on her stomach and stared at the screen. Every so often she heard a clicking noise as he adjusted something or other, or maybe he was taking photos. She didn't know and couldn't even guess. Triplets. It wasn't possible.

"Yep, three babies," David Helm said with a grin. "And they look great. Want to see them?"

"Please," she whispered.

He turned the machine a few inches until she could see the screen, but it was in black and white and made little sense to her.

"Here are the hearts," David said, using a pointer to touch the screen.

Tamara's mouth dropped open. She could see them! Three different beats on the screen. Her babies' hearts. Tears filled her eyes. "Can…can you tell if they're boys or girls?" she asked emotionally.

David moved the handset over her tummy again, stopping it here and there to study the image. "They're very tiny yet, and very crowded together. I really can't tell. In another month or so we should be able to answer that question." He wiped the remaining gel from her stomach. "That's it, Mrs. Sherard. You may get dressed now. The photos and data will be sent to your doctor."

"Thank you," Tamara whispered.

"Do you have other children?"

"No, this is my first." She managed a choked laugh. "My first three."

David Helm smiled. "You're probably feeling a little overwhelmed about now, but there are many, many women who would envy you. My wife, for one." He got up from the stool. "Would you like some help in getting dressed? It wouldn't be any trouble at all to have a nurse assist you."

"I can manage, thank you."

"Very well. Goodbye, Mrs. Sherard."

"Bye," she whispered as he walked out of the room.

After a stop at the hematology lab so another technician could draw vials of blood from her right arm, Tamara called Elliot Grimes, told him she had suddenly fallen ill and would not be back to work that day. She could not sit at her desk and think of her three babies; she needed to be alone to do that.

Tamara walked the floor of her apartment, wept at intervals and wished a hundred times that her mother was alive so she could phone her. It would be such an enormous relief to talk to *someone*.

Tamara sobbed into a handful of tissues. It wasn't that she didn't *want* her babies—Lord knew how much she already loved them—but how would she take care of three infants and work the long days her job demanded?

Sam's offer popped in and out of her mind. Sometimes it seemed to be the only answer, but Tamara's spirit repeatedly rebelled at that solution. She loved him and he didn't love her, it was as simple as that. As difficult as the future looked if she faced it alone, she could not bear the thought of living the life of a woman with a disinterested husband. And it would come to that—of course it would, she told herself. How could it not? Sam would be considerate at first, but that would gradually wane and she'd be trapped on his ranch, raising three babies in an isolated area while Sam wandered hundreds of miles to make a living.

It couldn't possibly work, and she was not going to become a jealous, harried woman because the man she loved was rarely home. Sam was too damned handsome for his own good, and she could see herself suffering agonies over nagging thoughts of him and other women. No, that wasn't for her.

But dare she completely discard Sam's offer? How *was*

she going to care for three infants and keep her job? Natalie's misery today was a frightening example of the reality of motherhood. Yes, millions of mothers held jobs, but how many of them had borne triplets?

Oh, if only she could go back and do it all again, she thought with an agonized groan and another onslaught of tears. So what if she'd been pregnant and unmarried? Had she bettered her situation by bringing Sam into it? She should have told Elliot Grimes the truth behind her request for a transfer, and then let anyone who was even remotely interested in her personal life know that she was going to become a single parent.

She suddenly remembered some of the frank discussions she and her mother had had during her teen years. More accurately, Tamara recalled Myra's passionately stated advice: *Tamara, any woman with a drop of good sense does not fool around with sex before marriage. But life being what it is today, it is possible you'll find yourself so attracted to some young man that you simply cannot resist temptation. For heaven's sake, and yours, use every precaution on the market. Believe me, there is nothing more humiliating for a family than to have an illegitimate child to deal with. Tamara, I'm sure I would love any child of yours, but please don't ever put me in that situation. I've always maintained a position of respect in this community, as did your father, and I would do almost anything to keep from tarnishing his memory and my own reputation.*

"My God," Tamara whispered. She'd been so completely saturated with disdain for unwed mothers that she had automatically, and rather frantically, looked for a way around it. *Any* way. Why hadn't she understood that before now?

By that evening, Tamara was admittedly a basket case. Her nerves were totally shattered, and she'd shed so many tears her eyes were swollen into slits. Coming home to be alone with her thoughts had definitely backfired. It would have been far better if she'd returned to work after her tests. At least at her desk she would not have been able to concentrate solely on herself and her problems.

If only there was someone to talk to, she thought while curled up in a ball of utter misery on one end of the sofa. Her sisters? Could she really bare her soul to either of them? They believed she was a happily married woman with a wonderful job. She'd *led* them to believe that fairy tale, and could she take it back now?

But could she go on like this? Tamara eyed the phone across the room. She was much too worried about other people's opinions. Her upbringing again, she thought unhappily. Maybe Sierra and Blythe *would* understand, because they had to have been brought up with the same advice and attitudes as herself.

Tamara's hands clenched and unclenched nervously while she debated calling her sisters, then she forced herself off the sofa and stumbled to the phone. She automatically dialed her mother's number in Coeur d'Alene. Blythe answered on the third ring. "Hello?"

Tamara took a breath. "Blythe, it's me, Tamara."

"Tamara, how nice to hear your voice. How are you?"

The horrible day Tamara had just put in suddenly defeated her. She began sobbing and just barely managed to blubber, "I—I'm…miserable."

"Oh, Tamara, calm down. Take some breaths. Talk to me, honey."

Did any other woman she know have a voice quite like Blythe's? It was low pitched and projected empathy and comfort, which Tamara absorbed like a thirsty sponge.

"Oh, Blythe, I've made such a mess of things," she moaned. "I didn't want you and Sierra to know. I wanted to be like the two of you, strong and…and perfect."

"Perfect? Tamara, I can't speak for Sierra, but believe me, I'm a long way from perfection. What do you mean, you've made a mess of things? What things? What's wrong?"

The dam broke. "Blythe, I forced Sam to marry me

because I was pregnant. I'm so unhappy I feel that I'm on the verge of a nervous breakdown. The final straw happened today. I learned—'' Tamara stopped to swallow the lump in her throat ''—that I'm going to have triplets.''

''Oh, how fabulous! Three babies. Oh, Tamara, don't you realize how lucky you are?''

It was then, at that precise moment, that Tamara thought of Blythe's childless marriage. Neither of her sisters had children, but it had never occurred to her to wonder *why* they didn't. From the excitement she heard in Blythe's lovely voice now, she understood immediately that her sister must have always wanted children.

''Tamara?'' Blythe said.

''I'm here,'' she answered in a painfully choked near whisper. ''I just did something terrible, didn't I? You wanted children and you didn't have any, and here I am, calling you to whine because I'm going to have triplets. Blythe, I'm so sorry.''

''You called because you're frightened, Tamara. I can hear the fear in your voice. Why are you so afraid, honey? You said you forced Sam to marry you, but forcing a man to do anything is almost impossible in this day and age. Tamara, there's more to this than what you've said so far. Is it that you don't love the father of your babies?''

In the back of Tamara's mind was how neatly Blythe had eluded admitting to wanting a child or children of her own. But Blythe's question about Sam, presented so gently, took precedence.

Tamara could be nothing but honest at this point. ''I love him, Blythe, I love him very much. But Sam doesn't love me.''

''Has he told you that?''

''Not in so many words, no, but neither has he said he *does* love me.''

''Even when you told him how you feel about him?''

''I—I never...''

"Tamara, I'm confused. You're living with a man you say you forced into marriage, and yet—"

"Blythe, we're not living together. We never have. Sam lives on his ranch and I'm still in my apartment."

"I'm beginning to get the picture. Let me ask you this. How did Sam react to the news of your having three babies instead of one?"

Tamara was also beginning to get the picture, from Blythe's point of view, and it wasn't very pretty. "I haven't told him," she said quietly, no longer teary.

And then Blythe said something that took Tamara completely by surprise. "Mother did her job very well, didn't she?"

"Pardon?"

"We're all so adept at keeping secrets." Blythe's voice was a whisper in Tamara's ear. "But I guess that's neither here nor there at this point. Tamara, if you really love your husband, get your fanny out to his ranch and tell him so. You think he doesn't love you, but how can you be so certain if you've never talked about it? Whatever you do, don't make the mistake of thinking you can read his mind. You can't, and neither can he read yours. With three babies on the way, you and Sam need to come to a solid understanding. I don't know Sam, but he married you when he certainly didn't have to, which makes him an honorable man in my book. Do you see each other at all?"

"Yes."

"Your doing or his?"

"His. But it's only because he wants his baby."

"He said that?"

Tamara's voice kept getting weaker. "Uh, no. But, Blythe, I can sense—"

"You can *guess*, Tamara. Unless you possess some sort of magic power, you can only guess at Sam's thoughts and feelings."

Tamara fell silent, and Blythe didn't intrude on her thoughts. After a few moments Tamara murmured,

"You're right. I'm so glad I called. You've given me a whole new perspective to reflect upon."

"Don't just reflect, Tamara, act! If you love Sam, don't lose him. For your sake as well as your babies."

After the sisters said goodbye and hung up, Tamara sat there thinking. She felt alive again, probably because once and for all she knew what she must do. Possibly she would have reached this conclusion on her own, but at the rate she'd been going it might not have happened for a very long time.

Pondering for several minutes how to approach Sam, she finally got up and went to find the piece of paper on which she'd written Sam's phone number and address. She knew how to physically locate his ranch, but she had never called him.

He was going to be very surprised, wasn't he?

She shivered slightly. This wasn't going to be easy. But for some time now, had *anything* been easy?

Chapter Eighteen

"Hello, Stubby, this is Tamara. Could I please speak to Sam?"

"Sam's not here, honey. He went back to work. Left before dawn this morning."

"Oh." Tamara's heart sank. "Did he say where he was going?"

"Let me think a minute. Yes, he said something about Lubbock."

"Lubbock is pretty big, isn't it?"

"Around two hundred thousand folks, I believe. Tamara, is it urgent you talk to Sam?"

"Extremely."

"Are you okay? I mean…"

"I know what you mean, Stubby. I'm fine and so is the baby." She couldn't tell Stubby about the triplets before she told Sam. "It's something else, Stubby."

"Glad to hear you're all right. Okay, listen to me a minute. Sam keeps pretty good records, and he's a man of habit. If he's in Lubbock, he's probably staying at the same motel he always uses. Do you get my drift?''

''Yes!''

''Okay. Now, you give me a little time to go through his records and receipts, then I'll call you back.''

''Thank you, Stubby. I'll be right here. Oh, you'll need my number.'' Tamara recited her phone number, said goodbye and hung up.

The next hour passed at a snail's pace, but finally Tamara's phone rang.

''Okay,'' Stubby said. ''I found two receipts for motels in the Lubbock area. Got a pencil?''

''Yes.'' As Stubby read off the names, addresses and phone numbers of the two motels, Tamara wrote them down.

''That's it, Tamara, all I could find.''

''Thank you so much, Stubby.''

''Good luck, honey.''

Before she could lose one drop of courage, Tamara dialed the first number on the paper. A man answered, ''Vic's Motel.''

''I'm calling long distance for Sam Sherard. Is he registered at your motel?''

''Sam? I know Sam. No, ma'am, he isn't staying here.''

''Thank you.'' Tamara broke the connection and dialed the second number. She asked the woman who answered the phone the same question. ''Is Sam Sherard registered at your motel?''

''Yes, ma'am, he is. Hold on and I'll ring his room.''

''Thank you. Oh, wait a minute! I—I'm going to be in Lubbock tomorrow. Can you tell me if Mr. Sherard is registered for tomorrow night, as well?''

''I'll check.'' Tamara virtually held her breath until the woman came back on the line. ''He registered for three nights, ma'am.''

Tamara breathed a sigh of relief. ''Thank you very much.''

"You don't want me to ring his room?"

"No, I'll see him tomorrow. Thank you again. Good night."

The idea to go to Lubbock had come out of nowhere, but she would much rather talk to Sam face-to-face than on the phone. She next realized that she didn't know how many miles lay between Dallas and Lubbock, and she got out her atlas to find out. "Hmm," she murmured. Three hundred eighteen miles, at least a six-hour drive.

Well, that meant another two days away from her job. After all, she had to make the return trip and it couldn't all be accomplished in one day. She felt guilty about taking more time off, but it couldn't be helped. She would call Mr. Grimes in the morning before leaving for Lubbock.

Sam drove into the motel's parking lot at six that evening. It had been a satisfying if tiring day, as he had a stack of orders to pass on to the people at Rowland. He'd already had dinner, and planned to take a shower and turn in early. There were dozens of assorted vehicles in the lot, which he ignored. Parking as close to his unit as he could get, he got out of his Jeep, stretched his back for a moment, then reached back for his leather case.

Walking to the door of his room, he inserted the key in the lock and turned it. The second he pushed the door open, he saw her. "Tamara!" His surprise was so apparent that she laughed.

Sam shut the door, Tamara got up from her chair and they stood there staring at each other. He finally shook his head. "I don't get it. What're you doing here?"

His remark and question weren't exactly encouraging. Tamara resorted to flippancy to conceal her wounded ego. "Oh, I just happened to be in the area and thought I'd drop in and say hello."

Sam gave her a pointed look. "You just happened to be in Lubbock. Yeah, right."

Her eyes flashed pure fire. "Well, why do you think I'm

here? I drove six hours to get here. I'd think you'd automatically know I came to see you!''

Sam set his case on the little round table in front of the
window, so confused by this turn of events that he honestly
didn't know what to say next. It had to be better than what
he'd already said, obviously, because Tamara wasn't at all
pleased with his initially shocked reaction to finding her
in his room.

''All right,'' he said. ''Let's start over. Tamara, I'm glad
to see you.''

Her eyes softened. ''Are you really?''

It was sinking in, her driving those many miles to see
him, her anger because he'd reacted to her presence without thinking, her softer expression when he'd said he was
glad to see her. Something very, very important was happening here, and he'd damned well better make the most
of it.

Moving closer to her, he smiled and touched her hair.
''You are the prettiest thing,'' he said softly.

''So are you, Sam.''

He didn't laugh. She was deadly serious, and he didn't
dare laugh. He probed the depths of her eyes, searching
for answers to nebulous questions.

''In case you're wondering how I got into your room,''
Tamara said, ''I told the desk clerk about my being your
wife. Hope you don't mind.''

''Why would I mind? It's the truth, isn't it?''

''Legally, yes. But there are all kinds of truths, aren't
there?''

''I suppose so.'' What was she getting at? Leading up
to? Should he kiss her? He wanted to, but she couldn't
have come all this way just to sleep with him. No, there
was something on her mind, something very big and very
intense. His stomach suddenly churned in alarm. She
hadn't lost the baby, had she? Oh, God, not that.

''How are you feeling?'' he asked anxiously.

''I'm fine. How are *you* feeling?'' She took a breath.

"Sam, I'm serious. How are you feeling about my being here?"

"I told you I was glad to see you."

Tamara backed away from him and moved to the other side of the room. The bed was between them, though she didn't appear to notice. But Sam did. He looked at that big bed and then at her, and he couldn't help thinking of sharing it with her.

She faced him in an abrupt turn. "Are you really glad or merely being polite?"

Sam frowned. "Tamara, what do you want me to say?"

She was silent for several seconds, then drew a shaky breath. "I want to know—I *have* to know—how you feel about me. Me, Sam, not the baby or anything else, just me." She watched him closely, and he didn't move a muscle. "Can you tell me?" she asked.

Sam could tell that she was losing confidence. Her unsteady voice was a giveaway, as was the tension in her stance. Well, he wasn't feeling so confident, either, he thought uneasily. She was asking him for something he wasn't emotionally prepared to dole out without second thoughts. A *lot* of second thoughts.

But hadn't he already been there and done that? Dare he keep his feelings private any longer? What if this surprise visit had something to do with her moving out to the ranch? What if this was her way of gathering information to help her make that decision?

"I can, but..." He looked away for a moment, then brought his gaze back to her. As much as he wanted to, he couldn't seem to totally eradicate the confusion that had struck him at the sight of her in his room. "This is why you came?"

"Yes, this is why I came."

"May I ask you something first?" For some reason he glanced at her left hand, and was stunned to see it denuded of all jewelry. She wasn't wearing the ring he'd given her, but neither was she wearing that fancy one of her mother's. What did *that* mean?

"Go ahead."

Sam's mouth was suddenly dry as a desert wind. But he was glad he'd noticed her ringless finger. It made it easier to ask, "Why is it suddenly so urgent that you know my feelings?"

"I have a very good reason—several good reasons, actually. In fact, if I added them up they would total four."

"But you're not going to tell me what they are."

"You're wrong. I *am* going to tell you what they are, but first I'd like to hear what you have to say."

Sam had never before felt the attack of nerves he was suffering at that moment. He couldn't begin to imagine her having four reasons for missing work and coming so far to put him on the spot like this, but worse than that, he'd never once said I love you to a single person in his entire life, and the thought of just blurting it out, with the lights on and Tamara looking him straight in the eye, scared the tar out of him.

But neither could he get all macho on her and toss off some nonchalant lie. This was it, their moment of reckoning. His plan had been to take it a day at a time, with his first step to a solid relationship being to convince her to move to the ranch. There they would gradually become closer. She would gradually understand how important she was to him, and one night while making love he would whisper in her ear, "I love you, Tamara."

That plan was in the ash can. There was no direction to go but forward. He had to risk his heart, his soul, his everything, and hope to high heaven that she didn't tromp all over them.

"Well?" she said quietly.

"Okay, you win. You want to know how I feel about you, here it is." Sam swallowed hard. "I love you."

She continued staring at him for a moment, then threw herself across the bed and began sobbing. Sam was so shaken up he didn't know what to do. Somehow he found himself lying on the bed next to her.

But then he was afraid to touch her. He reached out a hand and quickly drew it back. Why was she crying? Would he *ever* understand her? Did his loving her make her so unhappy she couldn't help crying? What had she wanted him to say? What had she expected to hear?

Feeling dejected and broken, he lay on his back and wished the earth would just open up and swallow him whole. Tears seeped out of his own eyes, and he hastily brushed them away. He'd risked it all and lost. Now she'd never move to the ranch. She'd get a divorce and he'd probably hardly ever get to see his child.

Without any warning at all, Tamara rose up and threw herself on top of him. "Oh, Sam, I'm the happiest woman in the world." She started sobbing into his shirt.

His arms came up from the bed and curled around her, but the deepest frown possible furrowed his brow. If she was so darned happy, why was she crying her eyes out?

Wait a minute. Was she happy *because* he loved her?

He suddenly felt as though the sun had just come out. "Tamara, do you *want* me to love you?"

She raised her head. "Well, of course I do! Didn't you ever catch on at all to how much *I* loved you?"

"No, babe, I didn't."

"Sam, I've been in love with you since that weekend in November."

"But you were going to move to Alaska and never tell me about our baby."

"Sam, the minute you drove away from the apartment that weekend, you forgot I even existed. Be honest. Isn't that true?"

He looked downcast. "I'm sorry you got that impression, sweetheart."

"I know you are. I'm sorry, too. Sam, we've been a pair of complete dolts."

He touched her tear-streaked face. "You're not a dolt."
He grinned then. "A little crazy, maybe, but not a dolt."

"I have been crazy, haven't I?" She threw her arms
around his neck. "Oh, I love you so much, and I came
here scared to death that you'd say something like 'Tamara, I want to stay married because of the baby, but I
don't love you and probably never will.'"

"Good Lord," Sam groaned. "I almost told you I loved
you half a dozen times, but I was so afraid you'd laugh,
or break off our relationship, that I always stopped myself."

She dipped her head, ardently kissed his mouth and felt
his hand go under her skirt. "You have the sweetest body
in this whole insane world," he whispered. "I want it."

She rolled to the side, yanked off her panties and opened
her legs. "What's mine is yours, my love. All yours. *Only*
yours."

"Oh, Tamara..." It was a cry of total and complete
surrender.

They lay cuddled together in the aftermath of truly glorious lovemaking.

"Sam," Tamara said in a dreamy voice, "there's something I haven't told you. Remember when I said that I had
four reasons for coming here?"

"I remember." Sam was drowsy and very close to falling asleep. This was how he wanted to fall asleep every
night for the rest of his life—first making love with his
wildly passionate wife, then holding each other until sleep
took them. Even drowsy as he was he was already thinking
of their next time, and he smiled in the dark.

"Aren't you curious about the other three?"

"What other three, honey?"

"My reasons, Sam." Tamara turned over and faced him.
"Wake up. This is important."

He yawned. "I don't even know your first reason, Tamara."

"You most certainly do. Think about it."

"Oh, finding out how I felt about you." He nuzzled his face in her throat. "Damn, you smell good."

"Sam, be serious! We have to talk."

His hand slid down her tummy to nestle between her thighs. "May I do this while we talk?"

"I thought you were sleepy." She grabbed his oh-so-clever hand and held it.

"I was until you turned over. Okay, I'm awake. Tell me about your reasons for coming to my motel room and seducing the hell out of me."

Tamara laughed. "Said the biggest seducer of all time. Okay, here goes. We're past one of my reasons. You love me and I love you. Sam, do you think that's a happy ending to our story?"

"It's sort of like that movie we saw together. Yeah, it's a happy ending. In fact, I'd call it a *very* happy ending."

"Well, try this one on for size. My other three reasons are..." Tamara held her breath.

"Are what?"

She said it in one long word. *"We'renotjusthaving-onebaby, we'rehavingthree."*

She'd spoken so fast that Sam only caught a few words. He chuckled. "Sounded like you said we're going to have three babies, but that couldn't be right, so slow down and..." It hit him then. Three reasons, three babies. He bolted up to a sitting position, reached out to switch on the lamp and then looked at her. "Was that what you said?"

"Yes," she whispered meekly.

"Three? Triplets?"

Her head bobbed on the pillow. "Triplets."

"And you were going to tell me even if I didn't love you?"

"Yes, I really was. You see, Sam, whether or not our marriage had a chance of working, I didn't think I could handle three babies by myself. I was going to ask for your help.''

Sam startled her by jumping to his feet and standing on the bed. ''Three!'' he yelled. ''Three at one time! Yahoo!''

''You're as crazy as I am,'' she gasped in the midst of a spasm of giggles.

Sam fell to his knees. ''So, with a crazy mama and a crazy daddy, what kind of kids are we going to have?''

''Crazy!'' they yelled in unison, and collapsed in a laughing, giggling heap on the bed.

The next morning was the most fun Tamara had ever had with a man. They tickled each other in the shower, they dueled with damp towels after drying off and they laughed about everything. Sam's laughter was music to Tamara's ears. He was witty and funny and as silly as she was. Why, oh why had he concealed this incredible side of himself so successfully that the people at Rowland called him Stoneface?

Just before they left the steamy bathroom to get dressed, something truly wonderful happened. Sam locked his hands behind her waist and looked deeply into her eyes. ''I never knew it before, but I do now,'' he said softly. ''Tamara, I've been looking for you all my life.''

Her heart nearly melted. Gently she touched his face. ''Oh, Sam, that's the nicest thing you could ever have said to me.''

''It's not a line, honey, it's the truth.''

''I know it is.'' She did know. They were no longer two separate people, but rather one love-saturated entity. At least it felt that way to her. She snuggled against Sam's warm, damp body and sighed happily. ''Now *this* is what I'd call a happy ending,'' she whispered.

''The end of our story is a long way off,'' Sam murmured, his lips moving in her wet curls. ''Till death do us part, Tamara. We're going to raise our babies and grow old together.''

"Yes, darling, yes." She felt Sam's hands move down her back to her hips, and she smiled serenely. They could not touch and hug each other without wanting more. She could feel a languorous desire developing in the pit of her stomach, and prayed to God that it would always be this way for them.

She had never been happier.

They didn't leave the motel room until noon, and they might not have left then if hunger for food hadn't gradually taken precedence over their hunger for each other.

Sam took her to a nice little café about a mile from the motel. They ordered mammoth breakfasts from a friendly waitress, then Sam drank coffee and Tamara drank herbal tea while they waited for their food.

It was Sam who started the conversation. "Did last night really happen or am I asleep and dreaming?"

Tamara smiled. "It happened, my love. I know it feels like a dream, but it's reality. Isn't it incredible?"

Their eyes met across the table of their booth. "I love you," Sam said softly—said it in broad daylight, in a public place. And though he'd spoken quietly, he realized that he really didn't give a damn if everyone in the café had heard him.

"And I love you," Tamara said.

"Tamara, we need to make some plans."

"I know."

Sam took a swallow of coffee and returned his cup to its saucer. "I'm not ever going to tell you what you should or shouldn't be doing, Tamara, but I would like to hear how you feel about keeping your job with three babies to raise."

"I think it's impossible," she said quietly, and saw the sudden gleam of pure joy in her beloved's eyes. She smiled. "Apparently you approve."

"You've made my day, honey." He grinned then.

"That was a dumb thing to say. You made my *life* last night—how could you make my day today?"

Tamara laughed. "I knew what you meant."

Sam sobered. "Tamara, if you want to live in the city, I'll sell the ranch and buy a house."

Her shock showed in every feature of her face. "You would do that for me?"

"I'd do anything for you, Tamara, anything."

She drew in a long, slow breath. "You love your ranch."

"I love you more." Again Sam brought his cup to his lips.

Tamara took a sip of her tea. This was unbelievable. He would actually give up his ranch if she said the word?

"No," she said quietly. "I would never ask you to do that, Sam. It doesn't matter where we live, as long as we're together."

"That's how I feel, too. Tamara, I want you to think about something. I'm gone a lot, sometimes for ten days at a time. You're going to be alone often, and you're not used to the seclusion of rural living."

"I'll *get* used to it, Sam. And do you think I'm going to be alone after our babies are born? I'm going to be so busy I probably won't have one spare minute to worry about myself." Her expression softened. "And I'll always be thinking of your next homecoming." After a second she added, "And Stubby's there. He's going to stay on the ranch, isn't he?"

Sam grinned wryly. "I don't think you could pry Stubby loose from that place with a crowbar. But that's something else to think about. He lives in the house, honey."

Their food was delivered, interrupting them for a few moments. They started eating, then Tamara picked up where they'd left off. "I don't know Stubby very well, having met him only that one time. But you know him. Should I be worried about being alone with him?"

"No, no, God no. Stubby's the salt of the earth. He likes

women, but his lady friends are all around his own age. Actually, I think the two of you would hit if off real well, but there again, it has to be your decision.''

Tamara reached for a piece of toast and sent her husband a beautiful smile. ''Very well, here's my decision. I'm going to work tomorrow morning and turn in my resignation. I will, of course, discuss very thoroughly with Mr. Grimes everything I've been doing on the job, so he can transfer my work to the best possible person. I think a thirty-day notice is called for because of my position in the company, but my apartment lease requires a thirty-day notice, also, so it will be a month before everything is finalized in Dallas and I can leave. However, during that period, I will start moving my things to the ranch, and any time off I have will be spent there so I can get to know Stubby and—'' she smiled again ''—also get to know the ranch.''

Sam could hardly contain his excitement. He leaned forward. ''I'll coordinate my own time off with yours so I can be there whenever you are. I want to show you the ranch myself, Tamara. It's so beautiful. You probably shouldn't get on a horse now, but—''

''Oh goodness,'' Tamara exclaimed, breaking in. ''I've never even been *near* a horse!''

''After the babies come, I'll teach you to ride. You'll love it, honey, I know you will.''

And what will we do with the babies while I'm out riding? Tamara thought it but she didn't say it. Sam was so happy right now, and she loved that look on his handsome face.

''Then it's settled,'' she declared.

Sam grinned. ''If you say so.''

''I do.'' Tamara reached for her purse and took something out of it. She held her hand across the table. ''I want you to do something for me.''

Sam looked puzzled. ''What is it, honey?''

''Put this on my finger.''

Sam held out his hand and Tamara dropped her wedding

ring into it. He drew back his hand and looked at the plain gold band. "Tamara, you don't have to wear this. I'll buy you a nice ring."

"I want that one. Sam, it didn't bother me to take it off and wear my mother's ring instead, because without your love that ring had no meaning. Now it does. Now it means the world to me. Please put it on my finger again." She stretched out her left hand.

Sam's eyes misted over. He slipped the ring on her finger and said huskily, "With this ring I thee wed."

"Thank you," she whispered, and wiped her eyes at the same moment Sam wiped his. "That was lovely," she said, after taking a moment to recover.

"You are the most incredible woman alive," Sam said, still emotional about that inexpensive ring meaning so much to her.

They started to eat again, and after a while Tamara said, "Sam, there's one more thing we should talk about."

"What is it?"

"Family, yours and mine." She saw him stiffen. "Please, Sam, no subject should be off-limits between us."

"I'll talk all day about your family, Tamara, but I don't want to talk about mine."

"You're not going to take me to meet them, or invite them to the ranch to meet me? Sam, my parents are gone, but you still have yours. They're going to be our babies' grandparents."

"Not if I can help it," Sam muttered. "You don't understand, Tamara. My family's not like yours. Hell, they're in a league all their own. How could they be compared to *anyone* else's family?"

She recalled him saying not ten minutes ago that he would do anything for her, and she almost reminded him. But she thought better of it and smiled instead. "All right, we'll do it your way for now. But I'm warning you, Sam,

I'm a stubborn woman, and someday I'm going to meet your family.''

He studied her beautiful face. "Is it really that important to you? Tamara, you're going to be very disappointed."

"Maybe so, but I still want to meet them." Sam looked so distraught that Tamara quickly added, "Someday, Sam. Please don't worry about it now."

"I don't want that hanging over my head, Tamara," he said. "If you're bent on meeting them, I want it over and done with. Can you take one more day off from work?"

"I don't see why not. But why?"

"We'll fly to Tulsa this afternoon and get it over with," he said stonily.

Sam's granitelike expression was back, and Tamara's heart nearly stopped. What in heaven's name was she doing? Whatever problems existed between Sam and his family were *his* business, and how dare she interfere like this? Maybe someday Sam would want to bring them all together, maybe not. But forcing him into it like she'd been doing was abominable.

"Sam, I'm sorry," she said with tears in her eyes. "We're not flying to Tulsa this afternoon, and I promise I will never mention your family again."

Sam visibly relaxed. "Thank you."

"If I've damaged our relationship...?" Tamara bit her lip.

"You've damaged nothing, but let's leave my parents out of things for now. I don't want them in our life, Tamara. You don't know how I grew up. I'll tell you about it sometime and we'll deal with it together, as we'll deal with everything from now on."

She nodded mutely and picked up her fork. While she ate she thought of her own family, her two wonderful sisters. Most definitely she wanted Sierra and Blythe to meet Sam. Once she was settled on the ranch, she would invite them to come for a visit. Sam would approve, she knew.

She suspected now that Sam's inordinate need for privacy had been a result of his upbringing. She was a product of *her* upbringing; why wouldn't he be the same?

Looking at her handsome husband across the table, she felt that uniquely marvelous sensation of loving and being loved. There was nothing else like it, and she must nurture and protect it as she was going to do with their babies.

Sam smiled at her and she smiled back. "This is really our happy beginning, isn't it?" she said.

His smile remained intact but an emotional mist formed in his eyes. "I like that. A happy beginning instead of a happy ending. Yes, my love, my dearest wife, this is our happy beginning."

And it was.

*   *   *   *   *

THE BENNING LEGACY *continues in*
August 1998 in Silhouette Desire.
Watch for Sierra's story—A MONTANA MAN!

The Benning Legacy

**An absorbing new cross-line miniseries in
Silhouette Special Edition and Silhouette Desire from
Jackie Merritt**

**Three sisters find that true love uncovers the secrets of
the past...and forges bright new tomorrows!**

Starting June 1998 in Silhouette Special Edition:

FOR THE LOVE OF SAM—June 1998 (Special Edition)
Spunky younger sister Tamara Benning had a sneaking
suspicion that there were long-buried Benning family
secrets. But she had a budding secret of her own....

A MONTANA MAN—August 1998 (Desire)
Tamara's older sister Sierra's adventure begins with the
Man of the Month

And coming this December in Special Edition,
the conclusion...the Benning family secrets
are finally unraveled in **THE SECRET DAUGHTER.**

Available at your favorite retail outlet.

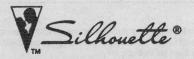

Silhouette®

TM

Take 2 bestselling love stories FREE

Plus get a FREE surprise gift!

Sizzling, Sexy, Sun-drenched...

**Three short stories by *New York Times*
bestselling authors will heat up your summer!**

LINDA HOWARD

LINDA LAEL MILLER

HEATHER GRAHAM
POZZESSERE

Experience the passion today!

Available at your favorite retail outlet.

Look us up on-line at: http://www.romance.net

PSUNSEN

FIVE STARS
MEAN SUCCESS

If you see the "5 Star Club" flash on a book, it means we're introducing you to one of our most STELLAR authors!

Every one of our Harlequin and Silhouette authors who has sold over 5 MILLION BOOKS has been selected for our "5 Star Club."

We've created the club so you won't miss any of our bestsellers. So, each month we'll be highlighting every original book within Harlequin and Silhouette written by our bestselling authors.

NOW THERE'S NO WAY ON EARTH OUR STARS WON'T BE SEEN!

OVER
5 MILLION
BOOKS SOLD
SPECIAL OFFER INSIDE

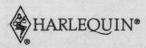
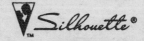

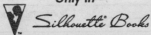